Fit to Die

Fit to Die

Karen Hanson Stuyck

Five Star • Waterville, Maine

First Edition, Second Printing

Published in 2006 in conjunction with Tekno Books and Ed Gorman.

Set in 11 pt. Plantin by Ramona Watson.

Printed in the United States on permanent paper.

Library of Congress Cataloging-in-Publication Data

Stuyck, Karen Hanson.
    Fit to die / by Karen Hanson Stuyck.
      p. cm.
    ISBN 1-59414-369-2 (hc : alk. paper)
    1. Overweight women—Fiction.   2. Women journalists—Fiction.   3. Personal trainers—Crimes against—Fiction. I. Title.
    PS3619.T89F58 2006
    813'.6—dc22   2005028626

For Steve and Danny

Acknowledgements

I want to thank the members of the Tuesday Writers' Consortium for their skillful help with this book—and for laughing at the right places. Thanks to Irene Bond, Patsy Ward Burk, Julia Mercedes Castilla, Louise Gaylord, Guida Jackson Laufer, Vanessa Leggett, Ida Luttrell, Jackie Pelham, and Sue Volk.

One

"You're cheating!" my husband Rob accused, his face blotchy with rage. With his thumb and forefinger he held up the evidence.

I stared at it for a minute, then shifted my gaze to him. I could see that he expected me to feel guilty, apologetic, but all I felt was pissed off. "You went through the trash?" I asked. "Scrounged through the garbage for a candy wrapper?"

He hesitated. Apparently this was not the way Rob's mental script proceeded. After a moment, though, he rallied. "It was a whole bag of Baby Ruths, Lauren! Thousands of calories!"

"So?"

"For God's sake, you're supposed to be on a diet."

"And you are—what? The Diet Police?" If I'd had another bag of Baby Ruths I would have eaten every chocolate bar right there in front of him.

The redness spread across Rob's face. "I am a concerned husband who worries that you're allowing your weight to jeopardize your health," he said in a voice frigid enough to quell hot flashes.

I raised an eyebrow. "I appreciate your concern, but . . ."

"And you're getting as big as a house." Meaning, I'm embarrassed to be seen with you, a no-longer-slim, no-longer-young woman who doesn't even make an effort to turn back the clock.

I glared at the balding, paunchy man I'd been married to

for nearly thirty years. "You're not such a prize specimen yourself, kiddo. It's not Hugh Grant I see across the kitchen table every morning."

Rob's color seemed to deepen a shade. "Well, I guess this is your lucky day, Lauren. You won't have to endure the unappetizing sight of me for another morning. I'm moving out."

Too stunned to speak, I stared at his back. I heard him stomp up the stairs, march into our bedroom, then slam shut bureau drawers. I felt as if I were a detached bystander, watching someone else's life.

I hadn't moved a muscle by the time Rob, a suitcase in each hand, stopped in the doorway to our family room. "If you have to get in touch with me, you can reach me at the office."

"Rob, my God, don't do this," I pleaded. "It was just a silly, insignificant argument. We've had hundreds of fights worse than this. We get over it, we make up."

"Not this time," he said, avoiding eye contact. "I'll get the rest of my stuff once I find a place." He moved away and moments later the front door slammed.

I sat there so long that the automatic outside lights had turned on before I realized I was sitting in the dark. I moved from the couch only when the phone started ringing. Could it be Rob, coming to his senses, calling to apologize?

"Lauren?" The alto voice was not my husband's.

"Hi, Meg." To my ears, I sounded amazingly normal. Not at all the voice of a woman whose husband of twenty-seven years and the father of her children, the man she'd put through dental school by working two jobs, had just walked out on her.

"What's wrong?"

I took a deep breath and then, to my horror, burst into tears.

"I'll be right over," Meg said. "Hold on."

She was at my house in ten minutes—enough time for me to gain some emotional control and splash my face with cold water.

"You look awful," Meg said when I opened the door. Dressed in gray wool slacks and a pale-gray cashmere sweater set, she, of course, looked terrific. Also concerned. She handed me two bottles of white Zinfandel. "Pour us some and then I want to hear everything that happened."

I did as she instructed.

"That bastard," she said when I finished my story. Sitting across from me at my butcher-block kitchen table, she shook her head in disgust. "He's cheating, you know. The Baby Ruths were just an excuse for a fight and the exit speech."

"What are you talking about? You haven't even laid eyes on Rob in the last nine months." Meg and Rob were not the best of friends. Rob thought that Meg, who'd been married and divorced three times, was a spoiled, self-absorbed shrew, while Meg found Rob a pompous bore.

"I don't have to see him to know. Rob has always been tediously predictable. I'll bet his girlfriend is young, trashy, and not too bright."

"And skinny," I added. The Anti-Me.

"That too," she agreed grimly. She picked up a bottle of wine and refilled both of our glasses. "Tonight you wallow in self-pity. But tomorrow"—she pulled a business card from her pocket and handed it to me—"tomorrow you call my divorce attorney." Meg's grin was positively shark-like. "She'll chew up Rob and spit out his bones."

11

★ ★ ★ ★ ★

I didn't follow Meg's advice. For one thing, I woke up with an incredible hang-over, and the prospect of launching any serious action in my present condition seemed too grim to contemplate. For another, I wasn't sure that I wanted to get a lawyer involved just yet. What if Rob, a pouty and temperamental man at the best of times, was having second thoughts? Maybe right now he was cleaning somebody's teeth and thinking, "I've made the old girl suffer long enough. I bet after this she'll think twice before she mouths off to me." Or perhaps (this was probably wishful thinking unless Rob had experienced a total personality transformation overnight) he was berating himself for jeopardizing a long-term marriage over a few Baby Ruths.

I took a tentative sip of coffee, waiting to see if the caffeine eased my headache. Unfortunately, no. I washed down three Advil with my coffee, then stretched out on the couch in the family room, pulling an afghan over me. I clicked on the television for company.

I fell asleep midway through *The View*, not awakening until the ringing of my portable phone roused me. "Hello?" I hoped that my voice did not betray to my husband that I was half asleep, not to mention hung-over.

But it wasn't Rob on the phone. "Did you phone my lawyer?" Meg's husky voice demanded.

"Not yet."

"Were you asleep?"

"Yeah, sleeping off all the wine I drank last night."

"You know what's great for a hang-over?" Meg was saying when I interrupted, "Got to go, Meg." I sighed, plopped down again on the sofa, and pulled the afghan over my head.

But I couldn't go back to sleep. Slugging down another

Advil with cold coffee, I tried to think of something to keep me occupied. The obvious choices—call Rob to talk things out, think about my options on what to do next, or phone Meg's attorney—were not appealing. Nor was contemplating what kind of job I could find after having spent the last twenty-three years as an unpaid caretaker of others.

Fortunately a story on the noon TV news caught my attention. Stan Harris, a local fitness club owner and the author of a best-selling diet and exercise book, had died—fittingly enough, while jogging. The title of his book was *Before and After*, and the television show ran clips of an interview they'd done with him a few years earlier when the book first came out.

"Why that title?" the interviewer had asked him, and Stan, a too-tan, hard-bodied type with thinning hair, was off and running. He'd been a fat kid himself, bullied and laughed at throughout his childhood and adolescence. But then, at age twenty, Stan had had his defining moment.

He'd discovered weight lifting and "The rules of proper nutrition. I changed from this miserable, three hundred-pound hunk of flesh," he said dramatically, holding up a photo of a very fat teenage boy with bad skin, "to this hunk." With a flourish he pulled out another photo, this one of a muscle-bound Stan competing in a bodybuilding contest. "And if I do say so myself, I don't think I look too bad right now for a fifty-year-old man."

I groaned and was about to switch channels when the camera focused on the attractive young woman sitting next to him. "And my wife, Terri, is another of the before-and-after stories I tell in my book," Stan said. The camera moved to Terri, a svelte brunette who looked a good twenty years younger than her husband. "Before she met me, this gorgeous gal looked like this." He held up a photo of a heavy young woman with downcast eyes. "Can you believe it? She tipped the scales at two hundred ten when she asked me to design a diet and exercise program for her. And look at her now! A size six who I couldn't help falling in love with."

What did she see in this guy? I wondered as the gorgeous gal flashed a toothy smile that didn't reach her eyes. Terri, we were told, now also worked at her husband's fitness studio.

"Didn't your first wife also have a weight problem before you were married?" the interviewer asked.

"Yes, she too slimmed down with my guidance. It's very exciting for me to take a miserable, self-hating person with zero self-esteem and uncover the dynamic, fit person buried under all that fat."

I wondered if his ex-wife shared his assessment of his effect on her. The story segued to a scene of yesterday's memorial service for Stan. A patrician-looking woman I recognized from her syndicated health column, "Ask Dr. Elizabeth," was giving the eulogy. "Stan," she said, solemnly scanning the room, "was a personal friend as well as an inspiration to all of us to find our healthiest selves."

By inspiring us to die jogging? I wondered. The camera panned to the front row of the church where the young widow sat next to a sharp-featured woman with short gray hair, an extremely heavy teenage girl who looked like Stan Harris, and a long-haired, sullen-looking young man. None of them seemed very upset that inspirational Stan was no longer with them.

It was probably my own sense of betrayal that made me envision these mourners as a group of murder suspects gathered together in the drawing room for the unmasking-the-killer scene in an old English mystery novel. Which of them had killed the tyrannical Henry Higgins-with-muscles who molded his chubby Eliza Doolittles into fit, "gorgeous gals"? Perhaps the two formerly-fat wives had done it together. An unrelenting regimen of carrot sticks and jogging could push anyone into committing murder, I thought as I dunked an Oreo into my coffee.

At 1:05, I decided to take action. This was Rob's lunchtime, the forty-five minutes when he propped his feet up, read the newspaper, and ate the sandwich that Iris, his longtime receptionist, had picked up for him at the downstairs deli. It was also the only guaranteed time during his workday when I could reach Rob by phone.

I drummed my fingers on the kitchen counter as the phone rang. Five, six, seven times. Finally an unfamiliar female voice came on the line. "You have reached Dr. Rob Prescott's dental office. We're not here right now, but please leave your name and phone number, and we'll get back to you." The voice was breathy and way too sultry for a dentist's office.

So where was Rob? And when had he got this ridiculous automated message? The woman on the tape sounded as if she was trying out a Marilyn Monroe imitation. I left my message: "Rob, it's Lauren. Call me." As I made myself a peanut butter and banana sandwich, I mentally rehearsed all the things I'd say when he called back.

But he never called. By 5:10 I was furious and, I had to admit, a little scared. Over the years Rob and I had had our share of arguments, but he had never not wanted to elaborate on why he was right and I was wrong.

I phoned again. This time a real person answered, the same breathy voice I'd heard on the answering tape. "Could I speak to Dr. Prescott? This is his wife."

"He can't come to the phone right now."

"He's with a patient?" Usually Rob didn't like to schedule patients after five unless it was some kind of dental emergency.

"No, he's not with a patient." She paused. "He just doesn't want to talk to you."

"Excuse me?" I was tempted to slam the phone down, but I reminded myself that the woman was only repeating Rob's message. "Where's Iris?" I asked instead.

"She no longer works here," the woman said smugly and hung up.

It was not a good night. I declined Meg's dinner invitation and spent the evening brooding. So what if Rob didn't want to talk to me? I wanted to talk to *him*. Unfortunately I didn't have a clue where he was staying, and a frustrating half-hour phoning every hotel and motel in the vicinity didn't provide any answers. Finally I ended up crawling into bed at 9:15, too depressed and exhausted to keep my eyes open.

I woke up the next morning feeling anxious and still tired. I was grateful that I had to spend the day at my volunteer job. Smiling, making change for customers at the Methodist Hospital gift shop, I could at least pretend that I was still the same friendly, wisecracking, and rather complacent woman who'd been doing the same job every Tuesday for the last ten years.

At 5:15 I pulled into my driveway, bone-weary and headachy. Maybe I'd have a bowl of tomato soup and some cheese and crackers for dinner, followed by the Baby Ruth I'd bought at the gift shop. Then I'd settle into the bathtub with a good mystery novel. Tomorrow I'd figure out what to do about Rob.

It took me a few minutes to register that something was different about my house. The pile of mail on the kitchen table had not been there when I'd left this morning. Knowing that Tuesday was my volunteer day, Rob must have come to get the rest of his things while I was gone. Feeling suddenly queasy, I wandered through the house. Then stopped dead in my tracks.

My once lavishly furnished living room was now empty, stripped of the antiques Rob and I had hunted for, the huge crimson and navy rug we'd bought on our trip to Turkey, the couch we'd had reupholstered before Katie's wedding last July. Even the paintings on the walls were gone; only picture hooks now marked their former places.

Heart thudding, I moved to the dining room. The long rosewood table and chairs, which this morning had occupied most of the room, were no longer there. Nor were the antique sideboard, my grandmother's silver service, or my Chinese porcelain collection. Dust bunnies occupied the floor space where the Oriental rug had lain.

Aside from the kitchen table and chairs, only the family room furniture—the comfortable faded couch and the matching chairs Rob and I had bought when we were first married—was left downstairs. The big-screen TV, VCR and stereo equipment were also gone, though the collection of framed family photos remained.

I hurried up the stairs, dreading what I'd encounter there. From the hallway the girls' rooms looked untouched. In our bedroom the half-empty closet revealed that Rob had indeed moved out. At least he'd left me our bed, though I wasn't sure that I'd ever want to sleep in it again.

Only when I moved into the bathroom did I see the note Rob had taped to the mirror: DON'T TRY TO CONTACT ME. YOU CAN KEEP THE HOUSE.

17

★ ★ ★ ★ ★

I arrived outside Rob's office the next morning at 8:05, five minutes after his normal starting time. I hadn't slept at all last night, my mind racing with everything I intended to say the minute I laid eyes on him, beginning with "What kind of sleazebag sneaks in with a moving van the minute his wife leaves the house?"

Of course I'd always known that Rob was stingy and obsessed with money. He'd only bought the expensive art, antiques, and rugs for our house in order to impress visitors. But on Sunday night when he'd told me he'd come back later for the rest of his things, it never crossed my mind that his definition of his "things" would include every valuable object in the house.

Rob's gray Mercedes was not parked in the usual space, but maybe he was hiding it in fear that I might decide to appropriate one of his prized possessions. I marched to the elevator, punched the button for the third floor, wishing it was Rob's beak-like nose. My previous depressed exhaustion seemed to have been replaced by adrenaline-fueled rage. When the elevator stopped at Rob's floor, I was ready—eager—for a fight.

Except Rob was not there to fight with. No one, in fact, was in his office. A hand-lettered sign on the locked door announced why: The office of Dr. Rob Prescott is closed for business.

I stared at the sign. Was the office closed for the day, closed for the week, or closed forever? And if the closing wasn't temporary, where the hell was Rob's new office? I took a deep breath, then pulled my cell phone from my purse and punched in Rob's office number. Behind the door, I heard the phone ringing until the answering message kicked in. It was the same breathy voice. This time, how-

18

ever, it said, "The dental office of Dr. Rob Prescott has closed. We are sorry for any inconvenience."

I stood there, staring at the door, too dumbfounded to do anything else. "That's a real shocker, isn't it?" asked a female voice from behind me.

I turned to see a nurse from the oral surgeon's office next door. "It sure is. Do you know where they moved to?"

She shook her head. "No one around here seems to know. Monday it was business as usual, and the next day the movers showed up." She sighed. "The guy's been in the same office for all the years I've been here. You'd think he'd at least stop to say goodbye, wouldn't you?"

"Yes," I said, "you would."

I could just imagine Rob gloating as he envisioned me gaping at his empty office. How diabolically clever he'd been: stealing every valuable piece of furniture and art we owned while I was at my volunteer job, and then closing his office and disappearing off the face of the earth—all before I even realized that our separation wasn't temporary.

Gripping my keys so hard they cut into my palm, I took one last look at the place where my soon-to-be ex-husband used to work.

"I'm not going to let you get away with this, you bastard," I muttered as I turned and headed back to my car.

Two

Besides taking the good furniture, art, and my grandmother's silver service, the bastard also emptied our joint bank account.

"Oh, I can't cash this," the bank teller told me, peering at the screen of her computer. "This account has been closed."

"Closed?" I repeated stupidly. "There was ten thousand dollars in it a few days ago."

The teller, a young woman with dyed-blonde hair and a bad case of acne, nodded. "There was ten thousand, two hundred and ten dollars in it. But that money was withdrawn yesterday."

"Shit!" I muttered under my breath. Could Rob get away with this—just walking in and taking whatever he chose? And what was I going to do without any money?

"Lauren!" The small, gray-haired teller waving at me lived at the end of my block. Just what I needed right now: a little neighborhood gossip. Feeling numb, I walked over to Stella's place at the counter.

"I think it's just terrible!" she began.

"What is?"

"Why what Rob did to you, of course—taking all your money. I was here yesterday when he came in," she said, lowering her voice and leaning toward me. "I wasn't paying much attention until the teller called over John, the bank manager. Apparently Rob tried to liquidate your checking account too, but John said he couldn't because only your

20

name was on the account. That made Rob mad; he said it might be your name on the checks, but it was his money."

"That worm!" How could I have stayed married to such a man? The only reason I had my own checking account was because Skinflint Rob wanted to monitor how much I spent each month on household expenses. "Uh, could you tell me, Stella, how much money I have in that account?"

I watched as she typed some numbers into her computer. She looked at me. "Only three hundred and one dollars and thirteen cents. I'm really sorry, Lauren."

"Thanks." I tried not to think about what I was going to do next as I stumbled to my car.

"That asshole!" Meg said that night when I told her what had happened. "Not one of my husbands pulled anything remotely as sleazy as that. Granted, a couple of them did their share of screaming at me when we discussed the division of our assets, but no one sneaked into the house and stole the couch."

I took a large sip of the margarita Meg insisted on buying me, along with a lavish meal at our favorite Mexican restaurant. "I can't believe Rob took all of our money. Not half—all! After I left the bank, I went home and phoned our mutual funds. He closed every one of them, Meg. If he could have taken the house with him, he probably would have that now too. How could he do this to me? What would make him so vengeful?"

Meg leaned over the plate of nachos to pat my hand. "The man has always been a cheap, selfish, narcissistic bottom-feeder. You were just too generous—and naive—to notice what I always saw in him: an unmitigated shit-heel."

I took another bite of my nacho. Meg was right. Even I, who until a few hours ago had loved the jerk, had realized how miserly and self-absorbed Rob was. I should have seen this coming. I should have prepared for it: found a paying job, socked away some of my own money, toughened up. But I hadn't, and here I was. "I don't even have enough money to make the next mortgage payment."

Meg watched appreciatively as a hunky young waiter set plates of fajitas in front of us. "I'll lend you some money. What you need to do tomorrow morning is call my divorce lawyer. She'll nail Rob's fat butt to the wall."

"First she'll have to find him," I said grimly. "Which is more than I've managed." That afternoon I'd phoned the landlord of Rob's office building, Rob's sister, and his dental assistant. The landlord ranted about Rob breaking his lease, and Marla, Rob's hygienist, said Rob told her he was taking early retirement and would send her back pay. None of them knew where Rob had gone.

"What you need now is a nice, high-paying job," Meg was saying between bites of her fajita.

I finished my margarita, wondering if it would be a major mistake to order a second one. "You're absolutely right. I'm afraid though that a job at the minimum-wage establishments which will hire me will not support my habit of paying my mortgage and utility bills while also eating regularly."

Meg shook her head in disgust, causing her temporarily auburn curls to cover her small, heart-shaped face. "You are so defeatist. You have a college degree, Lauren. And, as I recall, you used to work as a newspaper reporter, right?"

"That was twenty-five years ago. Newsrooms still had typewriters."

Meg sighed. "I guess I'm just going to have to find you a job. An interesting, good-paying one."

"You do that," I said. "In the meantime I'm going to

visit Rob's mother. If he told anybody where he's hiding, it's that old bat."

Mother Prescott did not look especially happy to see me the next morning when I showed up at her nursing home, but then she never did. "Lauren," she said, patting a seat next to her on the chintz sofa in the home's large recreation room, "What brings you here?"

She made it sound as if this was my first visit in a decade, but, in fact, I came to visit her once a week. Usually I tried to placate her, coax her into a better mood the way I'd once done with my cranky toddlers. Today, though, I wasn't up to it. "Rob is gone," I said, cutting to the chase. "He closed his office and moved out of our house."

I watched her closely for a reaction of surprise or shock, but she only nodded, her wrinkled face noncommittal above her gaunt body, which was dressed, as always, in a polyester pants suit (today lime-green). "He came to visit me before he left town. Told me he was going away for a long vacation."

"Where?"

Her cold, heavy-lidded eyes regarded me for a moment. "He didn't say, but he promised he'd come visit. And he said he'd paid my bills for the next several months."

Mama's boy. He wouldn't leave me a dollar, but he paid ahead on his eighty-five-year-old mother's nursing care! "Did he say when he'd visit?" I asked, trying hard to sound casual.

"No." My mother-in-law looked pleased that she couldn't—or wouldn't—tell me.

I stood up. "I have to leave now."

"But you just got here," she protested.

"I have an appointment," I lied.

As I turned toward the door, Mother Prescott got in her

parting shot. "I told Rob not to marry you."

I swiveled back to her, looking directly into those steely gray eyes. "Too bad he never listened to you."

On the way home I stopped at the grocery store. I bought bread, eggs, several cans of soup, and a giant bag of Baby Ruths: staples. Then I drove home, trying hard to believe that everything was going to be all right.

Dressed in a business-like black suit and black pumps, I arrived for my job interview with sweaty palms and a newly typed résumé. I smiled nervously at a skinny receptionist with blue hair and a nose ring. "I'm here to see Mr. O'Neal about the staff writer job."

Her eyes ran over me. "I'll tell Paul you're here."

I took a deep breath and sat down on an uncomfortable chair. Fifteen minutes later Mr. O'Neal still had not appeared. Meg had procured this interview for me; the editor-in-chief of *City Magazine* was a friend of a friend of hers. Had someone twisted Paul O'Neal's arm to see me? And was he now clueing me in on his displeasure?

I'd just decided to leave and find my own job interviews when the receptionist motioned for me to follow her. "Paul is ready for you now."

Paul O'Neal looked like a hulking, muscular Irish cop, the kind of part that a younger Brian Dennehy might have played in a movie. Except for his rumpled blue oxford-cloth shirt pushed up to his elbows, his disheveled salt-and-pepper hair, and incredibly messy desk, he did not seem like my idea of a magazine editor.

He rose to shake my hand, towering above me. "Have a seat," he said, indicating a tweed upholstered chair that had seen better days. "It's one of the few uncluttered spots in the office."

He scanned my résumé as I inspected a group of framed magazine covers and journalism awards hanging on his walls. Finally he looked up at me. "So tell me why you think I should hire you, Ms. Prescott."

I had prepared for this by reading a library book for "mature workers" reentering the job market. I knew what to say. "I think I can contribute a great deal to your magazine, Mr. O'Neal. I've lived in Houston for over fifteen years" (over thirty years actually, but the books advised not admitting your age) "and have been very active in community affairs. I have writing experience as a newspaper reporter and I also wrote my civic club's monthly newsletter."

"Uh-huh." The editor nodded, looking as if he were trying not to laugh. "Give me your idea for a magazine article for us, something timely we might run in one of the next issues."

"Well . . ." This was one I hadn't prepared for. Frantically I tried to think of something timely. "What about an article on Stan Harris, the fitness club owner who died last week?"

O'Neal raised an eyebrow. "That's your angle—he died?"

"No!" I hated this—hated this supercilious journalist for laughing at me, hated Rob for putting me in this position, hated myself for feeling so old, so housewifey, so professionally inept. "My angle is that Stan was married to a very heavy woman who he claims in his book to have transformed into a svelte, gorgeous babe. He supposedly did a similar makeover on his first wife. I'm interested—and I'd bet a lot of other people would be interested too—in how it feels to be someone's Pygmalion project."

O'Neal didn't say anything, but at least he no longer looked amused.

"Also," I went on, "I might go into what effect his death has had on his business. I mean it's not exactly inspiring when your fitness role model dies jogging at age fifty-two, particularly when he was always saying how exercise prolongs your life."

He nodded. "Might work. The real man behind the buff facade. Write the story for me as a freelancer. If I like what you turn in, we'll talk about a staff position."

I stared at him, wanting to explain that I'd been only suggesting an idea for a story. I had never intended to write it.

"No more than five thousand words—if you come up with some unique angle that no one else has. Otherwise keep it under thirty-five hundred."

Dozens of objections leap-frogged through my brain. What if Stan's widow didn't want to be interviewed? What if I didn't have 3,000 words to say about Stan Harris? And what if I'd forgotten how to write serious articles? But the memory of those amused blue eyes made me keep my doubts to myself. I always could back out of the project later—by e-mail.

O'Neal stood up. "I need the article in three weeks. Oh, and we pay ten cents a word."

Gee, I thought, standing up too, $350 might pay for a month's utility bills—if I made no long-distance phone calls. "I'll see what I can do."

"You do that," he said, dismissing me.

I took the elevator down to the lobby, wondering what other employment I could line up this week. Clearly this one was not destined to lead to a real job. I was halfway past a row of pay phones when I reconsidered. What the hell? At least I could give it a try. I found the name in the phone book, then—quickly, before I could change my mind—punched in the numbers.

A woman answered. "Harris residence."

"Could I speak to Terri Harris?" I suddenly realized how much I didn't want to go through with this. Please, God, let her not be home.

"This is Terri."

I swallowed. "My name is Lauren Prescott. I'm a writer for *City Magazine*. I don't mean to intrude on you at such a difficult time, but I'd like to write a magazine article about your late husband."

Silence.

I felt like one of those sleazy TV reporters who yell to a woman who just learned her child is dead, "How are you feeling right now?" I took a deep breath. "I thought I might interview you and maybe some other family members."

"You want to interview me?" she demanded, her voice clipped. "You mean like how I met Stan, lost weight, married him and joined the business?"

"Well, yes."

"Terrific!" she said. "Can you be here tomorrow at noon?"

Three

I arrived at my interview with a portable tape recorder and a list of questions, hoping that I would be able to bluff my way through this. The Harris residence was a three-story stucco home on a gigantic lot. The house that fitness built.

Terri Harris herself opened the door. She was dressed in lavender sweats and tennis shoes, a statuesque brunette with large, doe-like eyes who seemed somehow more vulnerable than she'd appeared on television. Also a little heavier—still slender, but with the rounded contours of someone who had to fight her tendency to blimp up.

"I thought we could talk and eat in the sunroom," she said. "It's my favorite room in the house." As she led me down a tiled hallway, I glimpsed an all-white living room—two long white couches, white rug, a glass coffee table holding a white flower arrangement.

"I can see why," I said. "It's lovely." The sunroom, at the back of the house, was a sunny, plant-filled room with comfortable-looking chintz chairs. Floor-to-ceiling windows overlooked a grassy hill leading down to a small lake. In the far corner of the property were a swimming pool and a tennis court.

Terri seemed pleased by my admiration. She glanced at a pine sideboard loaded with dishes and food. "I hope you're hungry. I'm ravenous."

I turned to gawk at the food: fried chicken, biscuits, potato salad, assorted fruit, and a plate of brownies. "This is

28

the way you eat and still stay so thin?" I asked as she poured two glasses of iced tea.

She smiled. "This is the way I eat now." She proved the point by eating with a gusto that astounded me. I, who had always considered myself a hearty eater, could not hold a candle to Terri, who polished off huge helpings of the delicious fried chicken and potato salad, three of the biscuits (I had two), and a generous portion of the fruit. We each had two of the truly decadent brownies.

"This food is incredible," I said, feeling more than a little bloated. "You said you frequently eat like this?" I clicked on the tape recorder for her answer.

Terri grinned. "Sometimes I eat like this. When Stan was alive the two of us were more likely to eat plain grilled chicken or fish, grilled or steamed vegetables, and a green salad dressed with vinegar. Occasionally we had fruit for dessert or a glass of wine." Her mouth tightened. "Other times I only had a big pitcher of water for dinner. Stan had me weigh in every day and when my weight went up more than two pounds, it was time for what he called a 'little fast.' The little fast could last for two or three days if the scale didn't move."

"That sounds like abuse," I said, genuinely horrified.

"It wasn't. Stan was doing the same thing himself—fasting, exercising until he dropped. He was convinced that his whole life had been transformed when he lost weight. He changed from a fat, miserable, bullied wimp to this muscular guy who other men looked up to and women suddenly tried to seduce. Fitness was almost a religion to him, and like a missionary, he wanted other people to experience what he had. Stan truly believed that fat equaled misery and fitness equaled happiness. It was that simple. And he was going to lead the miserable people to happiness."

I raised an eyebrow. "Even if that meant starving himself?" I made a mental note to find out if too much exercise and fasting could have brought on Stan's heart attack.

She nodded. "He said it was the price you had to pay. Whatever the cost, it was worth it to be fit and attractive."

"And you felt that way too?"

Terri shrugged. "Some days I did. For the first time in my life men were ogling me and I liked what I saw in the mirror. I could run a marathon, which I wouldn't have even been able to walk eight years ago. But other days, when I was dizzy with hunger or almost every muscle in my body was screaming, I kept wondering why I was torturing myself merely to look good. Because, don't kid yourself, while Stan was always going on about the health benefits of exercise, it was how those bodies looked that really mattered to him."

"And he himself was a case in point," I said. "He looked great, but obviously he wasn't really that healthy if he died of a heart attack at fifty-two." When Terri didn't respond, I added, "Did your husband have a history of heart disease?"

"Yes, Stan's father died of a heart attack when he was only forty. That was what got Stan interested in fitness. His daddy was fat and sedentary too, just like Stan was. But even when Stan lost weight and started exercising every day, he still always worried about his health. He was a real hypochondriac, always going to the doctor for something."

"Did his doctor find any evidence of heart disease?"

Terri shook her head. "Nope. His doctor always told him he was in perfect health. I used to think Stan was nuts to keep on believing that something was wrong—but then he turned out to be right, didn't he?"

I glanced at the list of questions I'd jotted down in a notebook. "Has Stan's death affected his business? I mean,

30

do clients say, 'Hey, exercising didn't help Stan live longer'?"

She scowled. "Exercise does help people live longer. When someone says that about him, I always tell them if Stan hadn't been exercising regularly, he probably would have died twelve years earlier at the age his father did."

"You're running the business now?"

"Yes. I'm continuing our program the way Stan would want me to."

"So he left the business to you?"

Terri's thin lips tightened. She looked as if she was considering whether or not to respond. "The details on that are still being worked out," she said. After a moment of strained silence, she smiled a not very convincing smile. "You wanted to talk about how Stan and I met?"

I marveled that a woman who had no qualms about telling a reporter that her husband systematically starved her did not want to answer a few simple questions about his business.

I only half listened as Terri launched into the Cinderella story I'd already read in Stan's book. Terri's version of their meeting was similar: shy, fat girl who all her life felt "invisible" comes to Stan for help in losing weight. He designs a diet and exercise program for her and takes a personal interest—a very personal interest—in her progress. "Stan made me feel so attractive and sexy. He bought me lovely clothes, strapless evening gowns, snug little knit dresses, even a bikini that I would never have been caught dead in before. And he told me constantly how great I looked, how fit and strong I was becoming, and how proud he was of me."

And he starved her to make sure she stayed that way. "I can't imagine that many women could put up with Stan's diet and exercise regimen for too long. Do you think that was why he and his first wife—a woman who he also helped lose weight—got divorced?"

Terri leaned forward, as if she was going to tell me a good piece of gossip. "Jane, his ex-wife, used to sneak Hostess Cupcakes into the house. One day Stan caught her eating them in her closet."

"And he divorced her because of that?" I asked, unpleasantly reminded of my own Baby Ruth–obsessed spouse.

"No, she divorced him. Jane told me they were fighting all the time about the kids, and she couldn't take it anymore." Terri glanced around as if to see if anyone was eavesdropping. "You do know about his daughter, Amber, don't you?"

I shook my head.

"She's huge." Terri spread her hands in illustration. "Amber despised Stan. She used to leave candy bar wrappers and empty potato chip bags around the house for him to see. And now that she's grown, she's started a magazine called *Flab Power!* They even had a story showing a lot of fat, naked butts, including Amber's. I thought it was kind of funny, but Stan was not amused."

I needed to get a copy of that magazine and talk to the daughter. "Did he get along any better with his son?" From what I remembered of the televised memorial service, the boy looked sullen, but thin enough.

Terri rolled her eyes. "Stan practically croaked when Stan Jr.—he calls himself SJ now—came out of the closet. Stan thinks of himself as this big macho man, and here his only son is marching, in drag, in a gay rights parade."

Maybe, on the other hand, Stan was done in by killer stress. "It sounds as if there was a lot of aggravation in his life."

A muscle at the corner of Terri's mouth twitched. "Stan used to say that he caused aggravation, he didn't experience it." Before I had time to follow up on that comment, she glanced at her watch. "I'm sorry, but I need to get moving. I'm teaching an exercise class in half an hour."

She was going to exercise after a meal like that? "Well, thanks very much for your time. Do you think his ex-wife and kids will let me interview them?"

Terri stood up. "Maybe. I don't know about Jane or SJ, but Amber would be delighted to have the publicity for her magazine. Maybe she'll even give you a photo of her butt— not a pretty sight."

I grinned. "I'll definitely talk to Amber," I said, standing up too.

Terri's eyes ran assessingly over my body. "I meant to tell you I have a great free-weights and aerobic class especially for women over forty. Come in for a free session. You can write about it in the article. I promise, if you stay with the program, you'll be thrilled by the results. Those upper arms will firm up, you'll have a waist again, and we'll even improve those abs."

"Uh, I'll get back to you on that. Thanks very much for the interview." I smiled weakly and, grabbing my tape recorder and purse, headed for the door.

The ringing of the phone jarred me from a deep sleep. "You weren't asleep, were you?" Paul O'Neal's deep voice asked accusingly, as if it were aberrant behavior to be sleeping at ten-thirty on a weeknight.

"Yes. What do you want?"

"I want to know what you've done so far on the Harris story."

I turned on the bedside light and propped the pillows be-

33

hind my back. "You always phone your writers in the middle of the night to chat about their stories?"

"I'm sorry. I didn't realize what time it was. But for the record, I seldom chat with my writers at all. Consider yourself blessed."

I was too out of it to think of any appropriately caustic retort, so instead I told him about my interview that morning with Terri.

He listened to what I had to say, only occasionally tossing in a question. When I was finished, he said, "It sounds as if Mr. Harris was not exactly cherished by his family. Have you arranged to interview the ex-wife and kids?"

"Not yet." What was this guy's problem? I'd just got the assignment a day ago, and the story wasn't due for three weeks.

"Well, get on it," he snapped. "I need the story for the next issue—five thousand words. Give it to me by the end of next week."

That woke me up. "Impossible! You said three weeks and thirty-five hundred words."

"Nothing is impossible if you set your mind to it. Part of being a professional journalist is being able to meet tight deadlines."

It was a cheap shot. "Why is this story suddenly so important to you?" I asked, awake enough now to be suspicious.

"I talked tonight to a friend from the coroner's office. He told me the autopsy of Stan Harris indicated that he may not have died of natural causes. He apparently had a huge amount of potassium in his system."

"Potassium? You mean he accidentally took too many potassium supplements?"

"Maybe. I know these body builders often take massive amounts of all kinds of supplements, but Harris took one hell of a lot of potassium. There's also a possibility that he wanted his death to look like a heart attack rather than suicide. From what I heard, his business was going downhill fast. He was on the verge of bankruptcy."

Which might explain why Terri had seemed so reluctant to discuss the business. Suddenly the repercussions of what O'Neal was telling me hit me like a sucker punch. "Wait a minute. You're saying that you want me to figure out how Stan died and then write five thousand words about it—all in one week?"

"You don't have to worry about what killed him. I'll write a sidebar on the autopsy results, the medical angle. I just want you to focus on what the guy was like, an in-depth personality piece, as well as whatever you can find out about why his business was going down the tubes."

"In one week?" I repeated.

"Well, maybe I could give you ten days," he said magnanimously.

I sat up straighter in my bed. "Not for ten cents a word."

"What?"

I hit the volume button on my phone. "You are changing the terms of our agreement—moving up the deadline and increasing the length of the story. I want more money: thirty cents a word."

"Twenty cents," O'Neal said, sounding extremely annoyed. "And it better be a damned good story."

"Oh, it will be." I mentally calculated the bills I could pay with a thousand dollars.

"I want a daily report on what you're getting," O'Neal growled.

Twenty cents a word! "Well, I guess then we'll be talking tomorrow. Lovely chatting with you."

He hung up on me.

I smiled. It took about ninety seconds for my sense of victory to be replaced by a stab of anxiety. How the hell was I going to pull this off?

Four

"How would you like it," Amber Harris asked in her gravelly voice, "if your father called you Fat Ass?"

"That's horrible," I said to the young woman with angry brown eyes and a round face that looked startlingly like her late father's. "What did your mother say when he called you that?"

"She told him to cut it out; he was hurting my self-esteem. Then he said my self-esteem would be a lot higher if I wasn't so damned fat. Eventually she told him she wanted a divorce. They were fighting all the time—about a lot of things, not just my weight—and she couldn't take it anymore."

"So how old you were you when they got divorced?"

"Twelve." She grimaced. "A great age to have your father tell you how unattractive you are."

I nodded. Twelve was a bad age for almost every girl, even if she was average weight and her father repeatedly told her that she was the spitting image of Julia Roberts. "Did you see him much after that—after your parents were divorced?"

Amber shook her head. "SJ and I were supposed to spend every other weekend with him. We did that for a while, but it was really awful. Dad's idea of a great time was to take us hiking or on long bicycle trips, even though he knew that my brother and I hated that outdoor stuff. It was as if he couldn't give up on making us over into the kind of kids he wanted us to be: athletic, great-looking, popular—a cheerleader and star football player instead of a fat, shy bookworm and an uncoordinated opera-lover whose only interest in football players had nothing to do with team sports."

"Was he any more tolerant of your brother than he was of you?"

She shook her head, causing her straight, shoulder-length brown hair to swing across her face. "He was probably even less tolerant. Dad at least believed that my flaws were merely cosmetic. Sometimes he tried to be nice to me, telling me how bad he'd felt when he was a fat kid, how mean the kids were to him. But SJ was different, not like Dad at all. When SJ came home from college announcing that he'd decided to become a nurse, and, oh, yes, he was in love with another man, Dad went ballistic. He saw SJ's sexual preferences as a reflection on him. What if it got out that Mr. Macho Man was the father of—in Dad's immortal words—'a pathetic fag'?"

A father whose overweight, unathletic children chose not to be transformed into his new-and-improved image. I glanced around Amber's neat, sparsely furnished apartment. Her dining room had been converted into an office for her magazine. The walls held framed copies of eight covers of *Flab Power!* A large metal desk was covered with photos and papers. Next to it were file cabinets and a table holding an impressive amount of computer equipment.

The question I most wanted to ask this smart, furious young woman was "What do you think your life would be like now if your father had accepted you the way you were?" But somehow I couldn't. The assumption that her work, her passion, was merely an attempt to thumb her nose at her father was undoubtedly too simplistic and also very insulting to Amber. "So how did your father react to your magazine?" I asked instead.

"At first it didn't bother him. He wrote me a patronizing little note about my finally using both my English and computer degrees—I was a double major. It was clear that he expected no one to read it. But when we did the photo spread of bare butts in the second issue, and more people actually bought copies, then he suddenly was offended. I'm getting these wonderful e-mails from people saying, 'This publication speaks to me! Finally someone gets what it's like to be obese in a weight-obsessed society,' and my father is saying, 'Amber, you are embarrassing me and embarrassing yourself.' "

As she recalled the conversation, red blotches spread across Amber's cheeks. "I said to him, 'Gee, Dad, you don't think you might have embarrassed me when you called me Fat Ass or embarrassed SJ when you called him a fag?'

"He started sputtering something about how he'd been only trying to help us, to motivate us to change so that we'd have happier lives. He didn't seem all that happy to me— torturing himself to keep from getting fat. It was eminent justice that he jogged himself into a heart attack."

I opened my mouth to mention the autopsy results, then closed it. I had a strong suspicion that Amber Harris did not much care how her father had died. She only cared that he was dead.

Glancing at her watch, Amber stood up. She was a tall, big-boned and very overweight woman, dressed in loose black pants and an oversized black shirt. "I'm sorry, I have to leave now. But I wanted to give you these back issues of *Flab Power!* before you go."

I opened the manila folder she handed me. On the cover

of the top issue was a large photo of a grinning Amber, wearing a polka-dotted bikini and holding a huge beach ball inscribed with the words, "FLAB POWER!". "Thanks. I'd like to read them."

I shook the hand Amber extended. "I wish I didn't have to cut this short," she said, "but I have another interview with *Living Large Magazine* in half an hour. If you have any more questions, feel free to call me."

So her father's death was netting her the media attention I sensed she'd been wanting for a long time. Maybe "Fat Ass" was going to get her revenge on Stan after all.

I thought about my own daughters and their father as I drove home. In contrast to Stan Harris, I supposed, Rob was not a bad father—a bit distant, perhaps, but affectionate enough when Katie and Emily were little girls and not too exasperated when they became teenagers. Basically Rob had viewed his role as supplier-of-the-cash, while mine was nurturer and hands-on parent, a division of labor which, in hindsight, cheated all four of us. If, for instance, I had been more career-minded or less convinced that my children's well being required my constant availability, I would probably not be lying awake now wondering how I was going to pay my bills. And if I hadn't fashioned myself as Supermom—a woman with no burning needs or problems of her own—I might also have some idea on how to break the news to my daughters that Daddy was now out of the picture and Mommy was feeling more like a helpless, over-the-hill victim than she cared to admit.

I took a deep breath. But this—like seeing the divorce attorney, locating my weasel of a husband, and applying for a bank loan to carry me through the next months—was something I was going to deal with later, after I'd finished this article. "Stay focused on the story," I kept reminding myself, trying not to think about how desperately I wanted—needed—this story to lead to a real, full-time, bill-paying job at the magazine.

At home I heated a can of tomato soup. Since Rob had left I'd basically given up on real cooking, instead making myself sandwiches, eggs, or something from a can when I was hungry. I was surprised how much I enjoyed not cooking. In fleeting non-panicky moments, I found the idea of rewriting my life to suit only me an exhilarating proposition: What would Lauren like to do? (If Lauren did not become bankrupt, destitute, and homeless before she could work out the details.)

As I ate my lunch I thought over my interviews. Stan's widow and his daughter had both portrayed him as a fitness-obsessed control freak. It could be an interesting angle for my article—the insecure man inside the buff physique—but I needed to talk to more people to make sure it was an accurate one. Amber had said that her brother was off work today, though she wasn't sure if he'd talk to me. Putting my dirty dishes in the dishwasher, I decided to find out.

Stan Junior answered his phone at the sixth ring, sounding groggy. He listened silently while I explained who I was.

"I don't have anything to say about my father," he said, an edge in his voice.

"I just got through interviewing your sister," I said in my coaxing-recalcitrant-children tone.

"Amber has her own agenda. Unlike her, I don't find it therapeutic to spill my guts in public."

Quickly, before he had a chance to hang up, I said, "I certainly don't want to delve into anything that makes you uncomfortable. But I was hoping that you, as a health professional, might give me your take on your father's physical condition before he died. For instance, had you assumed that he was in good health?"

I was almost certain he was going to brush me off, but instead he said, "Dad prided himself on being healthy, but in fact a lot of things he did—starving himself, exercising excessively, taking massive doses of vitamins and supplements—were actually detrimental to his health."

I scribbled furiously in my notebook. "What kind of supplements was he taking?"

"All kinds. Some of the stuff he'd take, like vitamins, were fine in normal doses, but Dad had to overdo those too, just like he did with exercise."

I could sense that SJ was about to end the conversation. "And he must have been under a lot of stress too, with those business reversals." It was a shot in the dark, but at this point I didn't have much to lose.

"Yeah, he was devastated that his precious exercise empire was going down the tubes. That damn gym was his whole life." SJ did not sound at all unhappy about his father's pain.

"Do you know what kind of problems he was having with the business?"

SJ snorted. "The problem was that people didn't want to exercise any more with an old coot like him. They wanted someone sexy, with-it, young. Dad just didn't seem to grasp that his old clientele had moved on to trendier gyms; he was so yesterday. But instead of accepting that and maybe starting some other business, he just kept coming up with these pathetic ideas for getting publicity."

"Like what?"

"Like finding another fat chick to transform: *Pygmalion, Part III*. Terri was not thrilled with that idea, not with

Dad's history of personal involvement with his makeover projects. But he didn't seem to care how Terri felt about it. He told me that he'd started writing another *Before and After*-type book, with someone else in the Terri role."

"Did he say who this new woman was?"

SJ gave a malicious laugh. "Oh, am I bad! I've already told you way too much."

Before I could ask him anything else he said, "Nice gossiping with you," and hung up.

I spent the rest of the afternoon transcribing my interviews. By the end of the day I was tired and in no mood to report to my snide editor. Instead of phoning, I decided to e-mail O'Neal; he'd get the information he wanted and I could avoid some unwanted sarcasm.

As I logged onto AOL, I thought how lucky it was that Rob had never learned to use a computer—the only reason, I was sure, he'd left our Macintosh behind. I smiled when I saw my younger daughter, Emily, had e-mailed. After sending O'Neal a brief description of my interviews, I opened Em's message:

Hey, Parents, What's going on? I got a strange, cryptic note from Dad and a check for ten thousand dollars. Does this mean you're disinheriting me and never want to hear from me again? Hope not, since I was planning on coming home soon to do my laundry. Love Ya Anyway, Your Smart Daughter.

So much for my dilemma about when to break the divorce news. Not entirely sure what I was going to say to Em, I picked up the phone.

Fortunately, she was in her dorm room. "Hi, sweetie, I just read your e-mail."

"What's the deal with Dad?" she asked. "I couldn't believe he sent me all that money."

The money he'd just taken from our joint checking account, I was willing to bet. But Em didn't need to know that. I took a deep breath. "Your father and I are getting a divorce. He moved out, closed his office, and from what I gather, left town."

"Jeez!"

It was the expression she'd used as a young girl, when she was stunned or hurt—one I hadn't heard her use in years. More than the news I had to tell her, that "Jeez!" made me feel suddenly teary. "I'm sorry, Em," I said, swiping at my cheeks with the back of my hand. "I know what a shock this must be to you."

"Where is he?" she asked after a minute. "Where did he move to?"

"I don't know. No one else seems to know either. Where was the postmark on his letter from?"

"Hold on." She returned to the phone a minute later. "I'm really sorry, Mom. I must have thrown it away. It was a cashier's check, by the way. But that doesn't help you figure out where he is, does it?" Em sounded as if she were crying.

"Don't worry about it, sweetie. It's not that important." I knew she wasn't crying about throwing away the envelope, but I wanted her to know that this—none of it—was her fault.

"But it is important," she said. "Dad left us, and we don't know where he's gone."

"No," I said firmly. "He left me, not *us*. His sending you the check and note was his way of telling you that he hasn't forgotten you."

"Are you sure it wasn't his way of paying me off?" Em

44

said angrily. "The final check before he departs from my life forever?"

A few weeks ago I would have insisted, with great confidence, that Rob would never write off either of his daughters—especially with no explanation and only a farewell check. But right now I didn't have a clue what he'd do or not do. Had I really known the man I'd lived with for over half my life? "I don't know, honey. I honestly don't know."

"It's just like Dad to think that money will solve everything. He sends me a big check and then I'm supposed to be okay with him walking out. Money was always the most important thing to him. That was all he really cared about."

How had she known that when I hadn't? I realized that what Em was saying was colored by her feelings of hurt and betrayal, but she was also relaying a hard-eyed, realistic appraisal of her father. I had certainly recognized that my husband was both frugal and extremely interested in making money, but I always told myself that this was proof of his strong desire to take care of his family. It wasn't until he pilfered every dollar in our joint accounts that I realized what Em seemed to have known all along: It was only the money that mattered to Rob.

"I'm sorry you had to hear it this way, Em. Is everything okay at school?"

"Fine." Which was more or less what she always said. When Katie, our older daughter, had been in college we'd heard about every minor crisis, every bump in her life. "The Drama Queen," Em called her older sister, with some justification. Emily ("The Brainiac," her doting sister called her) was just the opposite. Although she regularly e-mailed us, she seldom mentioned how she was feeling. I'd often worried that something might be going terribly wrong in my close-mouthed younger daughter's life and I wouldn't even know about it.

"I'm going to come home next weekend," she said.

"Great! I'd love to see you."

"And I'll find Dad."

"That would be helpful." I didn't have the heart to tell her that reading a couple of mystery novels a week did not qualify her as a bona fide amateur detective. "Bye, honey. I love you."

"Love you too. And Mom, what Dad did really sucks."

"Yes," I said, "it does."

I had just hung up the phone when it rang. O'Neal wanting to ask follow-up questions? Meg wanting to mother-hen me with free dinners and well-meaning but annoying advice? "Hello?" I answered warily.

"I want to speak to Dr. Prescott," a deep, unfamiliar male voice said.

"Dr. Prescott no longer lives here."

A pause. "This is important. It's business. How can I reach him?"

"I have no idea. But if you need dental work, I suggest you call Dr. Bob Dwyer. His number is in the book."

"I don't need dental work. I need to talk to Dr. Prescott. Immediately." Not exactly friendly to start out with, the man had turned actively surly.

"That makes two of us," I said. "I have no idea where he is."

"Listen, lady . . ."

I hung up. I bet the guy was some kind of bill collector. Probably Rob had given him the same "the check is in the mail" story he'd used on his former employees.

The phone rang again, but I ignored it. The caller didn't bother to leave a message on my answering machine.

I told myself that I was imagining the threat in the man's voice, that all the stress in my life was making me paranoid. It was time to take a well-earned break with a long soak in a hot bubble bath reading a nice trashy novel and sipping a glass of wine. I poured myself a glass of white Zinfandel to take upstairs, then gulped half of it and refilled the glass. Before I headed for the bathtub, I made sure that every door and window in the house was locked.

Five

Jane Harris was not what I expected. After my encounters with Stan's svelte, perky wife and his zaftig-and-proud-of-it, angry daughter, this woman looked like she could be the poster girl for average—neither fat nor thin, vivacious nor sullen. More than anything else, she looked tired. "I'm a nurse," she explained, "just finished a twelve-hour shift. Don't count on this being a long interview; I need some sleep."

She poured me a cup of coffee and we sat down at her kitchen table. "I really don't have much to tell you about Stan," she said. "We've been divorced for eleven years, and once the kids were grown, we didn't have much contact. Recently, though, he started phoning me just to talk."

"So you were friendly?"

Jane considered the question. "I guess you could say that. We were over being mad at each other, and we had a lot of shared memories—some of them good."

I hesitated. I liked this down-to-earth woman and felt awkward about violating her privacy. But that was what journalists did, wasn't it? Particularly journalists who wanted to make their mortgage payments. "In your ex-husband's book and in interviews he presented himself as a sort of Henry Higgins of fitness, a man who transformed obese people's lives. Didn't you meet him when you sought his help to lose weight?"

She nodded. "Yes, I was in his exercise class and I did lose quite a bit of weight, about thirty pounds. But it wasn't until years later, after he married Terri and got into big-time self-promotion, that Stan ever mentioned transforming me into a happy, thin person. That's all bullshit and I told him so. For one thing, I never had a major weight problem until I was twenty-two and broke-up with my boyfriend; all of a sudden I was eating everything in sight and of course I blimped up. Eventually I would have lost the weight, with or without Stan.

"But what I really hated was the way he equated being fat with being miserable. That just isn't true. Stan was miserable whether he was fat or thin. Amber, who certainly is overweight, isn't miserable at all. It would probably be better for her health if she lost weight, but I don't think being thinner would make her any happier. Unlike her father, she doesn't suffer from depression."

"Stan had serious depression?"

Jane nodded. "Clinical depression. He had bouts of it all his life."

"Was he especially depressed around the time he died?"

"The last time I talked to him he sounded very down about maybe having to lay off people at the gym. That was about a week before his death. He phoned one night just to see how the kids and I were doing, he said. It bothered him that he didn't have much of a relationship with either of them. But you already know that, don't you?" she asked, her eyes suddenly probing into mine. "You talked to them about their love-hate relationship with their father."

She made it sound like an accusation, as if I'd tricked them into revealing their feelings about their dad. I started to say that I hadn't heard much about the love part of their relationship with Stan, but then stopped myself. She probably just didn't want her family problems aired in *City Magazine*, and who could blame her? "They were both nice, bright, articulate kids," I said instead.

I could see the muscles in her face relax, her eyes soften. "Yeah, they're good kids."

"SJ mentioned that his father took a lot of vitamin supplements which could have been harmful," I said, hoping her ex-husband's health was a less touchy topic.

Apparently so. Jane nodded. "I know what you're getting at: all the potassium in his body. I heard about the autopsy report too. If you're asking if he was taking a lot of potassium supplements, I don't know. He might have taken them to balance the water loss from the diuretics he was always using."

"Could he have accidentally taken too much potassium?"

"I guess it's possible. An overdose of potassium can weaken the heart, cause an abnormal heart rhythm, and bring on cardiac arrest. Considering that Stan had a family history of heart problems, he might have been more susceptible to the effects." She yawned. "Listen, I'm sorry, but I really need to get some sleep. Maybe you should talk to Stan's physician, Elizabeth Stevens, about this."

"Ask Dr. Elizabeth?" I said, remembering now that I'd seen the physician/newspaper columnist give the eulogy at Stan's funeral.

"The very same," Jane said, standing up. "She may not tell you much, but she is always more than happy to talk to the press. Maybe that's why she and Stan were such good buddies."

I wondered as we walked to the door if Jane Harris had really gotten along as well with her ex-husband as she claimed. Was it just coincidence that she knew so much about the effects of potassium overdoses? And why had she seemed so nervous when she talked about my interviews with her children? Certainly it was possible that she was just a protective mother. Or maybe some sense of lingering loyalty to Stan made her reluctant to let the world know what a lousy father he'd been. But what if she was afraid of something else—some potentially damaging information her children might have let slip?

I sighed, making a mental list of all the people I still needed to interview. Probably I should talk to Dr. Elizabeth about Stan's health. Then I needed to find out more about Stan's alleged business problems. Maybe if I showed up at the gym someone might talk to me. Terri Harris had said I should come over to see their facilities—and get my free exercise session. The very thought of that made me shudder. To regain my equilibrium and feed my growling stomach, I pulled into a Jack in the Box and ordered a cheeseburger, fries, and large chocolate shake with some of the money that Meg had generously lent me. The meal made me feel better, though no more eager to get back to work on the story. Part of my problem was that I suddenly wanted to stop investigating Stan Harris's life and start investigating my own. With Em, the amateur-sleuth-in-training, coming home in a few days, I needed to get some of my own questions about Rob's disappearance answered. I had a sinking feeling that the longer I postponed dealing with this, the farther away Rob was getting—the trail, so to speak, was rapidly growing cold.

I'd intended to check again with his former employees and his mother's nursing home to see if any of them had heard from him. Rob's longtime receptionist, Iris—the loyal employee he fired to replace with the Marilyn Monroe imitator—lived near here in a big house she'd inherited when her mother died. Maybe I'd go visit her. I'd always liked Iris, a kind, dutiful woman who spent years nursing her sick mother. Rob always said that Iris mothered everyone in the office, so there was a good chance she'd stayed in touch with her old co-workers.

When I phoned, Iris invited me over for a cup of tea. I was at her doorstep before the tea had finished steeping.

A tall, thin woman with the perfect posture of a former ballet student, Iris showed me into an immaculate living room filled with expensive-looking English antiques. I sat down with the delicate china teacup she handed me, suddenly wondering what to say. "I was just in the area and thought I'd stop in to see how you were doing," I began lamely.

"That was sweet of you," Iris said. "Have you heard anything from Dr. P?"

I loved a woman who cut to the chase. "Unfortunately, no. Do you know anybody who has?"

"No." She hesitated. "I did talk to Marla a few days ago, and she said she still hadn't received her last paycheck."

Why didn't that surprise me? "Listen, Iris, I meant to call you earlier. I had no idea that Rob had"—I searched for the right words—"let you go until I talked to that rude new receptionist the day before they closed the office. I'm really sorry. If it makes you feel any better, Rob dumped me too."

Her eyes widened. "But you've been married forever."

I smiled grimly. Sometimes it had felt like that to me too. "Twenty-seven years."

My confession seemed to unleash a flood of words in Iris. "He told me that he didn't think I was a good fit for the office anymore. After ten years! Then he brought in this gum-chewing twenty-year-old kid. Apparently she was a better fit for the office."

"That's the only explanation he gave you?"

"Oh, I knew why he was getting rid of me. I'd been complaining about his new patients—how coarse and vulgar they were. But Dr. P. just said I'd better get used to them. With so many of his old patients moving out to the suburbs or going to these cut-rate dental clinics, he had to find new clients somewhere, he said."

"Who were these new patients?" I had heard Rob complain about his old patients leaving, but I didn't know anything about his new ones. When I asked about his practice, Rob had just said everything was fine and then steered the conversation to another subject.

"They looked and acted like thugs. But when I said that to Dr. P, he told me he was going to have to let me go. After all our years working together, he just hands me a month's salary, and says I don't fit in anymore!" She took a deep breath, trying to blink away the tears in her eyes.

I leaned forward to pat her bony hand. "I think that's what he decided about me too. I was no longer the kind of wife he wanted."

A series of expressions crossed Iris's thin face. Shock changed to recognition, then uncertainty.

"You know something," I said. Iris had the kind of face that couldn't conceal a lie even if she'd wanted to. "He was having an affair, wasn't he? I bet with that twenty-year-old receptionist."

"Kimberly?" She looked shocked. "Oh, no, not with her."

"With who then?"

Iris's expression changed to miserable. "Oh, Mrs. P, I don't know anything for sure. I don't want to damage anyone's reputation."

I took a deep breath. "Iris, my husband walked out on me, taking our money and disappearing without a trace. Nothing you tell me could damage his reputation any further. If you have any idea at all where he's gone or why, please tell me. I need to understand what's happened."

She hesitated then said, "It's Carol. They were always off whispering together. And whenever I came near them they stopped talking."

Carol Quaid, the frumpy, no-nonsense office manager who Rob had always called a "shrill, woman's-libber"? Granted, Carol was smart and hard-working and had just earned her MBA at night school, but she was also sour-tempered and humorless—not at all the woman I would have envisioned Rob having an affair with. "Carol Quaid? Are you sure?"

"No! I'm not sure!" Iris shook her head for emphasis, making her mousy brown hair cover her face. "I never used to think that Dr. P. even liked Carol. She was so bossy and abrasive. But all of a sudden they started spending a lot of time together, going out for lunch, kind of sneaking out so no one would notice. Of course I don't know what they were doing together . . ."

But she had a pretty good idea, if the blush crossing her face was any indication. "Would you mind, Iris, if I used your phone book?"

When she brought it to me, I looked up an address. "I think I'm going to make a call on Ms. Quaid on the way home." I stood up. "Thanks for the tea."

I drove to Carol Quaid's townhouse, wishing I had a gun. I wouldn't actually shoot the bitch, but I certainly would enjoy scaring her. Was it possible that Rob was living there with her, the two lovebirds holing up together, spending our money and enjoying my grandmother's silver tea service?

Rob's Mercedes was not parked in the parking spaces

behind her townhouse, but that probably wasn't significant. Although a scumbag, Rob was not dumb. He'd realize that people—me, for instance—would come looking for him and wouldn't want to make the search easy. I had no idea what kind of car Carol drove, so I wasn't sure if one of the three parked cars was hers. I certainly hoped so.

Trying very hard to look pleasant (I wanted the woman to open the door after all), I rang her doorbell. No one answered. For good measure, I knocked loudly on her door. Nothing.

A woman carrying a bag of groceries into the next-door townhouse called to me, "Oh, she's moved out."

"Carol Quaid?"

"Yeah. Moved out a few days ago."

"Do you know where she went?" I called to the woman, who was now unlocking her door.

"No idea. We weren't especially friendly. But from what I heard, she didn't even leave a forwarding address."

"Thanks." I hurried to the car before the waves of nausea overtook me.

Six

"You didn't call me," my editor accused, sounding very much like a petulant teenager.

My whole life was falling apart before my eyes. I'd just learned that my husband very likely had been having an affair with his dowdy, middle-aged business manager, I hadn't even begun to write the article that was due in three days, and Paul O'Neal was concerned that I'd forgotten to check in with him? "I e-mailed you," I pointed out, turning on the lamp next to my bed to check the time. Eleven-thirty! Was the man an insomniac? Or, like a vampire, did he only come out at night to prey on his victims?

"You didn't answer the e-mail I sent you."

Gee, maybe I had something else to do besides check my e-mails every hour. I wanted to slam the phone in his ear, turn off the light, and go back to a very satisfying dream in which Rob begged me to take him back. "Rest easy," I said instead, "I'm still working on the article."

"How are the interviews going?"

"Fine." I wondered if he checked up on all his writers like this or just the ones he thought incompetent. "Stan's wife said he had a history of depression and seemed down when she talked to him the week before he died."

"Interesting. Did anyone else corroborate that?"

"Maybe his doctor will when I talk to her tomorrow."

"See what she says about the potassium angle too—had she prescribed supplements or some other kind of medication that could have affected his potassium level? Oh, by the way, the coroner is supposed to issue his report tomorrow."

I yawned.

"Am I keeping you awake?" he inquired nastily.

"As a matter of fact, yes."

"Sorry, I always assume everyone is a night owl like me. Though maybe you should have a checkup. Women your age usually don't need that much sleep."

This time I did hang up on him. Women my age, indeed!

I woke up the next morning feeling edgy and out of sorts. The deadline for my article loomed, I still hadn't finished my interviewing, and all the phone calls yesterday to locate either my missing husband or Carol Quaid, his business manager and possible mistress, had uncovered nothing. Various staff members at my mother-in-law's nursing home assured me that Rob had not visited his mother or been in contact with the home. None of Carol's co-workers seemed to know—or care much—where she'd gone. Iris, at least, had known Carol's mother's name and address, but when I phoned Mrs. Quaid, no one answered.

I took a life-restoring sip of coffee, then punched in Mrs. Quaid's number. She answered on the first ring, a sharp-voiced woman who sounded impatient.

I swallowed a mouthful of coffee. "Mrs. Quaid, this is Lauren Prescott; your daughter Carol worked in my husband's dental office. I'm wondering if you know how I can contact Carol?"

A pause. "Why would you want to do that?"

A good, if not very polite, question. I had intended to say something evasive about needing to ask Carol about closing Rob's office, but somehow I knew this cranky woman was not likely to be helpful. "I have a check I need to give to her," I lied, hoping that Mrs. Quaid was unaware that Rob at this point was about as likely to hand me employee paychecks as hell was to freeze over.

Fortunately the mention of money seemed to pique Mrs. Quaid's interest. "Well, you could send the paycheck to my address, and I'll see that Carol gets it. She just moved and the post office is sending her mail to my house."

"Oh, dear, I wish it could be that easy." I hoped I wasn't laying it on too thick, but acting—or lying, for that matter—was not one of my talents. "Unfortunately, I have a document—a certified legal paper—that Carol has to sign in my presence before I can give her the check."

"Well, I never heard of such a thing."

Me neither. "I know exactly what you mean. These ridiculous regulations make everything so complicated for everyone except those greedy lawyers."

"You can say that again. Attorneys are ruining this country with all those asinine lawsuits. Like that woman who sued McDonald's when she spilled hot coffee on herself. Now I ask you, does that make sense?"

I suspected that I'd unwittingly launched a long-winded tangent. "I couldn't agree more," I interjected. "And to think poor Carol has to suffer because of them."

"Carol suffer? How?"

Talking fast so she wouldn't notice the gaping holes in my story, I said, "I just meant it isn't fair that Carol has to come all the way back here to sign the documents in my presence if she wants to get the check. Either forego a significant amount of money or travel thousands of miles just to sign a stupid paper—what a choice."

"Oh, she's not thousands of miles from here. It's just that I don't know when she's coming back. How big is this check, did you say?"

I grasped for a number. "Seven thousand forty-two dollars," I said, hoping that Mrs. Quaid viewed this as big money.

58

Apparently she did. "Well, I'll be sure to mention it next time I hear from Carol. Tell me your phone number so she can call you."

I took a deep breath. "The problem is that I'm going to be leaving town next week and I'll be gone for a month. I was hoping to tie up all these loose ends before I leave. Maybe I should call Carol myself to arrange a meeting."

"There's no phone at the cabin. I told Carol she needs to get a cell phone, but she's such a cheapskate she'd rather drive into town to use a pay phone. She says it's restful not to hear phones ringing all the time. I told her it would be restful for me to be able to contact my own daughter when I needed to."

"That is irritating," I agreed. "My daughters are like that too. I'm not supposed to call and interfere in their lives, but the minute one of them needs something, she sure is fast to phone me to ask for help." As long as I was stretching the truth, might as well give it a big yank.

"Isn't that the truth?" Mrs. Quaid agreed. "Just the other day I told Carol—"

Lord, I'd opened the floodgates. "Oh, dear," I practically shouted into the phone, "I just noticed the time. I'm already late for my doctor's appointment. It's been great talking to you, but I'll have to let you go."

"What about Carol's money?" asked Mrs. Quaid, bless her greedy little heart.

I pretended to consider the question. "Well, you know I do need to get all these business details taken care of. Where is this cabin? If it's not too far, maybe I can go there and drop off the check."

"I guess you could drive up there," Mrs. Quaid said uncertainly. "It's only one hundred twenty miles up north, and I don't think Carol was planning on coming back any time soon."

I grabbed a pen and jotted down directions to a stone cabin on the north end of Lake Arrowfoot.

"I hope Carol doesn't get mad at me for giving you her address. She's so anti-social sometimes. Said she needed to retreat from the world for a while."

"I'll be in and out in a few minutes," I assured her. As I hung up, I wondered if I'd find my missing husband retreating from the world with Mrs. Quaid's anti-social daughter.

I would have loved to jump in the car right then. Even if Iris had been wrong about Carol and Rob having an affair, I had a strong hunch Carol knew a lot more than I did about my husband's recent activities. Unfortunately, though, I had an interview in an hour with Stan's doctor. Hoping that Mrs. Quaid was telling the truth about having no way to phone Carol with the news of my arrival, I grimly made a list of questions for Dr. Elizabeth. As soon as I finished with her, I'd take a little drive up north.

Dr. Elizabeth Stevens was a tall, big-boned, immaculately groomed woman with extremely white teeth. With her blonde helmet of hair, artful makeup, and a loud, take-charge aura of confidence, she looked like someone who might have once been president of a University of Texas sorority. She ushered me into a large office. At one end stood a huge desk and impressive-looking computer equipment, while the other end held a dark leather couch, glass coffee table, and two matching leather chairs. We sat opposite each other, me on the sofa with my tape recorder on the table. Before we got started I admired the turquoise and mauve abstract oil painting on her wall.

"Thanks." She flashed her white teeth at me. "I got it last year on a trip to Santa Fe. But I know you want to talk to me about Stan."

I nodded, clicking on the tape recorder. "He was a patient of yours?"

"He started out that way. Before I had my newspaper column and the books, I was a family practitioner, but I haven't seen patients for years. Stan was a friend and a collaborator. After I took one of his exercise classes, I asked him to write the exercise chapter in *Dr. Elizabeth's Guide to Health*. Stan was very passionate about getting fit, very inspirational."

"Did he inspire you?"

She raised an overly plucked eyebrow.

"To get fit, I mean."

"Oh, yes, of course. Unfortunately, I don't exercise as much as Stan thought I should; I don't have the time. Though, when I told Stan that, he said that he always managed to find the time, even if it meant jogging at five a.m."

"You didn't think, as a physician, that his rigid adherence to so much exercising might be obsessive, even harmful?"

"He did sometimes seem a bit fanatical. But it was extremely important for Stan's self-esteem that he stay fit."

"And might not that obsession have killed him?"

"If you mean that he was jogging when he died, I guess you might interpret it that way. But it's equally probable that Stan's years of exercise actually prolonged his life. His father, after all, had a fatal coronary when he was only forty, and Stan was over fifty when he died. Until the autopsy results are announced, it's probably premature to say anything about the cause of death."

"I heard he had a large amount of potassium in his

system. Could that have killed him?"

Dr. Elizabeth's eyes narrowed. "Who told you that?"

"Oh, I think someone who worked at the morgue mentioned it. Do you know if Stan was taking potassium supplements?"

She shrugged. "I don't really know. Stan and I had a basic philosophical disagreement about vitamin and mineral supplements. I used to tell him that one could get too much of a good thing, but he just thought I was a typical overly cautious physician."

"Can you think of any medical reason he might have had so much potassium in his body?"

"Well, potassium supplements are sometimes recommended for heart or hypertensive patients or for people who take diuretics, which can deplete the body's supply of potassium."

"Several people mentioned that Stan often took diuretics." When she didn't say anything, I added, "And he did have heart problems, right?"

"He had a family history of heart disease, but I wasn't aware he ever had any symptoms. But, as I said, I hadn't been his personal physician for years."

"Do you know who was his doctor?"

"Mark Thayer, I believe, a fine internist."

I tried another tack. "His ex-wife mentioned that Stan suffered from chronic depression. Do you know if he was being treated for that?"

Dr. Elizabeth looked surprised. "He never seemed depressed to me, not clinically depressed."

I wondered if Jane Harris had exaggerated her ex-husband's moodiness because of their difficult marital history. It was also possible that Dr. Elizabeth hadn't known her dear friend as well as she thought.

I glanced at my watch. "Is there anything else you'd like to tell me about Stan?"

Dr. Elizabeth smiled. "Only that he was a terrific guy and a loyal friend. So upbeat and inspirational, a real proselytizer for the benefits of exercise."

Even if he did die while jogging. I clicked off my tape recorder. "Thanks for the interview."

"It was my pleasure. You will send me a copy of the article when it comes out, won't you?"

"Of course." Not that she'd said much that I wanted to quote. At least Jane Harris had been on the mark when she'd cited Dr. Elizabeth's love of publicity.

Grabbing my purse and tape recorder, I hurried out the door. I hoped my next interview subject was more forthcoming. And if Carol Quaid was equally tight-lipped? Well, I'd just have to find a way to make her talk.

I decided to stop at the house to throw a few things into an overnight bag before I headed out to Carol's cabin. I was turning onto my street when I spotted two familiar cars—a VW bug and a vintage BMW—parked in my driveway.

I ran into the house. "Em! Katie! What a wonderful surprise!"

They were sitting at the kitchen table, Emily sipping a cup of herbal tea, Katie drinking a Diet Coke. Em jumped up and gave me a hug. "I'm sorry," she whispered into my ear. "I didn't know you hadn't told Katie about Dad."

Oh, God. I glanced over at my older, prettier, sulkier daughter—the Drama Queen—who sat glaring at me. How could I tell her that I'd had so much on my plate that I'd simply forgotten to tell her about Rob? The last time we'd talked—about two weeks ago—her father had still been in residence. "Sweetie, it's so nice to see you!" I walked over to plant a kiss on the top of her head.

"And when were you planning on telling me about Dad?" she asked, her voice quivering.

A month ago I might have been moved by her distress— back in the days when I tiptoed around Katie's moods like a soldier navigating a minefield. But today I had too many other problems to deal with. "I would have told you the next time you phoned or e-mailed, the same way I told Em," I said briskly. "I'd love to stay and visit, but I was about to leave on a trip."

Katie, for once in her highly verbal life, was speechless. "Where are you going, Mom?" Emily, my practical daughter, inquired.

"I'm going to drive to Lake Arrowfoot to see Carol Quaid. I hope she can give me some information about your father."

Em stood up. "I want to come too."

"Okay. See if you can find that map of Texas we used to have around here."

Ten minutes later we were ready to go. "Hey," Katie called from her seat at the table, "what about me? I want to come too!"

"Then what the hell are you doing still sitting there?" her younger sister inquired.

Seven

It took only about fifteen minutes of silent driving for my girls to revert back to form. On the outskirts of town Katie tiptoed back to her original question. Realizing that guilt and hysteria were not working, she shifted emotional gears. "I do realize, Mom, that I haven't been so great at calling or writing. But I wish you'd called me. I wanted to be there for you—as a daughter and as another married woman."

"Oh, please!" Em said from the seat on my right. "I think I might gag."

Before they could launch that battle—"You've only been married for six months, you silly twit!"—

"You're just jealous because no one will ever marry you!"—I intervened. Shooting a warning glance at Em, I said, "That's very considerate of you, Katie. I guess I was so stunned by everything that I didn't know what to say."

Katie, to her credit, kept her questions to a minimum. I told her no, I had no clue her father was planning to leave me and close his office, and I really wasn't sure where he had gone. Katie listened attentively then said, "What I don't understand is why Daddy wrote Em and didn't write me."

"He didn't write me some long, emotional letter," Em said. "He just sent me a check for my college expenses and a note that said he'd decided to send me one big check instead of monthly checks. He didn't say anything at all about his leaving."

"But he didn't send me anything," Katie insisted.

65

"He already paid for your college," Em said. "He was just meeting his financial obligation to me. I suppose I should be happy that he even did that considering he took all of his and Mom's money."

"That's horrible," Katie said. "I mean we all know Daddy was cheap, but he never seemed so mean or greedy. This doesn't sound like him at all. Maybe he had some kind of psychotic breakdown. You know, like one of those quiet people who go off one day and shoot everyone in their family."

"Or maybe someone was threatening Daddy and he had to get out of town right away to save his life," Em said.

When I didn't say anything, she added, "Do you think he ran away with his office manager, Mom? Is that why we're driving all this way just to see her?"

"Oh, you can't possibly think Daddy is in love with her," Katie said before I could respond. "Carol Quaid isn't even pretty, or funny, or even nice. He always used to say what a man-hater she was."

I took a deep breath. "I don't know whether your father is at the cabin with Carol. I also don't know much about his relationship with Carol, except they apparently talked a lot. But I thought Carol might be able to tell me something about where Dad went or why he closed the office so suddenly."

"Right," Katie said, a little too quickly.

I glanced in the rearview mirror at her flushed, heart-shaped face. Did she think I was really making this trip to bring back my man? Perhaps she imagined me pleading with Rob, begging him to come back to me, to remember "all the good years" and "our two wonderful children." Or maybe, taking a more vengeful tack, she thought I was planning to kill or maim Carol and Rob in their little love nest.

(Never mind that I'd never owned or even knew how to shoot a gun.) For the first time I wondered if my daughters had decided to accompany me on this trip not out of support or simple curiosity, but rather because they wanted to talk their mother out of committing a double-homicide.

I bit down a few caustic retorts and turned the radio to the classic music station. I sighed with pleasure as Vivaldi's "Four Seasons" filled the car, blocking out, for a few minutes at least, the unwelcome discussion.

A good two hours later we were pulling into the tiny and not-very-picturesque hamlet of Arrowfoot. Em stopped a somewhat long-winded discussion of her Internet search for information on her father's whereabouts. "What a pit. Who'd want to spend a vacation here?"

Either someone who wasn't fussy about ambiance or someone who badly wanted to hide, I thought as I scanned the handful of weary-looking stores on the two-block main street: one grocery store, one gas station, one not-very-inviting-looking cafe, a dime store, and—I counted—three bars.

Katie, who'd fallen asleep in the back, sat up, yawning. "I'm hungry. I never had lunch."

"Well, you're in luck," I said, pulling into a parking space in front of the cafe. "I need to get some directions anyway, and this looks like the only place around to eat."

"You think it's safe to eat here?" Katie inquired, frowning at the restaurant's faded paint and red neon sign—EAT—in the window.

Em snickered. "Just don't order anything with mayonnaise in it, or meat, or probably, come to think of it, anything that requires any cooking."

"Maybe you two would feel more comfortable waiting in the car," I suggested as I stepped out of the driver's seat.

"Oh, no!" In rare unanimity, the two of them jumped out of the car.

Inside there were only two customers, a pair of very old men sitting together, smoking and drinking coffee, and one bored-looking waitress reading a newspaper. The waitress looked up when we came in. "Three for dinner?" she asked hopefully.

I smiled at her, but she didn't smile back. "Maybe just a late lunch."

She took us to a wooden booth two down from the old men and handed us a plastic-covered menu. "The dinner special tonight is meat loaf and three vegetables," she announced as if I hadn't spoken. Maybe she hadn't heard me. The apathy in her squinting eyes, her half-chewed-off orange lipstick indicated a woman whose high hopes for the day were to finish her shift and get a load off her feet.

"I will have a cheese sandwich," Katie announced, "and a bag of low-fat chips and a Diet Coke."

"You want a grilled cheese sandwich?" the waitress asked, peering at Katie over the top of her silver-rimmed half-glasses.

Katie seemed to seriously consider whether or not grilling the sandwich would land her in the hospital. "I don't mean to be rude," she finally said, "but the grill is regularly cleaned, isn't it?"

The waitress looked as if she was resisting the urge to lean over and smack my daughter. "Regularly," she snarled.

"Fine," Katie said. "I'll have it grilled."

Em did not meet the waitress's eyes. "A bowl of your vegetable soup, please, and some crackers, if you have them. And a glass of water."

It was my turn. "What do you recommend?"

"I recommend the meat loaf," she said.

"Well, then that's what I'll have. And a cup of coffee."

I thought I saw her expression soften a bit as she jotted down my order, but I could have been imagining it. I sensed this was probably the height of her goodwill toward me. "Excuse me," I said as she started to turn away. "I'm wondering if you could help us out with directions."

"Where you want to go?"

I told her what Mrs. Quaid had told me. "Someplace near the lake, Bolton Road, I think she said."

The waitress shook her head. "Hey, Bob," she called to one of the old men. "Ever hear of Bolton Road?"

He turned and regarded us with watery eyes. "That's that little gravel road near the lake. Some summer cabins up there, but everything's closed down now."

I pulled a pen and scrap of paper from my purse and hurried to the booth where he was sitting. "Could you give me directions on how to get there from here?"

"Nobody's there," he said, eyeing me suspiciously. "All those places are boarded up."

I took a deep breath. "I heard one of our"—I groped for a noun—"friends is staying there for a little while. We thought we'd stop to say hello."

He shook his head. "Ain't no one there."

"Well, I guess we'll just go to make sure as long as we're this close," I said in that maniacally cheerful voice women use with balky toddlers. "Now how do we get to Bolton Road from here?"

Reluctantly he told me. About ten miles down the highway before I turned off, meandering another five or so miles down back roads, at which point, I'd be beside the lake. A long way to drive into town to use a pay phone.

If, that is, Mrs. Quaid had been telling me the truth about Carol staying at the cabin.

"You ever hear about anybody still out at those cabins?" the old man was asking his companion.

"Nope," the man said.

I smiled weakly, thanked them for their help, and went back to our booth. "I have the distinct feeling," I told the girls as I ate the surprisingly good meatloaf and mashed potatoes, "that Mrs. Quaid might be on the phone right this minute with Carol, the two of them snickering about that gullible Prescott woman."

It was getting dark before we found Bolton Road, a gravel road full of huge potholes.

"Maybe we should turn back," Katie said as our car lurched out of a hole. "This is not the place where I want the car to breakdown. There's no one for miles."

A significant part of me agreed with her assessment, but I wanted to see for myself if I had indeed come on a wild-goose chase. "It should only be a little further, honey. If the car breaks down, I have my cell phone to call for help."

"As if they'd really come out here to get us," my older daughter groused. "That gas station probably won't even answer the phone until tomorrow morning."

"Oh, stop being such a wuss," Em said. She'd stocked up on candy bars at the cafe, and, having gotten her chocolate fix, was ready for adventure.

"I don't see any cabin," I said. The lack of any street or residential lights didn't help either. "We're almost at the end of the road."

"Over there!" Em called excitedly, pointing. "I bet that's it."

If it was, Carol Quaid was not wasting any money on lighting it.

Now that we were here I felt suddenly engulfed by uncertainty. What if Carol wasn't there? Or she was inside sleeping—and furious at being disturbed in her secluded hideaway. What could I do if she claimed to know nothing about Rob's whereabouts?

But Em had already pulled a flashlight from the glove compartment and opened the door. "Come on, you two."

More out of maternal protectiveness than anything else, I hurried after her, hearing Katie's footsteps behind us. Em was already knocking at the cabin door by the time I got there.

No one answered or made any other noise, even when Em started pounding on the door.

"See?" Katie said triumphantly. "No one's there. Let's go."

I sighed. "Maybe we should. There's no point just standing here pounding."

But as we turned back toward our car, the beam of Em's flashlight hit something large and shiny behind the cabin. A car! The three of us went to inspect it: a fairly new, dark-green Honda.

"What kind of car does Carol Quaid drive?" Em whispered to me.

"I have no idea." Could it be that maybe Carol and Rob had taken Rob's car out, perhaps to get groceries, and they'd be returning any minute? We stood there, paralyzed with uncertainty, while all the endless possibilities spun through my head. Maybe this wasn't Carol's car at all—or her cabin. Or maybe Carol and Rob had been here, stowed her car and then moved on.

I realized suddenly that Katie had walked back to the side of the cabin and was motioning for us to join her. "Look," she whispered, "that window up there is open a little. Maybe one of us could crawl in and look around. At least we might be able to figure out whether Carol is still here."

"I don't know," I said. "I think that's called breaking and entering." Wasn't this the child who, only a few minutes ago, hadn't wanted to get out of the car?

"Great idea," Em said. "Help me up and I'll try to crawl in."

"You?" Katie asked derisively. "I've had years of cheerleading practice."

But the people who'd boosted her to the top of the formation had been husky boys, not her skinny, unathletic sister. "Hey!" I yelled as Em leaned over and Katie scrambled onto her back. "This is dangerous!"

I watched, hands sweating, as Katie, crouching on Em's back, managed to push the window open. Then, grasping the window ledge, she pulled herself through the open window.

My heart pounded double-time until Katie's face appeared in the open window. "I'm okay," she called. "Meet me at the door."

We did. But when, finally, Katie unlocked the door for us, she looked frightened. "I didn't see anything, but there's a really terrible smell."

Em stepped inside. "God, what is that?"

I was afraid I knew, but hoped against hope that I was wrong.

Eight

We found Carol Quaid lying in her bed, looking, from a distance, as if she were sleeping. Only when we got closer could we see all the blood that had soaked through her pillow. And the bullet hole in her forehead.

"Don't touch anything!" I ordered my daughters, though they probably had as little inclination to touch Carol Quaid's lifeless body as I did.

Katie, in fact, looked as if she was about to be sick. "Why don't the two of you go outside to get some air?" I suggested. "There's nothing we can do here."

"What are you going to do?" Katie asked.

I pushed them gently out of the bedroom into the outer room—a combination kitchen/living room. It was, I noticed, almost as messy as the bedroom. "I'm going to call the police on my cell phone."

"I am not going out there without you!" Katie said, grabbing at my arm. "Who knows who's out there watching us?"

We compromised by all going outside. I didn't spot anyone lurking behind a tree, though, admittedly, I wasn't looking real hard as we hurried to our car. Once inside, all doors locked, I rummaged through my purse for my cell phone. Scanning the deserted road for anyone trying to sneak up on the car, I phoned 911.

"Now where on Bolton Road are you?" the police dispatcher, a woman, asked.

"At the end of the road—the west end—outside the

cabin. I, my daughters and I, are actually in our car. A tan Toyota. You'll see us right away." I knew I was babbling, but I couldn't help it. Once I'd started my story (skipping the part about how we actually got into the cabin), I seemed unable to shut up. "We wanted to stop by to say hello to Carol, and then we found her in her bed with a bullet hole in her head." It was as if the sheer rush of my words could push away the horror of what I'd seen.

The woman managed to interject that a police car was on its way and we should stay where we were, in the car.

From the back seat Katie tapped me on the shoulder. "Ask how long before they get here." I asked.

"Soon," the woman said. "Maybe fifteen minutes. Now let me get your name."

It was the slowest fifteen minutes of my life. By the time the squad car arrived, lights blinking, Katie had curled up into a fetal position on the back seat, while Em was crying quietly in the passenger seat. "What do we say about how we got into the house?" Em asked as she spotted the police car.

"Tell them the truth," I said. It was generally the best policy—wasn't it? On second thought, I added, "Though you might skip the part about wanting to snoop around in Carol's house."

Katie sat up. "We could say that I climbed in the window because when we saw Carol's car in the back, and no one answered the door, we were worried about her and wanted to make sure she wasn't sick or anything."

"Or dead," Em added glumly as two police officers walked over to our car.

It was a very long evening. After I had shown the officers where the body was and a number of crime scene technicians arrived to collect physical evidence, the questions began. The girls and I each had to give our version of events to a police officer. The younger officer took Em to the squad car for her interview, while the older one, a red-faced, paunchy man named Sergeant Murphy, questioned me in my car. Poor Katie, looking cold and miserable, paced outside near the car.

The sergeant started with the purely factual questions: "What exactly did you see when you entered the cabin, Mrs. Prescott? What time was this? Did you see anyone else near the cabin? Did you touch or move anything inside?" The first time around the officer seemed to accept my explanation of why we had all agreed that Katie should crawl through the partially open window. But once I finished he said, "I'd like to go back over a few things you said. Let's talk some more about why your daughter felt it necessary to crawl in the window. Was there some reason you thought Ms. Quaid would be ill or needing your assistance?"

I did my best, but even to me, my reasons—the car was sitting there behind the cabin, we had to drive back to Houston, Carol was out here all alone and I'd told her mother that I'd check on her—sounded lame.

Sergeant Murphy jotted down a few more notes. "Now I'd like to talk to your daughter—Katie, right?—the one who climbed in the window." When I didn't budge from the driver's seat, he added, "Alone. You'll have to wait outside while we talk."

Katie's teeth were chattering as we traded places. "At least you'll be a little warmer in here," I said, patting her reassuringly on the shoulder.

"Yeah," she said, looking as if she'd rather take her chances with the cold.

The younger policeman, a pale, round-faced man with

wire glasses who looked like someone Central Casting would have sent over for an officer role in the SS, was still talking to Em. Whatever he was saying, she didn't like it. As I walked by, she shook her head vehemently.

And you had to bring them here, didn't you? I accused myself as I walked. Even encountering Carol's body by myself would have been preferable to having my sweet, sheltered girls involved in a grisly crime scene.

Unbelievably, when finally we had all been interviewed, we still had to go back to the police station to make our "official statements." Following the police car back to town, I tried to calm Katie, who was convinced she was going to be thrown in jail.

"That policeman kept asking me all these questions I didn't know the answers to," she said. "What had I first seen when I climbed through the window? Well, it was dark and I didn't notice much of anything, except for that terrible smell. I just wanted to get to the door and let you and Em inside. And then he kept saying, 'Why did you break into a locked house? Do you always do that when someone doesn't answer the door?' "

"What did you say to that?" Em asked.

"I said that we came all this way to see Carol Quaid and we wanted to make sure she was okay before we went back to Houston. Then he asked, 'Why did you drive all this way to see her?' And I said, 'My mother had some questions she wanted to ask her about my father.' "

Em groaned. "Real smart, Katie."

Katie glared at her. "All I said was that Carol was Daddy's office manager, and he closed his office suddenly and disappeared with all of his and Mom's money. I didn't say that Mom thought Daddy might be here too, or that she suspected something might be going on between them."

Katie did not meet my eyes during the speculation about her father's romantic exploits.

"Gee, what if Dad killed Carol?" Em asked suddenly. "Maybe he was here and they had a fight. Maybe she pulled a gun on him, and they struggled and he accidentally shot her."

"You read too many detective novels," Katie told her younger sibling, but she was less scornful than usual.

"I did look around the place a little," I said, "to see if I saw anything of your father's—and I didn't." Which might only mean that Rob was smart enough not to leave his possessions lying on the kitchen table or that my sixty-second inspection wasn't very thorough.

The police station was a small, depressing place that fit well with the general aura of the town. But at least it was warm. Em and I waited on two battered wooden chairs while the police officers took Katie's statement.

Em went next. Katie, sitting down next to me, whispered into my ear, "The young one is really a jerk. And guess what? We have to come back tomorrow! I said we didn't have anywhere to sleep, and the old guy—the nicer one—said he'd call a motel right outside of town to get us a room."

Em's statement was shorter than Katie's, or maybe she just talked faster. "Your turn," she said to me.

I told the officers exactly what I'd said before. The younger guy waited until I'd finished, then said, "If you suspected that your husband was having an affair with Miss Quaid, maybe you killed her."

"Who said anything about Rob having an affair with her?" I asked, trying to sound indignant. "I certainly didn't."

He didn't answer the question. "It seems kind of strange that you'd drive all this way just to have a conversation with your husband's office manager."

"Not if she doesn't have a phone."

"What was so important about talking to her?" He leaned back in his chair, sneering.

I would have liked to lean across the table and smack that superior expression off his face, but it didn't seem like a wise move. "My husband has disappeared, taking our joint assets with him. Obviously I would like to see him to discuss that. Since he also closed his dental office, I thought that Ms. Quaid, his longtime office manager, might have a clue where he'd gone."

"They were especially close—Ms. Quaid and your husband?"

I was not going to let this baby-faced Nazi get to me. "Not to my knowledge, but she had worked for Rob for a long time, and I'd already spoken to everyone else from his office."

"Maybe you thought he was here with her," Babyface suggested. "Maybe the three of you came to warn her to stay away from Rob, and things got out of hand—say, the gun you just wanted to scare her with went off accidentally."

"And what gun is that?" I inquired.

"Or maybe all three of you intentionally killed her," he continued, ignoring my question. "A kind of vigilante thing."

The older cop, probably himself a father, sent the kid a look. "So you have no idea where your husband is?"

I shook my head. "None."

He asked some questions about Rob—physical description, type of car he drove, how long he'd been gone. He studied my face. "Do you think your husband might have killed Ms. Quaid? If she was the office manager, she could have had access to his money."

I started to say, "I haven't the faintest idea what my husband might or might not do." But then I stopped myself. "I don't think so. Rob has never been violent—cheap, dishonest, greedy, but not violent."

He raised a gray eyebrow. "Sure you might not have murdered him?"

I shook my head. "Nope, tempting as the idea might be. He's still the father of my children."

I had to sign my statement and then we were allowed to go—for a while. "The three of you need to come back here around eleven tomorrow morning," Sergeant Murphy said. He glanced at his watch. "Or I guess I should say this morning."

It was almost two a.m. by the time the girls and I walked into our spartan room at the Arrowfoot Motel. "How could they even think we killed Carol Quaid if we called them to report the murder?" Katie was asking.

"Lot of murderers do that," Em said. "They get a big thrill out of watching the police investigate. And of course they're also giving themselves an alibi."

I looked at the two of them, their faces pale with fatigue. "I am so, so sorry that I got you into this."

"Stop apologizing, Mom," Em said. "It's not your fault."

"No, it's my fault," Katie said. "I was the one who suggested climbing in that window. Mom probably would have just walked away when no one answered the door."

Would I have? I wondered. Could I have just driven away after no one answered the door? Or would I have figured that I hadn't come all this way just to knock on a door then turn around and go home? It was hard to remember what I'd been thinking at the time. It seemed as if last night was weeks, rather than hours, ago. "This is ridiculous," I told Katie. "The truth is this is the killer's fault—not yours, not mine. I just wish you hadn't been there to find the body."

"Me too," Em said.

"Me three," Katie said with the ghost of a smile.

I glanced at my watch and shuddered. "Come on, let's go to bed. We need to get a few hours sleep before we go back to the police station."

"You think I should call Brad?" Katie asked. "He's probably wondering why I didn't phone him the way I said I would."

"No!" Em and I answered simultaneously.

Katie's lower lip protruded, the first phase of the Katie Pout. But then she seemed to reconsider. Pulling off her sneakers, still in her sweats, she crawled into the double bed I was sitting on. "Okay," she said, "but I get to sleep with Mom."

"The police were in here asking about you," our waitress announced cheerfully when the three of us straggled into the cafe the next morning. "You want a booth again?"

"Fine." I wondered if her perkiness was caused by our misfortune or if she was just a morning person.

Katie was still talking on my cell phone to her husband. "Listen, Brad, I need to go now," Katie told her beloved as she walked to the booth. "Yes, sweetheart. Me too. It's awful without you." Another pause. "Now you won't forget to call that lawyer, will you? Bye, honeybun."

Em rolled her eyes at me but refrained from commenting.

"You three look as if you could use some coffee," the waitress observed.

I expected Em to ask for herbal tea or Katie to spout a

mini-sermon on the evils of caffeine, but instead they both did what I did—nod gratefully. Perhaps too-close proximity to a crime scene promotes a change in behavior because as soon as the coffee was brought, both girls ordered the breakfast special—two eggs, bacon, hashed browns, and toast—without special requests or questions about recent health-code violations. "Make that three," I said, sipping the exceptionally good coffee. "And a small orange juice."

"Quite an appetite today," the waitress commented.

Before Katie had a chance to retort that under starvation conditions even she would eat anything, I quickly interjected, "What did the police have to say this morning?"

The waitress held up one finger. "Three specials, scrambled," she yelled in the general direction of the kitchen, before turning back to me. "Tom Murphy wanted to know what time you were here yesterday. And he was real interested that you'd asked directions to that cabin on Bolton Road."

I bet he was. "I told him we left here around 4:30, but I was only estimating the time."

"It was 4:45," the waitress volunteered. "I remember because my shift ended at five." She looked at each of us hopefully. Now it was our turn to share some juicy information with her.

Em asked glumly, "Did the policeman tell you if they found the murderer yet?"

"Nope. This is probably the first time any of those guys was ever involved in a murder investigation."

"Isn't that great news?" Katie muttered.

The woman turned to her. "You're the one who climbed in the window?" she asked in a tone that seemed to imply, I would have thought you'd be afraid to break a fingernail.

"Yes, I was," Katie proclaimed in her snotty, I-am-a-cheerleader voice, which I had hoped she'd abandoned at her high school graduation.

"Good for you," the waitress said approvingly. "Didn't think you had it in you." Before Katie could respond, she added, "Better go check on your breakfasts."

The breakfasts she returned with looked large enough for three lumberjacks. The minute she set the plates on the table, the girls stopped sniping at each other and dug into the scrambled eggs. Nobody spoke again until we—each one of us—had cleaned our plates.

We left the cafe, feeling bloated but satisfied. "Good luck with your interrogation," the waitress called as we opened the door. I smiled back at her, hoping she was making a joke.

Only Sergeant Murphy—the good cop—was in evidence when we got to the police station. Maybe Babyface had the day off. "Hello, ladies. I hope you slept well."

"Just fine," I lied, though, from the looks of him, we probably had gotten a lot more sleep than he had.

He motioned for us to follow him to the small room in the back where we had each been interviewed ten hours earlier. "I just have a few more questions for you," he said after we'd all sat down around the pitted wooden table.

"My husband says I shouldn't talk to you without a lawyer present," Katie announced.

The sergeant raised a gray eyebrow. "What does your husband do for a living?"

"He's an engineer," Katie said, looking puzzled.

The officer nodded. "You might tell him when you see them that you've already given your official statement. Unless of course"—he sent her an inquiring look—"you want to change that."

Katie thought about it for a minute, probably running

through everything she'd said. "Well, no."

"In that case," he said, "don't waste your money on the lawyer."

"Does that mean we can leave this morning?" I asked hopefully.

He nodded. "Soon. I just have a few more questions about Ms. Quaid."

"I really didn't know her that well," I began. "She worked for my husband for maybe ten years, but the only times I ever really talked to her were at the Christmas parties, and she really didn't have a lot to say."

"Tell me what she was like."

Nondescript was the first word that came to mind, but I tried to be a little more specific. "Well, she was very bright, got an MBA at night school. Efficient, a good office manager. Single, maybe divorced, I'm not sure. Kind of stand-offish—civil but not very friendly. I heard that she was quite, uh, assertive."

"Dad used to say she was a real ball-breaking bitch," Katie, the girl who didn't want to talk without her attorney present, volunteered. "That summer I worked at Dad's office, everyone hated her."

"Why?" Murphy asked her.

"She was very bossy and a real know-it-all."

"Kind of person who makes a lot of enemies?"

Katie shook her head. "Enemies like 'You're the last person in the world who's going to be invited to my party.' Not 'I'm going to blow your brains out' enemies. She was annoying, but not that annoying."

Murphy looked at Em and me to see if we agreed. Em gave a palms-up "What do I know?" gesture. I said, "I can't imagine anyone wanting to kill her." Unless, of course, Carol was screwing around with their husbands too.

"Would you say that Ms. Quaid was a messy person or a neat one?"

"Neat doesn't begin to describe her," Katie said. "Anal is what she was. Every paper lined up perfectly on her desk."

The police officer leaned forward. "Then it seems unlikely that Ms. Quaid herself would have strewn her possessions all around the cabin?"

"I guess," Katie said uncertainly.

"The place was a mess," I said. "Do you think that whoever killed her threw all her stuff around?"

"Don't know. That's why I'm asking you."

"Maybe the murderer was looking for valuables to steal," Em said. "Like jewelry or money."

"Could be," Sergeant Murphy agreed. "Except he left her wallet, which had two thousand dollars in it." When Em gasped, he added, "I keep asking myself, what did she have that someone would want so badly he'd kill for it?" He turned to me. "Any chance Ms. Quaid might have stolen something from your husband?"

"He never mentioned anything to me about suspecting her of stealing." Of course there were a hell of a lot of other things Rob never bothered to mention. "And if she'd stolen money from him, why would he leave behind the two thousand dollars?"

"Maybe he wanted something else. You sure you don't have any idea where your husband is?"

I forced myself not to snap, "If I knew that would I have come to this godforsaken hole to look for him?" Instead I said, "None at all. If you find him, I'd appreciate your letting me know."

He nodded. "Okay. I've got all of your addresses and phone numbers, so you can go home now."

That was it? A few hours ago he hadn't seemed so benign. I couldn't resist asking him, "What happened since last night? How come we're not your chief suspects anymore?"

He took the question well. "Two things: the medical examiner said Ms. Quaid had been dead for two to three days, and Jenny Sue at the cafe said you were in there asking directions to Bolton Road around 4:30. I guess you could have asked directions just to cover your tracks, but we small-town cops"—he sent me a look—"aren't that jaded."

I smiled weakly and stood up. Like puppets, the girls jumped out of their chairs. "Well, I guess this is goodbye."

Sergeant Murphy nodded. "Stay in touch," he said.

Nine

Someone's very annoying cell phone awoke me from my nap. Feeling groggy and disoriented, I opened my eyes. Em, her brow furrowed in the expression of intense concentration she seemed to bring to most activities, was still driving the car. A hand tapped my shoulder. "Hey, Mom," Katie said from the back seat. "Hand me your purse. That might be Brad calling."

"Haven't heard from him in the last forty-five minutes," Em muttered under her breath.

I managed to locate my purse and hand the still-ringing phone back to Katie. Was there any possibility of getting back to sleep while she cooed endearments to her beloved?

"Oh," Katie said into the phone, her tone suddenly cooler. "Just a minute." She handed the phone back to me. "It's some man," she whispered.

"Are you finished with the story yet?" a familiar voice inquired.

"Not quite." Not quite started it either.

"You do realize the deadline is Monday?"

My first decent sleep in days was interrupted for this? "And you, I hope, are aware that today is Saturday?"

After about sixty seconds of hostile silence, Paul O'Neal sighed. "I didn't call to fight with you. I wanted to see how the article was coming and to tell you that I read the autopsy report on Stan Harris. It said he died of cardiac arrest caused by excessive potassium."

"He had a heart attack because of too much potassium?"

I could hear a paper rustle in the background and then, obviously reading, he said, "Hyperkalemia—excessive potassium—makes the heart dilate and become flaccid. This causes an abnormal heart rhythm, which leads to cardiac arrest. Apparently Stan took potassium tablets to balance the water loss from the diuretics he used to look thinner."

"Someone I interviewed—either his ex-wife, who's a nurse, or his buddy Dr. Elizabeth—said Stan took dangerous doses of vitamin and mineral supplements."

"Of course there's a possibility he didn't overdose on his own."

"What do you mean?"

"The coroner says someone injected Stan between his toes. Maybe it was a shot of potassium."

I shuddered. "I can't imagine why anyone would choose that particular spot for an injection."

"Maybe Stan was hoping to hide the puncture mark. I guess he even could have been trying to make a suicide look like a heart attack, though that's one hell of a bizarre way to kill yourself. A guy I talked to at the medical examiner's office said that if Stan got a high enough dose of injected potassium, he probably died within five minutes."

"He died on the jogging trail, right? Could someone have accosted him and given him a shot?" Though it was a little hard to imagine some burly killer tearing off Stan's sock and jogging shoe to inject him and then, once Stan was dead, replacing his footwear.

From the corner of my eye, I could see Em turning to stare at me. "I'll tell you in a minute," I whispered, pointing meaningfully at the road ahead.

"That's a possibility, I guess," O'Neal said. "But the coroner said he didn't see any signs that there'd been a struggle."

"So is he ruling it a suicide? Getting a shot between your toes doesn't sound like an innocent mistake about potassium doses."

"So far all he's done is notify the police, who've started an investigation. Unfortunately, Stan had been dead a few hours before another jogger found his body."

"Doesn't anybody die a nice natural death anymore?" I muttered as much to myself as to him.

"Mother!" Katie was tapping my shoulder again. "What is going on?"

I waved her away. Didn't children ever outgrow their need to interrupt their mother the minute she got on the phone?

"Where are you anyway?" my editor asked. "I hear other people talking."

"In my car with my daughters, somewhere north of Houston. We drove to a cabin to talk to my husband's office manager and instead found her body."

"Is there a story there—in you finding the office manager's body?" he asked. "How did she die?"

"Shot. And no, I don't see it as a story." No wonder people said journalists were ghoulish. "I'll call you when I finish the Stan Harris article."

As I put the phone back in my purse, I told the girls, "It was an editor nagging me about the article I'm writing. I'm sure the conversation sounded a lot more interesting than it was." I closed my eyes. "Wake me when we get home."

I'd been awake for all of five minutes when Em pulled into the driveway. We were just getting out of the car when a tall, gray-haired woman hurried toward us. Apparently she'd been sitting in the ancient white Cadillac parked in front of the house.

"Who's that?" Katie whispered.

"I have no idea," I said, though, for some reason, the woman looked vaguely familiar.

"Mrs. Prescott?" When I nodded, she said, "I'm Eileen Quaid, Carol's mother. We talked on the phone."

Up close I could see the resemblance to her daughter, both tall with sharp features, both projecting an air of no-nonsense determination. Except this woman's brown eyes, so like her daughter's, radiated intense grief. I touched her arm. "I am so sorry about Carol."

Her face was so close I could smell the coffee she'd been drinking. "I need to know what happened. Everything. You must tell me."

I didn't have the heart to tell her that I couldn't give her the information she so desperately wanted: who had killed her daughter or why. But I invited her inside anyway, ignoring her puzzled looks at my empty living and dining rooms, ushering her back to the kitchen. "Would you like some tea or coffee?" I asked after we sat down at the table.

"Coffee, if you have it," she said as she set down a large canvas tote bag on the floor.

"I'll make it," Katie said quickly. She and Em had been hanging around in the doorway, obviously hoping to eavesdrop.

"My daughters were with me when—" I considered my words—"when I went to the cabin." I introduced them, and she nodded absently in the girls' direction.

"Tell me what happened to my daughter."

I took a deep breath. "We got to the cabin a little before five yesterday afternoon. No one answered the door when we knocked, but we noticed a car parked behind the cabin. A window was open so we thought we should check to see if Carol perhaps was ill and not able to get to the door." It sounded highly suspicious to me—Gee, ma'am, when you didn't answer the door, we thought we'd crawl in your window to see if you were okay. But my explanation didn't seem to faze Mrs. Quaid. Or more likely it just wasn't the part of the story she was interested in.

"So I crawled in the window and let Mom and Em inside," Katie said, handing us each a mug of coffee. "But I didn't see anything except a big mess everywhere—lots of stuff on the floor."

"But Carol is very neat," Mrs. Quaid said. "She never could abide a mess, even when she was a little girl."

"It looked as if somebody had been searching for something," I said. "Dumping everything on the floor."

Mrs. Quaid shook her head as tears coursed down her cheeks. "I told her not to go there. I told Carol at this time of year nobody else would be at the lake; she'd be all alone, isolated. But she said that was what she wanted—to be alone."

Why? I wanted to ask. If all she'd wanted was a little solitude, why couldn't she have been alone in her town house? Why was it so important to Carol to be at an out-of-season summer cabin with no one else for miles? But it seemed insensitive to ask now, and I doubted if Mrs. Quaid knew anyway.

"Tell me the rest," she said. "About finding Carol."

I told her, omitting the nastier details.

"She was in bed?" When I nodded, she said, "The policeman said she'd been dead for two days before—before you found her. He said she hadn't been beat up or sexually assaulted. I asked about that."

"Maybe she was asleep and never felt anything," Em said. "Maybe a burglar thought no one was home and when he saw her there asleep he shot her."

"I hope she was asleep." Mrs. Quaid turned to me, her eyes narrowed. "You didn't all drive up there to give Carol a check." It was a statement, not a question. "Why did you want to see her?"

I could feel my face grow warm. "I was hoping she'd be able to tell me something about why my husband closed his office and just disappeared. I wanted to ask her if she knew where he was."

"Why would Carol know that?"

"She'd been his office manager for years. I thought she might know something about his business that I didn't." There was no reason to mention that I'd half expected to find Rob hiding out with her at the cabin.

Mrs. Quaid nodded. "She did know a lot about business, and not just your husband's. She was a CPA, you know. Besides working for your husband, she had her own freelance accounting business, keeping the books for a few small businesses, doing their tax returns. Eventually she wanted to do that full time."

"I didn't know that," I said.

"Yes, Carol is"—she stopped, swallowed before correcting herself—"was a very ambitious woman."

We all sipped our coffee in silence for a few minutes until Mrs. Quaid said, "The last time I talked to Carol she told me that if anything happened to her, I should go to her bank safe-deposit box—she left me the key when she went to the cabin—and use the information I found there."

Em gasped. "She expected something to happen to her?"

Mrs. Quaid shook her head, looking suddenly weighted down with fatigue. "I didn't think so at the time. I told her that I'd finally gotten around to having a will made, and that was when she mentioned her safe-deposit box. I thought she was just telling me that was where she kept her will."

"What did she keep there?" Em asked.

Mrs. Quaid reached down to pick up her big carryall. She pulled out a long white envelope. On the front of it, written in block letters, was the heading ROB PRESCOTT.

With a trembling hand I took the papers Mrs. Quaid pulled from the envelope, not sure what to expect: love letters? Proof of embezzlement? Written threats? But what she'd handed me was the dental records of two patients I'd never heard of, along with their full-mouth X-rays. I scanned the pages, looking for some clue why Carol kept this information locked in her safe-deposit box. Had Rob accidentally killed or injured a patient or committed some other act of gross malpractice? I saw no evidence of it. Both men, a Vinny Scalia and Leonardo Lorenzo, had only been patients for about the last six months. Mr. Scalia had been in once to have his teeth cleaned and Mr. Lorenzo had come in twice, for teeth cleaning and to have two cavities filled. I glanced at the X-rays, seeing nothing noteworthy about them either.

"I don't get it," I told Carol's mother. "What's the significance of this?"

She shrugged. "I thought you might know."

"There wasn't anything else in the envelope?" My husband's current address and phone number, for instance, would be helpful.

"That was it." She hesitated. "There were several other envelopes as well in the safe-deposit box. It's possible the information Carol wanted me to use was in one of them."

"Envelopes with other people's names?" When she nodded, I said, "Was there any kind of threat in them, some reason to think Carol might feel this person meant to harm her?"

"Not really," Mrs. Quaid said. "Carol was always a very private person. She didn't reveal much, not even to me." She studied her coffee mug. "I probably shouldn't be telling you all this. Carol would have wanted me to keep these matters confidential."

In other words, she wasn't going to disclose the names on the other envelopes. I tried another tack. "Was there anything else in the box besides these envelopes?"

Mrs. Quaid's face reddened. "Only a few personal mementos and some money."

"A lot of money?" Katie asked. As both a business major and passionate shopper, she was acutely interested in the subject.

"Quite a bit." Mrs. Quaid peered into her mug as if searching there for the exact number. "About twenty thousand dollars."

Quite a bit indeed. Particularly for a CPA who, presumably, was aware of more profitable places to park her money.

"Maybe it was the money, not the stuff in the envelopes that your daughter wanted you to use if something happened to her," Katie said.

Mrs. Quaid seemed doubtful. "Maybe if I go talk to the other people, I'll have some idea what Carol meant."

"The other people whose names are on the envelopes?" Em asked.

Mrs. Quaid nodded, clearly reluctant to reveal more. As she tucked the papers and X-rays back into Rob's envelope, I suddenly noticed a photo that must have been in her bag. I tilted my head to get a better look at the picture of a tall, muscular woman in a bikini who seemed to be flexing her biceps. "That isn't Carol, is it?"

Mrs. Quaid smiled and nodded, holding the photo for us

to see. "It was in the safe-deposit box too. Carol got very serious about fitness this year."

"Boy," Katie said admiringly, "talk about abs of steel! She must have really worked out."

"She did. She worked out with a personal trainer two or three times a week. She was very proud of the progress she'd made."

"I can see why," Katie said, still studying the photo. "Did she work on machines or with free weights?"

"Machines, I think." Mrs. Quaid dug in her carryall and pulled out two more photos. One showed a plumper Carol in a swimsuit. Obviously it was the "before" photo. In it Carol's body appeared soft and flabby, and she had a stooped, tall-girl posture—a far cry from the confident-looking Amazon in the later picture.

I pointed to the "after" photo. "When was this taken?" Since Carol had been lying in bed wearing a loose, flannel nightgown the last time I saw her, I had no idea what her body had recently looked like.

"Oh, just a few months ago. Stan, her trainer, told her he'd use her before-and-after photos in his new book."

"Not Stan Harris?" I asked.

She nodded sadly. "Carol was just devastated when he died. He was such an inspiration to her; he really encouraged her."

I nodded. "Many people said that about him." Among other things. "I'm writing a magazine article about him."

"Oh, really?" she said, looking interested. "Carol did accounting work for him in exchange for personal training at his gym. They were working on some new marketing plan for his business when he died."

I hesitated, then decided to plunge in. "I heard that Stan was having business problems."

"Well, I don't really know about that, except Carol told me she was helping Mr. Harris to turn his business around."

"Did she say how they were going to accomplish that?"

Mrs. Quaid shook her head. "I don't know all the specifics. Carol said she advised him not to take an offer to sell out to one of those fitness chains. She really believed that he could make the business profitable. She was extremely enthusiastic about the project." The memory of Carol's enthusiasm was apparently too much for her. Eyes welling with tears, Mrs. Quaid said, "I need to go. I have lots of arrangements to make."

We all stood up to walk her to the door. "Let me know if there's anything I can do," I said.

She nodded, then hurried to her car.

Neither one of us, I thought as I watched her drive away, had gotten the information we so desperately wanted.

Ten

I knew I should start writing my article, but I just wasn't up to it. For one thing, there was still a bit more background research I wanted to do. I glanced at my watch. "Anyone interested in coming with me to Stan Harris's gym?" I asked the girls.

They both decided to accompany me. Katie announced that she would be an invaluable asset because she was "very knowledgeable about fitness facilities," while Em said pointedly that she'd uncover some vital information while Katie worked her pecs. And I wondered if I might have been better off going alone.

The gym was not as impressive as it looked in the photos in Stan's book. In contrast to some of the glitzier facilities I saw in TV ads, with their indoor tracks and Olympic-sized swimming pools, Stan's place seemed small and plain and rather dated. Also empty except for a skinny, bored-looking young woman sitting at the desk and two gray-haired women riding the exercise bikes.

I explained to the woman at the desk that I was writing an article on Stan.

"Terri isn't here," she said. "We're closing for the day in about half an hour." She looked as if she were counting the minutes.

"You don't have much exercise equipment," Katie said, walking back from a sixty-second inspection of the facility.

The woman sent her a look. "We have enough for serious exercisers. I teach several low-impact aerobic classes. You don't need a lot of equipment for that."

"No, you don't," I said quickly. "I read Stan's book. He seemed to get some very impressive results with his clients."

I could see the woman unbend a bit. Behind my back I waved at Katie to go away, which she, of course, ignored.

"Yes, the important things," the exercise instructor said pointedly, "are motivation and of course making sure that the client is using correct form to prevent injuries—not shiny new equipment."

Katie, to her credit, did not respond.

I smiled and asked, in what I hoped was a pleasant, chatty voice, "When Stan Harris was alive, did you have more business?"

She thought about it. "More business than this, sure." She glanced around, to make certain the clients weren't in earshot. "But things have been going downhill since that new gym down the street opened. They just went faster downhill after Stan died. The rumor is that we're going to close soon, that Terri is planning to sell the gym."

"I heard something about Stan having a new marketing plan to revamp the place," I said.

She shrugged. "Stan always had a new plan—a new book, a new class, a new free-trial offer to bring people in." A lot of good it did us, her expression said.

"Do you know who Terri is selling to or when?"

She shrugged again—apparently a favorite gesture. "No, Terri is not into sharing secrets with the employees. I hope she waits until after I find a new job."

I could see that her interest was flagging. She checked her watch and glanced at the two exercisers, who were now getting off their bikes and talking to each other.

"Do you happen to know a woman named Carol Quaid?" I said. It was a long shot, but why not ask? "I understand she worked out with Stan quite often."

The question seemed to pull her back into the conversation. "Oh, yes, she and Stan worked out a lot." Her smile was distinctly malicious. "I suspect that was the main reason Stan and Terri were getting a divorce."

The three of us had just walked in the kitchen when the phone rang.

"This is Terri Harris," the no-longer-perky-sounding widow announced when I said hello. "I want to see the article you wrote about Stan."

It certainly hadn't taken the woman at Stan's gym long to report back to her boss. "I haven't finished it yet," I said.

"Well, I want to see it when it's done, before you turn it in to the magazine."

Don't hold your breath on that one, honey, I thought, but did not say. As a general rule, journalists do not show their stories to the subjects of their interviews. The interviewees have too much of an inclination to rewrite the story—omitting their tactless quotes or any less-than-flattering observation of the author.

When I didn't respond, Terri added, "I understand that you were snooping around my gym."

What happened to the affable, upbeat woman I'd interviewed only a week ago? "Actually I went there to see you. You may recall that you invited me to come for a free exercise class."

A pause. Either Terri was trying to remember if she had offered me a free class or she was considering her conversational options. "That's right," she said in a friendlier voice. "I guess I should have told you that I don't work on Saturday afternoons. Our clients tend to come on weekdays."

In other words, the two people I saw exercising were not

indicative of the gym's usual level of business—which might or might not be true. "I guess I should have called first before I came."

"It would have saved you a trip."

Such a considerate woman, always thinking of others. "While I have you on the phone, let me ask you a few more questions for the article."

"Okay." She didn't sound thrilled at the prospect.

"I heard a rumor that you were thinking of selling the gym. Any truth to that?"

"Absolutely not! Who told you that?"

"Gee, I don't remember. I've spoken to so many people in the last week."

"If you print that, I'll sue."

I took a deep breath. "I also heard about the autopsy report on your husband, that his death was caused by an overdose of potassium."

"Stan must have taken too many potassium pills," his widow said. "He was always stuffing handfuls of vitamins into his mouth. He thought he knew more than the doctors."

"Someone also apparently had recently given him some kind of injection." When she didn't say anything, I added, "Do you know anything about that?"

"No idea."

No concern either, I thought. Or curiosity. Even if your marriage was falling apart, you shouldn't be totally indifferent to your husband's death. I wouldn't be if Rob, that bastard, died.

I remembered one of my old journalism professor's Cardinal Rules of Interviewing: Ask the hard questions last. "By the way, Terri, where were you the morning Stan died?"

"At work getting ready for my six a.m. step class."

"Lots of people around the gym at 5:15 in the morning?"

"No. I don't get there until 5:50, and neither does anyone else."

"So you and Stan didn't drive to work together?" The jogging trail where he'd died was less than a mile from their gym. It would have been easy to drop Stan off for his jog on her way to work. After he was through with his run, Stan could have had a cool-down walk to the gym.

"No, we always took separate cars. What are you getting at anyway with all these questions? Are you implying that I killed Stan?"

"No. In fact I never said that anyone killed Stan."

"And you damn well better not," she snapped. "I think I'm going to call your editor right now. I don't like your attitude one bit."

"I'm sure Mr. O'Neal will enjoy hearing from you," I said sweetly.

Slamming down the phone in my ear was apparently Terri's idea of an appropriate response.

Paul O'Neal phoned about fifteen minutes later. "Terri Harris is very annoyed with you," he said, without pre-amble.

"I gathered that."

"She is insisting on reading your article before it's printed to make sure that you're not slandering her."

I sighed. "And what did you say?"

"I said that it is not our policy to show articles to the persons who are interviewed, though I'd make sure that she received the magazine as soon as it came out. And I think I also mentioned that if your statements in the article were untrue as well as malicious, this was called libel, not slander. But since our magazine made a point of checking the stories for accuracy, the word she was really searching for was 'embarrassing,' which, while unpleasant, was not illegal."

I grinned, wishing I could have heard the conversation. "And what did Terri say to that?"

"Something about speaking to her lawyer. I didn't really catch every word since she slammed the phone down in my ear seconds later."

"She did that to me too."

"Nasty habit." He paused. "I'm eagerly anticipating reading this unfair, vitriolic article of yours. When exactly can I expect it?"

"Soon. I promise I'll let you know the minute it's done." When he made irritated noises, I reminded him that I needed to get back to writing my article.

"I'm pleased that you managed to work it into your busy schedule."

I couldn't think of a sufficiently scathing retort, so I just hung up. Hopefully O'Neal would interpret this as an overwhelming impulse to crystallize my thoughts on Stan Harris.

So, finally, it was time to Just Do It. No more procrastination, no more vital, but time-consuming trips. I had to bite the bullet, take the plunge, write the damn article. I circled the house, getting myself ready to begin. "I am not to be interrupted," I told my daughters as I made myself a peanut butter and banana sandwich, "except for a life-threatening emergency."

"Okay," Em said. "Katie and I were thinking of driving to the nursing home to visit Grandma. Maybe she's heard from Dad."

"Good idea." I placed my sandwich and a large handful of potato chips on a plate. "Oh, is that the mail?" I asked, as Katie walked in carrying a pile of envelopes.

"Yeah, there's several things for you—besides all these bills." She handed me a large brown envelope and a bright yellow flyer.

The flyer was for a weekend workshop, taught by Amber Harris, called "Fat Power! Love Your Body—No Matter What Shape You're In." On the top of the page Amber had written "Thought you might be able to use this in your article."

The oversized envelope contained a glossy photo of a smiling Dr. Elizabeth, either air-brushed or from an earlier decade of her life, and a lengthy and no doubt impressive curriculum vitae. She too had included a personal note: *"Ms. Prescott, I enjoyed our visit. Thought this might be valuable as background info for your article. Best, Dr. E."*

I poured coffee into a thermos, shaking my head. Threats, notes, and blatant self-promotion, all in one day. Too bad no one had thought to send me lavish gifts.

I bid my girls goodbye and carried my plate and thermos to the study. Fortunately, I had already transcribed my tape-recorded notes of the interviews. Now all I had to do was figure out the parts I wanted to use, arrange them enticingly, and write the damn article. I sipped my coffee, thinking through the various approaches I could use. *Before and After: The Life and Death of a Self-Made Fitness Professional*—a basic factual, chronological account? Or maybe a warts-and-all portrait of an ambitious but insecure entrepreneur who believed that success meant losing the fat? Or how about *The Suspicious Death of an Aging Fitness Fanatic*? (Wouldn't Terri be consulting her attorney about *that* one?)

Not many of the people I'd interviewed had seemed especially fond of Stan. He'd been unable to love or accept his children because they weren't what he wanted them to be—thin, fit, and heterosexual. Both of his wives had started out as his personal-like creations, former fatties whom he shaped up and rewarded with their own photos in his exercise book. But one had divorced him and the other was apparently having major marital problems. Was one of these persons Stan's killer?

I turned on my computer and spoke my writing mantra out loud: "It doesn't have to be good. It just has to be finished." Then I started writing.

I was still at it three hours later when someone knocked on the study door. "Go away. I'm writing," I yelled.

"We've got pizza," Katie yelled back.

Well, maybe a little break would make me more productive. I finished the sentence I was typing then joined the girls at the kitchen table where a wonderful-smelling veggie pizza served as centerpiece. I helped myself to a slice, then asked, "So how was your visit with Grandma?"

"Boring," Katie said.

"Unproductive," Em said. "The only time she heard from Dad was right before he closed his office. He phoned her to say he was leaving town for a long vacation—he didn't say to where. He said he'd continue to pay her bills while he was gone. And"—she blushed—"he told Grandma you and he were getting a divorce."

I knew all of this already, but it still irritated me. The idea of Rob grabbing every nickel and piece of furniture he could steal from me while assuring his greedy, mean-spirited mother, "Don't worry, Ma, I'll still spring for your over-priced nursing home," made me want to slash the tires of his Mercedes—if only I knew where it was parked. I also suspected that Grandma might have given the girls an earful of Rob's complaints about me. "So she doesn't know where he is either?"

Em shook her head. "Though she thinks he'll show up after his 'vacation' is over."

"Maybe she's right," I said. "He only paid her bill for two months ahead—I checked at the billing office. Maybe he plans on coming back after that." Or maybe he'd just send another cashier's check, after he made sure the old bat was still alive.

I wondered suddenly if the phone in the nursing home's offices had Caller ID. Could I cajole or bribe someone to watch for Rob's new phone number and then give it to me? I was certain that eventually he would telephone the home. Sentimental as he was about his mother, Rob was way, way too cheap to send a big check without first making sure that Mommy hadn't croaked. "What do you think . . ." I began and then, abruptly, stopped.

Katie had turned on the little kitchen TV to the local news. An anchor with bushy blond hair was talking about an elderly woman who had just been found dead—shot—in her home in a quiet Houston neighborhood. "Police suspect foul play," the anchor was saying as a picture of a covered body being carried out on a stretcher filled the screen. "The woman's name is being withheld until her relatives can be notified."

I stared at the television. No, it couldn't be. Could it? Oh, God, yes it could. With a trembling hand, I pointed at the screen. "That's Carol Quaid's mother's house."

Eleven

I told myself I had to be mistaken. Surely my brief glimpse of the dead woman's home on our old black-and-white TV was of another rather nondescript brick ranch house, not Mrs. Quaid's. Older subdivisions were filled with dozens of such basic three bedrooms/two baths. My exhausted brain had just leaped to an irrational association between the unidentified murdered woman and Eileen Quaid, the grieving mother I'd talked to earlier today.

Em put down her slice of pizza. "What if whoever killed Carol murdered her mother too?"

"It was probably just a house that looked like Mrs. Quaid's," I told my daughters. But just to reassure them—and myself—I looked up Eileen Quaid's phone number and called her.

The phone rang five times before Mrs. Quaid's recorded voice informed me that she was sorry to miss my call, but she'd call back if I left a message. I hesitated. What could I say? "Hi, it's Lauren Prescott. Just calling to see if you're still alive." Perhaps I'd be better advised to phone again tomorrow. After getting the terrible news about her daughter's death, Eileen could very well have gone to bed early. I glanced across the table at my own two daughters. If anything happened to one of them, I knew I might never get out of bed again.

I started to hang up, but a voice from the receiver—an insistent, male voice—stopped me. "Hello? Hello?"

"Yes." Suddenly I felt slightly ridiculous. "Is Mrs. Quaid

there?" I only wished I'd thought ahead to what I'd say when she came to the phone, peevish about being bothered at such a late hour.

"She isn't available. Who is this?"

Was the man her son, or maybe her brother? A boyfriend perhaps? "This is Lauren Prescott. Will you just let her know I called?" Maybe by the time she phoned back, I'd have thought of something to ask her.

"What is this call in regard to?" the man asked.

What business was that of his—whoever he was? "I've introduced myself. Now who are you?"

"This is Police Sergeant Andrew Wolfe, ma'am."

I took a deep breath before asking the question I wasn't sure that I wanted answered. "And what are you doing at Eileen Quaid's house?"

"There's been a homicide. Mrs. Quaid is dead."

For the second time in twenty-four hours my daughters and I gave our statements about a murder to the police. Sergeant Wolfe, a paunchy, middle-aged man with the red nose of a serious drinker, arrived within twenty minutes at my house, accompanied by a younger homicide detective, Officer John Watts, a lean black man with cold eyes. Wearily, I led the two of them to the kitchen table where Em and Katie were sitting.

"Now let me get this right," the detective said, as he sat down across from me. "You were the people—you and your daughters—who found the body of Mrs. Quaid's daughter?" His eyes bore into mine, as if, by sheer force of will, he would elicit a confession.

I had the insane urge to giggle nervously and say, "That is an incredible coincidence, isn't it?" but I took a deep breath and managed to restrain myself. "Yes, that's why

Mrs. Quaid came to our house this afternoon—she wanted to find out what we knew about Carol's death." Seeing his raised eyebrow, I added, "Which, unfortunately, was nothing. When we found Carol she was already dead."

He sent me a look that said he knew I was guilty—of something. "Did Mrs. Quaid blame you for her daughter's death?"

"No." I sent him my own arctic glare. "She as well as the Arrowfoot police knew I had nothing to do with her daughter's death. The medical examiner determined that Carol had been dead for several days before we found her."

"Before you say you first saw her," the detective said.

Why was it always the young officers who wanted to play the Bad Cop? I wondered, remembering the Nazi Youth clone who'd tried to bully me only yesterday. "The fact that I was right here and Carol Quaid was over one hundred miles away when she died makes it rather unlikely that I had an earlier look."

"Are there witnesses who can verify that you were here?"

I thought back over the last few days. "Yes, several. I was interviewing people for a magazine article." I watched as he jotted down their names in a small notebook, raising his eyebrow when he wrote down the part about my visit with Mrs. Quaid.

Now, apparently, it was Wolfe's turn to ask questions. "What time was it when Mrs. Quaid arrived at your house?"

"I think it was around 1:45. We'd just got back from Lake Arrowfoot when she showed up."

"Did you notice anyone following her?"

"No. I didn't see anyone outside waiting when she left either, about half an hour later." I glanced inquiringly at my girls.

"Me neither," Em said. "But I wasn't really looking for anybody."

Katie just shook her head.

"Do you know what time Mrs. Quaid was shot?" Em asked the police officers. "I mean, was it right after she left our house?"

The two of them looked at each other. Finally Watts spoke. "If she left your house by 2:30, it was several hours after that."

Em glanced at me. "Didn't Mrs. Quaid say something about going to see the other people whose names were in Carol's safe-deposit box?"

I could see the detective stiffen. "Do you know who those people are?"

"No, she didn't tell us," I said. "But she was carrying this huge brown envelope in her purse. She pulled out another smaller envelope with my husband's name on it. I had the idea there were other things that she'd found in Carol's safe-deposit box, too."

"What kind of things?" Watts asked.

"I have no idea. The stuff about Rob was two patients' dental records and their dental X-rays. And no, nothing seemed unusual about them, and I don't know why Carol bothered to keep the information."

"Maybe your husband could tell us that," Wolfe suggested.

"Maybe he could," I said, trying not to sound too bitter. "The problem is that we don't have a clue where he is."

After my bare-bones explanation about my husband's disappearance, Emily eyed the officers. "Why don't you put out an APB to find Dad?"

The detective raised an eyebrow—apparently one of his favorite gestures. "You think your father is somehow connected to these murders?"

Emily shrugged, looking quite nonchalant, I thought, for

someone who might be implicating her own father in a murder. "Oh, Daddy probably didn't kill anybody, but Carol Quaid was his office manager and she was keeping some of his files in her safe-deposit box, so maybe he'd know something about what's going on."

Daddy probably didn't kill anybody? Was my daughter horrifyingly cynical or had I missed something about my husband's basic character? Or maybe Emily thought that suggesting her father was involved in a homicide was an easy way to elicit police help in locating him.

Wolfe wrote down the pertinent information about Rob, then looked at me. "You sure this guy just didn't decide he wasn't going to hand over half his assets to you in a divorce settlement?"

"He didn't want to give me a cent, the stingy bastard! He emptied all our accounts and took everything he could cram into a moving van. Probably right now he's setting up a new life in Tahiti."

Em scowled at me. "But that still doesn't explain why Carol Quaid had Dad's dental records," she said to the officers. "Or why both of them left town right after Dad closed his office. I would think you'd want to find him and question him."

"And while he's in town, your divorce attorney can conveniently get her hooks in him?" Watts said to me.

Oh, good, a surly, suspicious, and divorced cop on the case. Just what I needed. "It occurred to me," I said, ignoring his question, "that if you find Mrs. Quaid's purse, you'll have the other envelopes with the names of the people she was intending to visit."

"What did this purse look like?" Sergeant Wolfe asked.

I shrugged. "It was big, a tote bag, I think. I wasn't paying much attention."

Katie sighed, rolling her eyes at me. "It was dark brown, Mother, a Louis Vuitton knock-off." When the officers looked at her blankly, she said, "A dark-brown purse with a pattern of tan logos all over it." Apparently, she couldn't help herself from adding, "Not a new look."

"I was just thinking," Em said to Sergeant Wolfe, "that Carol Quaid was also killed in her house—well, cabin actually—the same way her mother was. Was Mrs. Quaid lying in bed like her daughter was?"

The sergeant shook his head. "No, she was in the entry hall."

"Any sign of a struggle?" Em asked. "And do you know if it was the same caliber bullet that killed Carol?"

"That's classified police information," Watts said before the sergeant had a chance to share any more details. He glowered at Em. "You seem extremely interested in this investigation."

"I am," she said.

"She's always been a big mystery reader," I said, trying to telepathically signal her to shut up.

"Where were you today between 4:15 and 6:30?" the detective asked Em.

She thought about it. "We—Katie and I—were visiting our grandmother at her nursing home from about 4:15 until about 5:45. Then we stopped to pick up a pizza at Pizza Hut; it was probably a little after 6:30 when we got home."

"That's right," Katie said. "It was the Pizza Hut on Stanway. I talked to the manager—Fred Page—for a few minutes; we went to high school together."

The detective made a few notes, then turned to me. "What about you?"

"I was at home in the study, writing a magazine article."

"Can anyone verify that?" he asked.

"I can," Katie said. "She was in the study typing when we left. I could hear her pacing around and kind of muttering to herself."

I could feel myself blush. "That's the way I begin to write."

"And she was still in the study when we got back," Em said. "Because I called through the door that we had pizza, and she came out to eat with us."

"But no one else saw you during the hours your daughters were out of the house?" the detective asked me.

"Not unless they were peeking in the study window."

"So you're saying that you didn't step out of this house from 4:15 until 6:30?" he said.

"That's what I'm saying."

He looked as if he wanted to go knock on my neighbors' door to ask if anybody had seen me leave the house. But all he said was, "Well, I guess that's it for now." He stood up. "We might want to talk to you ladies again."

"Fine," I said, even though it wasn't.

The minute the two of them left, Katie said, "I want to get out of here. Everybody we meet—or try to meet—gets murdered."

"Tell me about it," Em said. "All the time we were talking I kept thinking that if Mrs. Quaid was shot because of some incriminating information she was carrying around in those envelopes, whoever shot her might think we know the same secret."

"And how would we know that?" I asked.

"Maybe the killer thinks she told us. Maybe he was following her and saw her stop at our house. Of course her death might have nothing to do with those envelopes, but if the killer was following her, for whatever reason, he still might think that Mrs. Quaid confided in us. And the bad

111

news is that this guy sounds pretty casual about killing people who irritate him."

Katie shuddered. "You are seriously creeping me out. I think we should all leave tonight. Mom, you can come home with me. You can stay with Brad and me for a while—until the police find the killer." She looked at Em. "If you want to, you can come too. We've got a futon in the guest bedroom."

Em shook her head. "No thanks, I need to get back to school."

"Well, I can't go," I said to Katie. "I need to finish my article. And can't you two wait until tomorrow morning to leave? I don't like to think of you on the road so late."

"You can't stay here alone, Mom," Katie said. "You can finish the article at my place. E-mail your article to my computer, and then you can finish it there. You can e-mail it to your editor when you're done."

"Sweetheart, I'm fine here. I need to finish my article on my computer. I appreciate the invitation, but truly, I'm not in any danger."

The sound of the doorbell made us all jump. Who would be at our door at this hour?

"Maybe it's the killer," Katie whispered.

"Don't be silly," I said, more out of habit than conviction. I walked to the front door, the girls right behind me, and peered out the peephole. "It's the police." I opened the door to Officer Watts and Sergeant Wolfe.

"We forgot to tell you," Wolfe said, "that you should plan on staying in town."

"But I have to go home to Dallas, to my husband and my work," Katie said.

"And I have to go back to school in Austin," Em said.

The sergeant glanced at Watts.

"It's okay if the two of you go tomorrow if you leave us your address and phone numbers," the detective said. "It's just your mother who needs to stay in town."

"Why?" Em asked, before I could say anything. "She was planning on going to visit my sister for a little while. You'll have the phone number."

"Well, she's just going to have to delay her visit," Watts said. "Whether you and your sister stay here with her is up to you."

He got the girls' addresses and phone numbers then turned to leave. "Good night, ladies," he said. "Be sure to lock your doors."

Twelve

Monday morning Em was already sitting at the table eating a bowl of Cheerios when I wandered into the kitchen. She pointed to the counter. "I made coffee."

"Bless you." I'd stayed up half the night working on my article, falling asleep around 3:30. The resulting four hours of sleep hadn't done me much good.

Em allowed me a few sips of coffee before she hit me with her theory. "Maybe the police think the three of us killed Carol and her mother and then set up Dad as the main suspect."

"What?"

"Oh, you know. Maybe we killed these women—because Carol was sleeping with Dad, or she was helping him hide from us, or for some other reason I can't think of—and then used the murders to manipulate the police into locating Dad for us. Once they found him, you could get back the money and furniture he stole from you."

Katie walked into the kitchen, yawning. "You need to stop reading all those mystery novels," she told her sister.

"And you need to start reading something other than fashion magazines."

I held up my palm. "I can NOT take this before I finish my first cup of coffee. So either hush or go argue somewhere else."

The girls glared at each other, but they hushed.

An hour later they were both gone. It was sweet of the girls to stay Sunday to "make sure you're safe, Mom," but, truth be told, I was glad to have the house to myself again. Sipping coffee, I reread my finished article. I couldn't gauge if the article was good or not, but I sensed it was at least adequate. I wished I'd had time to interview more people. Surely Stan Harris had had more deep-seated beliefs than fat is bad and fitness is good. But the deadline was today, and I was turning the article—good, mediocre, or truly lousy—over to my editor.

I took a quick shower, dressed in a dark wool pantsuit, and, manuscript in hand, headed to the downtown offices of *City Magazine*. I didn't trust e-mail to deliver my story; I was handing this baby over in person.

The receptionist looked up from the paperback she was reading. "I'm just here to deliver my article," I said, handing the manuscript to her. "Could you see that Mr. O'Neal gets it?"

"Hold on a minute." She glanced at the top page. "Paul," she said into the phone. "Lauren Prescott is here to drop off her article." She nodded and returned my story. "He says he wants to see you. Go on in."

The man looked just as rumpled and disorganized as the last time I'd seen him. The collar of his blue oxford-cloth shirt was unbuttoned, his navy and red striped tie was loosened, and his thick salt-and-pepper hair looked badly in need of a trim. He was moving a pile of manuscripts off a chair in front of his desk when I came in. "So, Ms. Prescott, you finished the article." He motioned for me to sit in the chair.

"You sound surprised," I said, handing him my story.

"Quite the contrary." His eyes scanned the first page of the article. "Since you were reassuring me almost daily that you would meet the deadline, I chose to believe you."

If he was so damn reassured, then why had he found it

necessary to check in with me every ten minutes? And did I have to sit here watching the man read my article—my first paid, professional writing in over two decades?

He seemed to sense my discomfort because he stopped reading and glanced over at me. "You hungry?"

His eyes, I noticed for the first time, were a startling shade of blue—Paul Newman eyes. I shrugged. I was always hungry, but it was not information I intended to share with him. "You're going to offer me a muffin while you read my article?"

He smiled. "No, I was going to offer you lunch. It's almost noon and I'm starving."

When I hesitated, he said, "And if you can hold out for a few minutes, I'll read your article first and we can discuss it over lunch."

"Fine," I said, not very graciously. "But I don't want to watch you read it."

He nodded. "Come back in fifteen minutes." He was already starting to read as I left his office.

There was a pile of *City Magazine*s on the coffee table in the waiting room. I sat down and pretended to read one of them.

It was a very long fifteen minutes. I reread the same paragraph without understanding a word as I envisioned all the scathing remarks Paul O'Neal would heap on my writing talent in general and this pathetic article in particular. When finally he emerged from his office, I practically leapt to my feet. No way was he going to humiliate me in front of any witnesses.

"Ready to go?" he asked. When I nodded, he told the receptionist he'd be back by 1:30, then held the outer door open for me. "How do you feel about Italian food? There's a good restaurant about a block away."

"Italian's great." I followed him into the empty elevator and took a deep breath, "However I'm much more interested in your opinion of my article."

He nodded. "You write well, but the article is a little soft."

"Soft?"

"I have the sense that you think Stan Harris was a Grade-A Prick—self-involved, narcissistic, a lousy, insensitive father—but you're afraid to say it."

"You want me to say he was a Grade-A Prick?"

"No, I want you to show it. You're a reporter, not an editorial writer."

The elevator door opened and the two of us got out. I was sorely tempted to turn in the direction of the parking lot, get into my car, and drive to the safe haven of my home. The last thing I wanted to do was sit in a restaurant for an hour while this guy tore apart my fledgling effort at Real Journalism. But pride or sheer stubbornness forced me to follow him out the building onto the sidewalk.

"It seemed as if you were leaving out the juicy quotes from the article." He glanced sideways at me. "But of course I might be wrong."

He wasn't wrong, and he knew it. We walked half a block before I asked him, "Are you trying to tell me that the article is bland and boring?"

"Not at all. What I'm telling you is that it's basically good, but could use some polishing and a few harder-hitting quotes. You just need to learn to be less polite."

At least it sounded as if he intended to run the story—and, I presumed, to pay me for it. So why did I feel so disappointed? Had I really expected him to tell me it was a brilliant piece of journalism?

Even though I didn't feel much like eating, I was glad we

were finally at the restaurant, a wonderfully garlicky-smelling, red-and-white-checked tablecloth kind of place. At Paul's insistence we ordered salads, garlic bread, and the spaghetti carbonara he said was the restaurant's specialty. "I'm famished," he said. "The last time I ate was lunch yesterday."

"You forgot to eat?" It was something I rarely forgot to do.

"I got carried away with finishing an article." He shrugged. "There was coffee and a few stale donuts at the office."

"Doesn't your wife mind you working those kind of hours?" I asked, remembering his evening phone calls from his office.

"My ex-wife has not been concerned about my working hours for the last ten years."

"Is that why you got a divorce? Because of your workaholism?"

He looked startled, then grinned. "That's the last time I encourage a woman to be less polite. But in answer to your question, no, the fact that my wife was having an affair with her boss was more of a precipitating factor. I didn't become a workaholic until later."

"To fill the lonely hours?"

He nodded. "Something like that." He waited until the waiter set down two huge plates of spaghetti in front of us. "What about you?"

"I'm not a workaholic," I said, answering the part of the question I felt comfortable discussing. "It's not my addiction of choice."

He expertly twirled spaghetti with a fork and spoon. "What is?"

I considered. "Probably chocolate."

118

"Any specific kind or all types?"

I swallowed a mouthful of delicious spaghetti. "All kinds, I guess, though, to tell you the truth, my personal and admittedly unsophisticated favorite is Baby Ruths."

He nodded. "That is kind of juvenile. I'm an M & M man myself."

"Plain or with peanuts?"

"Plain, of course. I'm a purist."

We finished our meals in a surprisingly companionable silence. I could only eat about half my spaghetti, but Paul cleaned his plate. "Weren't you hungry?" he asked.

"It was delicious, but, unlike you, I refuel several times a day."

He shook his head. "Such a conventional woman." When the waiter appeared, Paul asked, "Sure you wouldn't like a hot-fudge sundae or a cappuccino?"

I laughed. "No thanks. I need to get home to sharpen up my article."

We walked back to his office building. "Thanks for lunch," I said as we reached the parking lot.

"I enjoyed it. And don't worry too much about the rewrites. I sense you have hidden depths of journalistic ruthlessness just waiting to be tapped."

"Exactly what I wanted to hear," I said and headed for my car.

A police car was parked in front of my house as I turned into my driveway. Oh, lovely, my old friends Wolfe and Watts had come for another chat.

"What can I do for you, officers?" I asked as I stepped out of my car.

"Could we come inside for a moment, ma'am?" Wolfe asked. "We have a few more questions."

Did I have the option to say no? Several consecutive nights of virtual sleeplessness had suddenly caught up with me. The only thing I wanted to do at the moment was take a well-deserved nap. "Will it take very long?"

"Only a few minutes," Wolfe said, following me to the house.

In the kitchen, I poured myself a cup of coffee and, yawning, asked if they'd like a cup.

They both declined. "Long night?" Watts asked.

"I stayed up until 3:30 finishing my magazine article." You know, the article I said I was writing when you thought I was murdering Mrs. Quaid.

Watts nodded. "I've pulled some all-nighters myself. I'm going to law school at night. They can really wipe you out."

"They sure can." Was he playing the Good Cop now?

We all sat down at the kitchen table. "We need to ask you what kind of car your husband was driving when he left."

"A black Mercedes. I don't know if he's still driving it, but it's no longer in our garage."

"You know what model it was?"

I shook my head. "It was one year old, a sedan. But I have no idea what model it was. I'm not much of a car person." Which might explain why I was driving a ten-year-old Toyota while my husband was cruising around in a new Mercedes.

"And you haven't heard from him since he closed his office and left town?"

"No." I took a sip of the coffee and grimaced at the bitterness.

"Do you know of any connections your husband might have to the Lake Arrowfoot area?"

That jolted me awake. "No, except that was where Carol

Quaid was staying—in a cabin on Lake Arrowfoot." They were apparently waiting for me to expand on my answer, but I didn't know anything else. "Why are you asking this? Did you find Rob's car?"

"Maybe," Watts said. "Someone told the Arrowfoot Police that he remembered seeing a dark-colored Mercedes parked outside Ms. Quaid's cabin."

"When did he see it?"

I could feel the detective's eyes on my face. After a pause, he answered. "Last Wednesday afternoon."

I stared at him. The medical examiner had determined that Carol Quaid died last Wednesday afternoon or evening.

I felt as if someone were giving me vital information in a language I didn't understand. "Wait a minute," I finally managed to say. "Are you telling me that somebody saw Rob's car at Carol Quaid's cabin on the day she was murdered?"

"We're not sure if it was your husband's car," Watts said. "The witness didn't get the license number or see the driver."

"Did this witness say how long the Mercedes had been there?" Might the car's driver, for instance, have been hiding out with Carol at her cabin for the last several weeks?

Watts shook his head. "He didn't see when the car arrived or when it left. But he said it was the first time he saw any car other than Ms. Quaid's Honda at the cabin."

So if the car was Rob's he probably had only been making a short visit. The question, of course, was why. Had he gone there intending to shoot Carol? Or had he come for another reason, but he and Carol started arguing and things got out of hand? Or maybe Carol was already dead by the time Rob arrived, and instead of phoning the police, as his law-abiding wife had done, he'd just decided to get the hell out.

"Does your husband own a gun?" Wolfe asked.

"Not that I know of." But I had the growing suspicion there were many things I didn't know about Rob.

"Can you tell us anything about your husband's relationship with Ms. Quaid?"

"Well, she was his office manager for ten years."

"What about any personal relationship? Did you have the sense that they were . . . close?" Wolfe glanced away, his ruddy cheeks growing redder, as he asked the last question.

For some reason I was touched by his embarrassment. "I never thought they had anything other than a professional relationship. I always had the idea Rob thought Carol was smart and competent but he didn't like her." I hesitated.

"But something happened to make you alter your opinion?" Watts asked, his eyes on my face.

Gee, Officer, the fact that the man walked out on me after more than two decades of marriage—that "something"—made me alter a hell of a lot of my long-held opinions. In fact many of those beliefs—about Rob, about marriage and fidelity, about the wisdom of ignoring ugly truths about the people I loved—would probably never be the same again. I took a deep breath, trying to squelch a spontaneous brush fire of emotion. It was not—I reminded myself—these two men I was angry with.

"After Rob left I talked to a woman who'd been a receptionist in his office, and she said she thought Rob and Carol might have been having an affair." Before one of the officers had a chance to ask the next question, I answered it. "And yes, that was why I drove up to Lake Arrowfoot Friday to see Carol. I thought that Rob might be staying at the cabin with her, or at least she might know where he was."

The detective raised his eyebrows. "You must have been very angry with Ms. Quaid for breaking up your marriage."

I didn't take the bait. "I was certainly angry with Rob, but I just thought Carol might help me find him. I'd talked to everyone else I could think of, and nobody seemed to know where he'd gone."

"You didn't blame her for having an affair with your husband?"

"Mainly what I felt was desperate for information. My husband emptied out all our bank accounts and took almost every valuable object we ever owned, and I was broke—am broke. At this point all I want is my share of our joint money. I hoped Carol might be a means to get it."

Watts didn't look as if he was buying this explanation. But all he said was, "Do you have a recent photo of your husband? The Lake Arrowfoot Police want to show it around in case somebody there remembers seeing him."

I thought a moment. "Probably the most recent one I have is from my daughter's wedding last summer. I'll get it for you."

Leaving them in the kitchen, I headed for the den where a series of framed family photos stood on the bookshelf. Rob had taken all our oil paintings, but he'd left the photo of himself walking his elder daughter, a radiant, beautiful bride, down the aisle. I found a duplicate of the photo in our album and carefully removed it. Before taking it to the officers, I studied the picture. Were there signs even then that this tuxedo-wearing father of the bride was not the man I always assumed he was? Didn't those eyes seem a bit vacant, and that smile appear not quite genuine? Perhaps I was just imagining that, interpreting past events to conform to later realities.

I returned to the kitchen and handed the photo to Wolfe.

He glanced at it. "Thanks. We'll fax it to the Arrowfoot Police. Maybe show it around Mrs. Quaid's neighborhood."

I was startled. "You think Rob might be in town?"

"We don't know where he is, ma'am, but sooner or later we're going to find him."

Watts stood up. "If you see your husband, please call one of us immediately." He handed me a business card. "He may have nothing to do with these deaths, but we also might be dealing with a dangerous and desperate man."

Dangerous and desperate? As I followed the officers to the door, it occurred to me that only a few weeks ago I would have scoffed at the notion that Rob was even remotely dangerous. But now I didn't know what to think.

"By the way," Watts said, "I meant to tell you we found that big purse of Mrs. Quaid's at her house."

"Did you get the envelopes I told you about?"

"Nope. Only thing in her purse was her wallet."

"You didn't find a big brown envelope or a smaller envelope with my husband's name on it somewhere else in the house?"

He shook his head. "Not in her car either."

Had Mrs. Quaid hidden the envelopes somewhere for safekeeping? Or had whoever shot her also taken the information Carol was keeping in her safe-deposit box—perhaps killed her because of that information?

The two men stood. "We'll be in touch," Watts said as they left.

Suddenly freezing, I wrapped my arms tightly around myself. I made very sure the deadbolt was locked before heading back to the kitchen.

I had intended to take a long nap as soon as I got home

and then get to work on rewriting my article. But now I felt too wired to sleep and too preoccupied with the Quaid women's murders to focus on anything else. What if Rob had been at Carol Quaid's cabin on the day she was killed— and what if he hadn't come just to trade nostalgic dental stories?

The police thought that Rob might be here in town. If he'd actually killed Carol, what else was he capable of doing?

Thirteen

"Well hello, stranger," a familiar alto voice said when I answered my phone. "Your daughter is very worried about you and wants dear Aunt Meg to intervene."

"Which daughter are we talking about?"

"My attentive goddaughter—the one who keeps me better informed than my supposed best friend."

Touché. "I'm sorry, Meg. I've just been so busy lately trying to finish my article and deal with everything else that's happened." I was confident that Katie had already filled her in on all the details. "Did Katie seem very upset? It was horrible for the girls to find Carol Quaid's body like that."

"She seemed more concerned about you. She wants you to move into my place because she thinks you're in danger staying there alone. And I graciously replied that I'd love to have you."

I sighed. "Katie is a worry-wart."

Meg laughed. "Lord, I don't think I've heard that word since the fifth grade." She paused. "But why don't you come spend the night anyway? Think of it as a sleepover for grownups."

I was tempted. "I'd love to, but I need to rewrite my article. I had lunch with Paul today, and he said it wasn't hard-hitting enough."

"It's Paul now, is it?"

Somehow she seemed to be missing the point. "That is his name. What do you want me to call him, He Who

Makes Me Rewrite My Article?"

"A couple weeks ago you were calling him That Jerk O'Neal."

"It's what I might be calling him again next week if he doesn't accept my rewrites. He did say, by the way, that the article was basically well written."

"Of course it is. Everything you write is well written. Now would you prefer that I come spend the night at your house? You can do your writing, and I'll do something quiet."

"That's very sweet of you, but Katie really was over-reacting. I'm perfectly safe here." I hoped. "Did I mention that the police just told me someone spotted a black Mercedes at Carol Quaid's cabin on the day she died, and now they're looking for Rob?"

Meg shrieked. "They think Rob is the killer?"

"Well, let's just say they're very interested in talking to him. Apparently they're even looking for him around here."

There was a pause. "You don't think he killed anyone, do you?"

"No, but I didn't think he'd run off with all our money and good furniture either."

"Lauren, you know I've never been a fan of Rob's. In fact, if asked to pick adjectives to describe him, the ones that come to mind are selfish, cheap, pompous, humorless, anal, self-absorbed . . ."

"I get the picture."

"And amoral. The man has the ethics of a newt. How-ever, even I do not think he's a murderer. I wouldn't have any problem believing that he robbed or cheated those women, but I just don't see him shooting them. This was a man, you may remember, who covered his eyes during tor-ture scenes in movies. He was, excuse the expression, a total wuss."

I snickered. "He was, wasn't he? Remember how upset he was when that movie *Marathon Man* came out, the one with Laurence Olivier as the sadistic dentist who tortured Dustin Hoffman with a dental drill?"

Meg groaned. "Do I? I think he must have talked non-stop for almost an hour about how that movie sent dentistry back forty years, and how his patients always told him how gentle he was. It was probably the longest conversation we ever had in twenty years—made me happy that he usually ignored me."

I grinned, remembering that night and how Meg started calling him "Gentle Rob" behind his back. "Just talking to you has made me feel better. If you, who always thought the worst of Rob, don't think he's a killer—well, that's good enough for me."

"Oh, he's a bastard, but not a homicidal one. You sure you don't want me to come over tonight to dispense some more down-home wisdom?"

"It's tempting, but I'll have to pass. I really have to finish my article."

"No, we certainly wouldn't want to disappoint Paul now, would we?"

"I'll call you when I'm finished," I promised.

I had barely put down the receiver when the front doorbell rang. The police returning for another chat?

I peered through the peephole and mentally groaned. Terri Harris stood on my front porch, looking impatient. What was she doing here—coming to my house to demand to read my story? I was tempted to pretend I wasn't home, but knowing Terri, she'd probably skulk around the house to peek in my windows.

I opened the door. "Terri, what a surprise."

She smiled, revealing very white teeth. "I stopped by to

let you know, before you read it in the newspaper, that I just sold the business to the National Gyms syndicate. I didn't admit it before because I wasn't sure the deal would go through."

So instead she'd lied that she wasn't even considering selling. "Will they continue to run the gym under the new ownership?"

"I'm not sure about the details, but our gym is closing in two weeks. The syndicate may remodel it and then reopen as a larger, more modern facility."

That was fast. "Were you and Stan planning to sell before he died?"

The question seemed to fluster her. "Uh, no, this was my decision."

I remembered my editor's recent admonition about getting tough. "In other words, your husband wouldn't have wanted you to sell his gym?"

She glared at me. "It's my gym now." Before I could ask another rude question, she said, "I also wanted to tell you that Stan's death has officially been ruled an accident. All the potassium pills he was taking along with the potassium in the salt substitute he used sent him into cardiac arrest." She sighed. "Poor Stan was taking huge amounts of diuretics so he wouldn't look bloated in the advertising photos. But the diuretics made him lose too much potassium and then he had muscle cramps and dizziness. So that was why he took all those potassium supplements." She shook her head sadly. "Bless his heart, my sweetie's vanity ended up killing him."

So Stan's death was being called an accident. "What about that puncture mark between his toes? Was Stan injecting himself with potassium as well as taking the supplements?"

Terri shrugged. "I don't know anything about that. He

could have given himself an injection—he wasn't queasy about needles or anything. I remember he sometimes used to give himself some vitamin shot for energy. Stan's doctor testified that she warned him about overdoing the diuretics and extra potassium, especially with his family history of heart disease. But, as usual, Stan didn't listen. He always thought he knew more about his health than doctors did."

"Which doctor," I began. But Terri had already turned away.

"Got to run," she called over her shoulder. "Send me a copy of your story when it comes out."

I watched her jog the few yards to her silver BMW, knowing I should be happy that she'd given me new information and some good quotes for my article. But my main reaction as I watched her drive away was distaste. Her syrupy hypocrisy made me, for the very first time, feel sorry for the late Stan Harris.

The PR woman at National Gyms, Inc. was surprisingly helpful, particularly when I mentioned that I might be willing to give her company a plug in my *City Magazine* article about Stan Harris. Yes, she said, they had purchased Stan's gym this week. They would probably use the location for building a new National Gyms facility; she had heard no discussion of remodeling Stan's existing structure. "It's a prime location, you know. That was why we approached Mr. Harris in the first place, but at that time he wasn't interested in selling."

I listened for a few minutes to the woman's description of the glorious new gym the company was planning to build on the site, a huge, high-rise facility filled with "state-of-the-art exercise equipment," an indoor jogging track, and an Olympic-sized swimming pool. From what I knew about him, Stan would have hated everything about it.

"When did you say that your company first approached Mr. Harris?" I asked. I could sense the wheels spinning in her head: what did that have to do with anything?

"I'm not sure," she said, her voice noticeably chillier, "sometime in late fall, I think."

"A few months before he died then?"

"I guess." The topic clearly did not interest her.

"But after Mr. Harris died, in early January, you decided to approach Terri Harris to see if she was interested in selling?"

"No, actually she approached us. I'm not certain of the exact date. Mrs. Harris said the gym was too much for her to keep up. And, off the record, I don't think their facility was doing very well financially. Their equipment, their whole approach was, well, rather dated."

"But I'd heard that Mr. Harris had been planning a major renovation, significantly expanding the gym."

"I wasn't aware of that."

I sensed I wouldn't be getting much more useful information out of her. "How much did your company pay for the Harris gym?" As she started to protest, I added—bluffing—"It *is* public record, you know."

To my surprise, she bought it. Who knows, maybe the selling price actually was a matter of public record. "In the one million dollar range."

I thanked her for her cooperation and hung up. Well, well. Terri certainly hadn't wasted much time in unloading her late husband's beloved gym! I wondered suddenly how much of the million dollars she would pocket herself. Had she been Stan's sole heir or would Terri have to share the money with Stan's children? Of course if there were substantial debts to be paid, maybe there wouldn't be much money for anyone to inherit.

Perhaps Jane—the first, and to my mind, nicer Mrs. Harris—would tell me about Stan's will. I phoned her number, but only her answering machine responded. I left a message that I had a question for my article and would appreciate her calling me whenever she got in.

She hadn't phoned back by 10:15 when I finally finished my rewrites. Maybe she was working the night shift at the hospital again. If she phoned tomorrow, though, I could still use the information.

I read my article one more time. It did seem better— faster paced and certainly more opinionated. Terri Harris, I suspected, would not be pleased by her portrayal.

I e-mailed the new-and-improved story to Paul O'Neal, then, impulsively, picked up the phone and dialed his office. Paul had told me to call anytime if I had a question, and he had often phoned me at night from the magazine. But this time he wasn't there. His phone rang until his voice mail picked up. I hung up without leaving a message, surprised at how disappointed I felt that he wasn't there to discuss my story.

It was time for the long, hot bath that I'd been promising myself. I'd always loved reading while stretched out in warm, scented water. When my children were very little, my bath-with-a-book had been about the only time in the day that I could call my own. But tonight not even my favorite lavender bath salts and a P.D. James novel could help me relax. I kept straining to hear unwelcome noises: a door being forced open or the sound of breaking glass from downstairs.

It's just your over-active imagination, I told myself when the sounds of someone walking by on the sidewalk outside made my heart race. I was reminding myself of Katie at three years old. She had vehemently insisted—despite repeated under-the-bed inspections with her parents—that a monster was under her bed. I ran some more hot water and tried hard not to think about the monster that had entered Mrs. Quaid's house two nights ago. Probably until then she too had felt safe in her own home.

Finally I managed to fall into a fitful sleep. I awoke feeling groggy and headachy. The joint funeral service for the two Quaid women was scheduled for this morning, and I wanted to attend.

Dressed in my black wool suit and black pumps, I drove to the large Methodist church near Mrs. Quaid's home.

I parked and was walking to the church when I heard someone behind me call my name. It was Elizabeth Stevens—Dr. Elizabeth—heading toward me.

"Lauren, how are you doing?" she asked, peering sympathetically into my eyes. "I heard that you were the person who discovered Carol's body."

The first time I met her, I'd been impressed at how good she was at empathy, but today her easy warmth seemed less credible. Maybe my sleep deprivation was making me cranky. I mumbled something about of course my daughters and I had been terribly shocked.

She patted my shoulder. "It's often beneficial to discuss painful subjects with others."

And sometimes it isn't. "Yes, I'm sure that's true," I said. "Now how do you know the Quaid women?"

She blinked, looking momentarily confused. "Carol was in the same graduate program as I was. We both were getting MBAs on the weekends. I didn't know her all that well, but she was kind enough to help me with the homework.

Carol was much, much better at math than I am." She shook her head. "It's hard for me to process that someone who was so healthy and energetic is now dead."

Fortunately we had reached the church entrance. "Nice seeing you again," I lied and headed inside, hoping she wouldn't choose to sit next to me.

There were already a respectable number of mourners seated in the sanctuary, a stark, blond-brick place with high ceilings and very little in the way of ornamentation—a setting that seemed right for the blunt, plain-spoken Quaid women. In the middle of the church I spotted Iris and Marla, Rob's former receptionist and his dental hygienist, sitting next to a young woman with long dark hair who I didn't recognize. Iris waved at me to come join them.

"Isn't this terrible?" she whispered, after sliding to make room for me on the pew. "Two women in the same family—and in the same week!"

"Yes, it is terrible."

I smiled at Marla, who was leaning toward me. "Have you heard anything from Dr. P?" she whispered.

I shook my head. "I take it he hasn't sent you your last paycheck either."

"Not yet." She smiled weakly, trying not to look angry, but not quite succeeding.

I could relate, though I was well aware that my empathy didn't help either of us to pay the mortgage.

The service started then. The minister, an earnest, prematurely bald man with wire rim glasses, spoke of the tragedy of the deaths of these "two good Christian women." Apparently Eileen Quaid had been very active in the church, as a Sunday school teacher and as women's guild president.

I scanned the mourners, most of whom seemed quite

elderly. They were probably Mrs. Quaid's friends. But at the very back of the church I noticed two familiar faces: Officer Watts and Sergeant Wolfe. Noticing my scrutiny, Wolfe nodded at me. I nodded back, wondering if they expected the women's killers—or killer—to come pay their respects to their victims.

The very thought made me shudder. "But we must not dwell selfishly on our own sense of loss," the minister was saying, "but instead we should rejoice for these fine women, knowing that they're now in a better place, at home with their Lord."

I could hear some muffled sobs as a soloist sang "Amazing Grace." The song made me feel a little teary too, as I remembered the grieving mother who'd been so desperate to make sense of her daughter's death.

There was a luncheon in the church fellowship hall after the service. Iris and Marla wanted to attend it, but I didn't, so I told them goodbye in the church corridor. "If you hear from Dr. P, you'll let us know?" Marla asked after mentioning that she still hadn't been able to find another job.

"You bet. And if you hear from him—"

"I will call you immediately. And then"—she smiled grimly at me—"one of us can phone the police."

I walked to my car, thinking of all the money Rob had managed to steal from those around him. If the police did locate him, would they find his money too? Or would Rob have already hidden it somewhere, in some secret Swiss bank account? Knowing my dear husband, he'd probably rather go to prison than hand over a dollar.

I was so absorbed in my thoughts that at first I wasn't aware that someone was trying to catch my attention. "I've been calling your name," the young dark-haired woman from the church said accusingly. "I wanted to talk to you about your husband."

"Rob?" I said, inanely. Was this another person who Rob owed money to?

She nodded. "Your husband is really, really cheap."

"Tell me about it." I looked at her. "Have we met?"

"No, but we talked on the phone. I'm Kimberly Moss, Rob's receptionist."

Ah, the snotty, Marilyn Monroe imitator. Her voice was less breathy and little-girlish than I remembered, or maybe that was just an act she reserved for the phone. She didn't look the way I expected. Scrawny, with no visible bustline, she had long, straight, center-parted hair and the remnants of adolescent acne on her pale skin. The only thing I'd guessed right was her age. "Did Rob not pay you your last paycheck either?" I asked.

"No, he gave me that. What I meant was that he was cheap about everything that didn't affect him. If it was for him, then he'd splurge and buy the best. He'd buy himself this aged Scotch and get me some generic beer that even a wino wouldn't touch. I don't know how you put up with him all those years."

I'd been wondering that myself, but at the moment I had more pressing questions. "And what was your relationship with Rob—besides being his receptionist, I mean?"

She shrugged. "We were together, briefly, after he left town."

She was so nonchalant about the whole thing that, for one of the very few times in my life, I was speechless.

Kimberly didn't seem to notice. "The last straw was when he bought me cubic zirconium earrings for my birthday and tried to convince me they were diamonds."

I shrugged. What did she want from me, sympathy? "He

once bought me a new iron for my birthday, so I'd do a better job of ironing his shirts."

She rolled her eyes. "What a schmuck!"

"So where is Rob now?"

"He was at this god-awful place in Mexico, right over the border." She sighed. "He told me we'd go someplace in the Caribbean—beaches, pina coladas, that kind of thing. Sounded great to me. But then Rob found out how expensive the Caribbean is and how cheap Mexico is, so he decides we should live there. But after a week in this cockroach heaven—where I got this incredible diarrhea, not to mention the cubic zirconium earrings—I told him adios, I could do a lot better than him. 'People who are as lousy in bed as you are, should at least give good gifts,' I said."

Despite myself, I snickered. "You know I thought he was having an affair with Carol Quaid."

She looked shocked. "Oh, God, no. She was much too old for him."

I could feel myself stiffen. "Carol was a good ten years younger than Rob was."

She shrugged. "It wasn't just her age. He really didn't like Carol. It was almost as if he was afraid of her."

"Afraid? Do you know why?"

"He always said what a ball-breaking bitch she was, but I always thought it was more than that. If he hated her so much, why didn't he just fire her?"

"But you liked Carol?" The two of them seemed incongruous friends.

"Hell, no, she was a bossy, motor-mouthed bitch."

"Uh, so why did you come to her funeral?"

She looked offended. "Office loyalty, of course. She *was* a colleague, after all."

Okay. I had a feeling that she had already told me everything of interest, but I tried one more time. "So do you think Rob might still be in Mexico?"

She shook her head. "No, he was getting kind of paranoid. Someone sent him a letter—I don't know who—and it really freaked him out that they'd been able to locate him. I bet he's moved on to some other cheap rat hole by now."

So much for that, I thought, feeling even more discouraged about ever getting back the money Rob had stolen from me. "I've got to get home." The home that might be taken away from me unless I found Rob or a well-paying job in the very near future.

"Hold on," she said, touching my arm. "I want to tell you something. Rob told me how he'd taken all your art and furniture." She wrinkled her nose. "That sucks, and I told him so. It's one thing to want to leave a dead, boring marriage, but that's no reason to spit on your ex. My mom, who's been married four times—my dad was her third husband—always told me that you can see how a man eventually will treat you if you watch how he behaves toward his wife."

I raised an eyebrow. "Interesting theory."

"So I just wanted to tell you that Rob put all the stuff he took from your house into this big storage place on Tenth Street. Said he didn't have time to sell it before he left town. Maybe you can go there and get the stuff back."

I looked at her. So it was okay to take someone's husband but not her big-screen TV? I took a deep breath. "Thanks."

"You're welcome," she said, then turned and walked back toward the church.

Fourteen

It was easier than I'd anticipated to find the storage facility where Rob had stashed our valuables. Convincing the jerk on the phone that I had any legal right to the stored contents wasn't so simple.

"You don't have the key to the storage room, you don't have any rights," he said. "Our clients are entitled to their privacy."

"What if the client stole the objects in storage?" I asked. "Rob Prescott, my husband, is trying to hide the furniture he illegally took from me."

"That happens a lot," he said, sounding bored. "We can't go into the room either. You seem not to get this— Prescott has the key to the storage room."

"You mean if my husband stops paying rent for this stuff you'll just let him store it there for free?"

"In the case of non-payment, we do enter the premises."

"So you do have a key!"

"Which we do not use except in extraordinary circumstances. We're kind of like a big safe-deposit box at a bank. Anyway, according to our records, Mr. Prescott has paid through the end of next month."

I wondered if that fact was significant. Did Rob intend to come back to town next month to retrieve the furniture?

I took a deep breath and tried another tack. "I'm sure you don't want to get into trouble for knowingly helping a thief to hide stolen goods. What if I come by, with proper identification, and take only half—my half—of the furniture and art? That way I won't have to call the police."

He snickered. "No, then your husband would call the cops. Listen, lady, we don't get involved in this divorce crap. Take my advice and either get yourself a good lawyer or else go steal the key from your husband's pants."

I hung up on him.

I was still fuming when Meg dropped by "to see if you're still alive."

I told her my story. "The thing that really burns me is that now I know where my grandmother's silver service is, but I can't get it back."

Meg shook her head. "For God's sake, why didn't you talk to me before you called the storage place?"

"And you could have done—what? Phone the storage guy pretending you were Rob, giving permission to let me in the storage room to take whatever I want?"

"Oh, ye of little faith." Meg glanced at her watch, then pulled her cell phone from her purse. "I hope I can still catch him."

"Him who?" I whispered.

She shook her head, holding one finger to her lips. "Nellie!" she exclaimed with the manic enthusiasm of a Miss America contestant, "it's Meg Peters. How are you? Those twin grandbabies of yours must be three years old by now." A pause. "Four? Well, that's an easier age, isn't it? Three year olds are a little too close to the terrible two-and-a-halves, as I recall."

I rolled my eyes. Meg's personal experience of three year olds consisted entirely of taking my children for short but very expensive trips to the toy store. By the time she'd acquired a stepchild, in her second marriage, he'd been well past the preschool years.

140

"Any chance that I might be able to speak to His Honor if he's not already in court? He's not? Great, I promise I'll only take a few minutes."

His Honor apparently agreed to talk because a minute later Meg said, "Well hello, Darlin'. I do know how busy you are, but I have a little favor to ask. Unfortunately, the situation is rather urgent, and you are the only person I know with the power to solve it."

I stared at her. My irreverent, feminist friend had seemed to morph in front of my eyes into a husky-voiced vamp whose faint Texas accent had turned into something straight from "Steel Magnolias." And who the hell was Darlin'?

Meg listened for a moment, a faint smile on her face. Then suddenly she shrieked with laughter. "Oh, you're so bad! No, this has to do only with your legal expertise."

Lord, was she shameless! Unfortunately she also was observant enough to notice my eavesdropping and turning her back on me, walked out of the room. I could hear a throaty laugh before a door closed.

Well, I had my own phone calls to make. Jane Harris had returned my call when I was out. Maybe I could end our phone tag.

She answered on the second ring, sounding tense.

"Mrs. Harris, this is Lauren Prescott again. I'm sorry we keep missing each other. If you have a few minutes—"

"I'm on my way to work," she interrupted. "I can give you three minutes."

So I'd skip my subtle lead-in. "I want to find out about Stan's will, who he left his assets to."

"Terri gets the house and half of Stan's share of his business. Amber and SJ—Stan Junior—each get a quarter of his business."

"So Amber and SJ were involved in selling the gym?"

"More like Terri talked them into it. Apparently business at Stan's gym hadn't been very good lately, and Terri convinced them it was better to cut their losses and sell the place while they still had an interested buyer."

I knew my interview time was running out, but there was an undercurrent in her words that puzzled me. "You sound disapproving."

She hesitated, then asked, "You won't publish what I tell you?"

"Not if you don't want me to."

"I can't prove anything—I may be totally off-base—but I think Terri is screwing my kids out of money that should rightfully be theirs. Behind that perky cheerleader exterior is a money-grubbing bitch. It took Stan a long time, but finally even he realized how ruthless Terri really is."

"So why did he leave almost everything to her?"

"He died before he had a chance to change the will. Last time I saw him, Stan told he was going to leave everything to the kids. And he planned to divorce Terri. There was someone else he was in love with—he didn't tell me who, but he said he wouldn't be surprised if he married her someday."

"When did Stan tell you all this?"

"About a week before he died." She gave a little gasp. "Didn't realize how late it is. Got to go." She hung up before I could say goodbye.

Meg walked back into the kitchen, looking smug. "Well, I've got everything worked out for you," she said. "Now all we have to do is find a couple of hunks with a truck."

"Hold on a minute. What do you mean you've got it all worked out for me? And who the hell is Darlin'?" The hunks with a truck could wait until later.

She grinned at me, looking, if possible, even more pleased with herself. "In approximately two hours a police officer will deliver a court order to the stubborn man at the storage office. It will legally force him to unlock Stan's storage room and allow you to retrieve your stolen goods. Which is why we need the hunks with a truck."

I stared at her. "How'd you manage that? And—again— who is Darlin'?"

"Russ, my stepson. You remember him, the wise-ass, red-haired kid who always spent the summer with Russell and me. I always used to tell him with a mouth like his he should become a lawyer."

I did, as a matter of fact, remember Russ, a smart, skinny kid who seemed to spend all his time either arguing or reading. And I remember thinking a few years ago when he was elected to the bench that he'd make a fine judge. "What was all that stuff about 'Oh, dear, you are so-o bad'?" I asked, trying my best to imitate her exaggerated Southern drawl.

Meg rolled her eyes. "What a potty mind you have! For your information, Russ was merely recalling some of the pranks he used to play on me."

"I do not have a 'potty mind.' I was merely asking a simple question."

Meg raised an eyebrow. "Okay, and now I'm asking a question: When are you going to get off your ass and find us some movers?"

"What about professional movers?"

"Too late. They need more notice."

I tried to picture all the muscular men I knew who might be available and willing to help. The only one who came to mind was my fit and agreeable son-in-law, who, unfortunately, lived five hours away. But his wife, on the other hand, had a lot of old boyfriends. I phoned Katie at work.

"It's great that you're getting the furniture back!" she said when I explained the situation. "Let me call around to see if I can find someone to help you move it back home."

"Thanks, honey. But if you can't find anyone, I guess Meg and I can put the stuff in our cars." I hung up the phone, ignoring the glare Meg was sending my way.

"Have you lost your mind? How could the two of us shove your dining room table, sofa, and antique sideboard—among other things—into our vehicles? Particularly when old Meg, as you may recall, has a bad back."

I shrugged. "I've been thinking that I really don't need much of that furniture anymore. I'm kind of getting used to the minimalist look. The only thing I really want back is my grandmother's silver tea service."

Meg shook her head, looking disgusted.

"What's your problem?" I asked.

"Number one: I didn't go to all this effort for you to retrieve only your grandmother's tea set. Number two: You have to get over this unselfish, self-sacrificing, I-have-no-needs-of-my-own mindset. It's unhealthy. You are entitled to these items, Lauren. Your loving husband stole every decent piece of furniture you own, your art, and your financial investments. You are merely retrieving them."

"Hold on one minute! What do you mean by that no-needs-of-my-own crack?"

Meg sighed and glanced pointedly at her watch. "This is hardly the time for this conversation."

"Like hell it isn't."

She sighed again, but this time she also sat down on a kitchen chair. "I was merely suggesting that you be more selfish, more focused on your own self-interest."

"It sounded to me as if you were suggesting a lot more than that," I said, impaling her with my malevolent glare.

Meg did not even have the grace to look embarrassed. "Okay, maybe I am. I guess I'm saying that you have always seemed to perceive your role in life as being a caretaker of others. That was fine when your daughters were little and needed you every minute. But right now those traits are not serving you well. Rob may be a self-absorbed, greedy pig, but you let him get away with it. You let him walk all over you."

I could feel my hands clench into fists. I'd never hit anyone since I'd become a grownup, but there was a first time for everything. I settled instead for yelling. "Damn you, Meg, that is so unfair! What was I supposed to do—post a guard at my house to prevent Rob from taking my furniture? Should I have confiscated the money from our accounts before Rob had a chance to get to them?"

"No, but you should have at least contacted a divorce attorney instead of sitting around waiting for—what? Rob to come to his senses and return home to you?"

"That is such bull—"

She raised a palm. "You want to hear this or not?"

I was not entirely sure that I did, but I shut up and let her finish.

"It's true no one could expect you to predict that Rob would walk out on you. But it's just as true that had you built a life of your own—gone back to work after the girls were grown, had a real bank account in your own name that Rob couldn't get into—you would not have been so totally vulnerable when Rob had his midlife crisis."

I stared at her, feeling hurt and angry and betrayed. Had she, my supposed best friend, been thinking all these years that I was some kind of pathetic Donna Reed clone, some throwback to the 1950s? Or was this just twenty-twenty hindsight—a revelation formulated only after Rob left me penniless? "I am not about to justify my life choices to you, Meg, but I do want to say that this reeks of blaming the rape victim for being raped: 'it never would have happened if she wasn't wearing so much makeup and out alone at night.' "

Meg's eyes flashed. "I am not blaming the rape victim. I'm just suggesting that every woman should take a self-defense class."

The ring of the telephone startled both of us. I picked it up. "Hello?"

"Mom, I've solved your problem," Katie said, her voice high with excitement. "I've got hold of Brad's brother Jason, and he and his buddy will bring a U-Haul to that storage place. You need to call him to set up the time."

I wrote down the name and phone number she gave me. "Thanks, honey."

"I think it is so cool that you're stealing back your furniture! Won't Dad freak when he goes to pick up the stuff and all he finds is an empty storage room?"

"I bet he will," I said, trying to sound more enthusiastic than I felt. "Bye, sweetheart."

I dialed Jason's number and made the arrangements. As I replaced the receiver, I told Meg, "The hunks and the truck are going to meet us at the storage place at four."

The man I'd spoken to at the storage facility was not at all pleased when presented with the court order allowing me to retrieve my stolen goods from the premises. But eventually, after ranting a bit and phoning his boss, he reluctantly opened Rob's storage unit and allowed Meg, my two volunteer movers and myself inside.

Everything was there: my dining room table and eight matching chairs, the living room furniture, art, assorted antiques, the big-screen TV. I glanced from object to object, remembering our twenty-fifth anniversary trip to Turkey when Rob and I bought the two Oriental rugs, the Sunday afternoon drive in the country when we'd stopped at a roadside antique store and found the pine sideboard, the Father's Day when the girls and I had surprised Rob with the big-screen TV. It was as if each piece of furniture represented a day or a specific event in my married life, and Rob had decided that he alone was entitled to all the memories.

"You want us to load up everything, Mrs. Prescott?" asked Jason, a friendly, muscular young man who looked a lot like his older brother. He and his friend Sam had arrived with a rental truck that appeared big enough to hold the entire contents of my house.

"Not everything. Some of this is my husband's." I ignored Meg's groan and looked around at the assembled marital property. "Leave the TV, that pair of wing chairs, those antique tables over there, and that étagère—that big ugly bookcase," I added when Jason looked confused. The wing chairs had always been uncomfortable and I'd always hated the Victorian antiques, which Rob had insisted on buying.

"But load up the dining room table and chairs, those rugs, the sideboard, the sofa, and, yeah, maybe that lamp too." My guests and I couldn't sit in the dark, could we? We probably couldn't all squeeze onto one sofa either. "Oh, hell," I said, "take those two armchairs over there too." Considering that just a few hours ago, I'd been considering taking only my grandmother's tea service, it was interesting what a hard time I was having deciding what to leave for Rob.

The boys picked up the sofa and started backing out the door. I walked over to where Meg was kneeling, critically inspecting several paintings.

"Some of this stuff you should be glad to get rid of," she said, wrinkling her nose at a large abstract painting that Rob claimed was a great investment. "Though, of course, you could always sell it. Some pretentious schnook with more money than taste would probably give you a good price for it."

"No, I have to give some things to Rob." In fact, I rather liked the painting, but I decided to leave all the "investment art" for my husband. Rob could afford some new furniture to complement his art collection.

"Why would you want to leave anything for Rob?" Meg inquired. "As I recall, he took all your money. Maybe he'd buy some of this overpriced art back from you."

"Because it's the right thing to do." I whooped in delight as I discovered my grandmother's silver tea service packed in a cardboard box, feeling as if something very important had been returned to me. "Also," I said, glancing over my shoulder at Meg, "I want to have at least a few things left in storage so Rob will continue to be charged rent."

Meg nodded her approval. "That's more like it." She picked up a floor lamp and together we went to load our finds in my car.

By seven that night, all the items I'd chosen to take were at my house, and were back in my house in their room of origin.

I smiled as I inspected my living room which now contained a couch, floor lamp, Oriental rug, and two upholstered chairs that hadn't been there a few hours ago.

"It's definitely an improvement," Mcg agreed.

"Yes, it certainly is." I suddenly noticed Jason and Sam,

who were standing in the doorway, looking bored but too polite to complain.

I hurried over to the boys. "Oh, guys, thank you so much. You saved my life." Impulsively, I gave each of them a hug.

They grinned at me. "Glad to help, Mrs. Prescott," Jason said, and the two of them turned toward the door.

"Wait!" I said. "Let me pay you for your time and for the truck rental." Fortunately, thanks to a loan from Meg, there was some money in my new checking account.

Jason shook his head. "That's okay," he said. "Katie's already taken care of everything." He waved as he turned toward the hall. "See you."

"Now isn't that sweet of Katie?" Meg said when the boys had left. "And except for calling me 'ma'am,' those boys were nice too."

I was about to ask her what she wanted the boys—mere children—to call an aging woman like herself when the phone rang. "Let me get that. I bet it's Katie."

But it wasn't. "This is Amber Harris," a familiar, petulant voice announced. "I'm calling to make sure that you're not going to publish all those mean things I said about Dad."

"I didn't write anything you didn't say."

"That's not what I'm worried about." She hesitated. "See, a lot of things have changed since you interviewed me."

"What things?"

"I'm having a career shift. I'm going to discontinue the e-zine and workshops and focus more on writing books."

I still didn't get it. "Do you mean that you want me to put that in the article—that you're writing a book?"

She sighed, that oh-God-you're-so-dense sound familiar

to all parents of adolescents. "No, I want you to take out the shitty things I said about my father. Terri gave me Dad's new book manuscript to finish, and I'll get all the royalties from it as part of my inheritance. As Terri said, I'm the real writer in the family so it makes sense for me to finish it. Also I decided it was pretty tacky of me to speak ill of the dead."

Particularly when you were now trying to write a book hawking the same exercise and diet philosophy that a week ago you'd called "totally masochistic." Unfortunately for Amber, I'd been pretty liberal with my use of her disdainful comments about her father's fitness-at-any-price ideas. "Maybe having your problems with your father aired will promote interest in the book. They always say that conflict sells books."

"Not this book," she said grimly. "Right now Dad and I are officially co-authors of his *Before and After: A Follow-up*, and his editor would have a stroke if she read about me criticizing him. Also, for the record, Dad and I may have had our differences of opinion, but we still loved each other. I was just in a bad mood the day you talked to me. I don't want you publishing any of the crap I said."

"I've already turned in the story. It's out of my hands."

"That's bull. Until the magazine is actually printed, you can make changes. Delete my whole interview if you want. You can certainly do that."

So much for my attempts at reconciling Amber to the inevitable. I was still annoyed with Paul for not giving me any feedback about the rewrites he'd been so eager to get. He had sent me an e-mail saying he received the story and would get back to me when he finished editing it, but that was all. "I'm not the person to complain to, Amber. You need to talk to my editor, Paul O'Neal." I smiled as I gave her his phone number and e-mail address.

Hanging up, I said to Meg, "Let's go eat." It might be a good idea to be out of the house when O'Neal's phone call came.

The two of us drove in silence to a neighborhood Italian restaurant. "I know I hurt your feelings before," Meg finally said. "I'm sorry."

"It's okay. The part that hurt was that it was true, not that you said it. I should have gotten a job a long time ago and set aside some money of my own. And I should have called the divorce lawyer days ago."

"Shoulda, coulda, woulda," Meg said. "I should have picked better husbands, got an MBA instead of an art history degree, chosen fruit juice and vegetables instead of margaritas and chicken-fried steaks, and, God knows, I should have stayed away from technology stocks. The point is, what are we going to do now?"

"Consume a deep-dish supreme pizza and a bottle of Chianti between us?" I suggested.

Meg sighed dramatically. "My pearls of wisdom wasted on philistines." She pulled into a parking space in front of the restaurant. "Though pizza and Chianti sound good to me."

I touched her arm. "And tomorrow—I promise—I'll call your lawyer."

The combination of the hours of moving furniture, the rich food, and several glasses of wine made me fall asleep on the ride home. "Hey, Cinderella, it's time to get out of the coach," Meg said, shaking my shoulder. "Sure you don't want to spend the night at my house?"

"No, that's okay." I tried hard to rouse myself. "Anyway, I want to enjoy my new old furniture." Hunting through my purse, I finally managed to find my house key. "And thanks, Meg, thanks for everything."

She smiled. "You'd do the same for me."

"Sure, if I had your money and connections."

"And chutzpah," she called as I got out of the car.

"That too," I said, waving goodbye.

I didn't sense that anything was wrong until I opened the screen door. Then I saw it. Obscene red smears—red paint? dried blood?—on my front door. Staring, I felt my stomach start to churn. Someone had left a message for me while I was gone: *WATCH YOUR BACK, BITCH.*

Fifteen

Who? I asked myself over and over again. Sitting at the kitchen table, drinking a Diet Coke to relieve my queasiness, I tried to decide who I knew angry enough with me to resort to painting threatening graffiti on my door. Was it Rob, who somehow found out that I'd retrieved our possessions from his secret hiding place? Or maybe Amber Harris, pissed off that I wasn't willing to change her disdainful remarks in my article about her father? Or Terri Harris, who might have heard that I was asking indelicate questions about her husband's will and the hasty sale of Stan's beloved gym?

It could be any one of them. Each was hot-tempered and seemed emotionally immature enough for such a stunt, and both Amber and Terri might feel that they couldn't confront me in person for fear I might include the incident in my article. And what about the message, "Watch Your Back, Bitch"? What if the message was not just an idle threat? Maybe the graffiti artist had been the person who killed Mrs. Quaid—someone who perhaps imagined that Mrs. Quaid told us about all the incriminating information she'd found in Carol's safe-deposit box as well as the other people she planned to question that day. Now that was a very, very scary thought.

The ring of the telephone made me jump. Had the door painter decided to call to reinforce the written threat? I hurried over to inspect my caller ID box.

I picked up the receiver. "Hello, Paul," I said. "Did you finish editing my article?"

"Yes, I did. Did you sic that Harris girl on me?"

"Yup. You are the editor. What did you tell her?"

"That I'd take her concerns under advisement."

"How did Amber react to that?"

"I'm not sure. It wasn't an extended conversation." He paused. "Your article, by the way, is better—pithier, less Pollyannaish. I have a much better sense of what an insecure tight-ass old Stan was."

"Great."

"What's wrong?" he said quietly. "You sound upset."

I started to deny it, to claim I was just tired in order to get him off the phone, but instead, to my horror, I started to cry. "I—I've got to go," I said between sobs and hung up.

I was still crying when the phone rang again. Oh, God, it was Paul again—not the person I wanted to talk to at the moment. I blew my nose and let my answering machine take the message.

His message was brief. "If you do not call me back within the next five minutes, I am coming over to your place." He hung up.

I called him back. "I'm sorry. It's been a difficult day. Maybe we should talk about the article tomorrow."

"Please tell me what's wrong. Maybe I can help."

"I doubt it." How could I ever face him again? Crying on the phone—exactly the thing to convince an employer to hire you.

"Try me."

Could the man possibly be more pig-headed? Reluctantly I told him about the message on my front door. "I just came home and saw it a few minutes before you called. I guess the shock just hit me."

"Something like that would shock most people. Who do you think did this?"

"Don't know. It could be Amber or Terri Harris or my husband, who will be very annoyed whenever he discovers I retrieved a lot of the furniture he took from the house. Or it could be whoever killed the two Quaid women."

"Why would the killer bother with you?"

"He—or she—could assume, wrongly, that I know something that incriminates him as the murderer. My daughters and I, after all, found Carol Quaid's body and were some of the last people to see her mother before she was killed."

O'Neal whistled softly. "At least someone who warns you to watch your back doesn't seem like an immediate threat."

"How'd you figure that?"

"Because if your painter wanted to harm you, he'd have done it—waited in the bushes until you got home, not defaced your door and left."

It sounded reasonable. "Maybe it was just some teenage prank," I said hopefully.

"Could be, but I doubt it."

I sighed. Well at least I liked the no-immediate-threat part. "I'm really awfully tired, Paul. Could we talk tomorrow about my article?"

"Okay. How about tomorrow morning? Is nine too early for you?"

"No, it's fine." I could sit at the kitchen table in my bathrobe, cradling the phone on my shoulder while I drank coffee and took notes.

"I'll bring breakfast. Can you make coffee if I pick up some bagels?"

"What?" I felt as if somehow I'd missed a crucial piece of this conversation.

"Are you capable of making coffee?"

"Of course I can make coffee. That's not—"

155

He didn't let me finish the thought. "Fine. I'll be at your place at nine." He hung up before I could add any objections.

To my surprise, I fell asleep immediately and slept soundly until my alarm woke me at eight.

I was downstairs making coffee when I heard a noise at my front door. Definitely not a knock, more like a scraping sound.

Heart pounding, I rushed to the door. Had the vandal returned to add a postscript?

I peered out the peephole, then yanked the door open. "What are you doing?" I asked Paul O'Neal.

"What does it look like I'm doing?" He held up a large sponge and a spray bottle of cleaner. Dressed in a flannel shirt and blue jeans, he looked like Brian Dennehy playing the part of the local handyman. "Unfortunately, your messenger used oil-based paint. You're going to have to repaint the door."

In the bright light of morning, the warning seemed more annoying than threatening. "Does this mean you decided to skip the bagels?"

He shook his head and reached down for a bakery sack, a manila folder and a camera at his feet. "I come prepared."

I stepped aside to let him into the hall. "You're going to commemorate our meeting with photos?"

He shrugged. "I took a picture of the door in case the police ever need to see it."

My buoyant mood of a few minutes earlier deflated like a punctured tire. In case there was another incident, he meant, the kind that couldn't be painted over.

I led him to the kitchen and peered into his paper bag. He'd brought an assortment of bagels.

"I didn't know what you liked, so I bought two of everything."

I toasted two cinnamon raisin bagels while he poured the coffee. I wasn't very hungry, but it seemed rude not to eat. Who knew? Maybe this would be my last breakfast.

We sat down at the kitchen table. "Good coffee," Paul said. "Now tell me why Terri Harris would be angry with you. I didn't see anything in your article that should upset her that much, unless she's sensitive about criticism of her late husband."

"Hardly. Terri only seems sensitive about things that directly impact her or her money. But I'm not sure that she really is angry with me. I do know that she hated me asking questions about how well Stan's business was doing, but she said that was because she didn't want anything to derail her negotiations with National Gyms. Maybe I just thought of her as a suspect because I don't like or trust her, and she doesn't like me either."

Paul spread cream cheese on his bagel. "You think she'd write 'Watch Your Back, Bitch' just because she doesn't like you? Either she's a very disturbed woman or there's something else going on."

"Terri is very purposeful, very focused. She wouldn't threaten me just out of spite. She'd have to think that scaring me would stop me from poking around anymore in her life. She was very angry when I asked an aerobics instructor at Stan's gym how business was. So I could certainly see her being upset to learn I was asking about Stan's will and details about the sale of the gym."

Paul raised an eyebrow. "Find out anything interesting?"

"As a matter of fact, yes. Jane Harris, Stan's ex-wife, said he told her he intended to divorce Terri and cut her out of his will. And the PR woman at National Gyms told me that they'd originally approached Stan, who refused to sell the gym. But as soon as Stan died, Terri approached National Gyms saying she was the owner now and she was willing to sell."

"It sure gives her a good motive for getting rid of Stan, doesn't it? Let's say here's Old Stan clinging nostalgically to a failing business, refusing a good offer to sell. Then, after years of putting up with this fitness tyrant, Terri learns that Stan is about to dump her. She sees this very small window of opportunity to solve all her problems—get rid of Stan before he changes his will, sell the business before National Gyms loses interest. Was she Stan's sole heir?"

"No, she got the house and half the gym business. Stan's two kids split the other half."

"And that is why Amber wanted to take back all the nasty things she told you about Daddy?"

I shook my head. "Not exactly. She said Terri suggested that Amber, as the writer in the family, finish Stan's new diet-and-exercise book, and Amber could keep the royalties as part of her inheritance. I suspect Amber suddenly realized that bad-mouthing her father's fitness philosophy might cut into her profits."

Paul shook his head. "Don't tell me Amber is leaving the Fat Power revolution for the enemy Skinny camp."

"More or less." I suddenly thought of something I hadn't considered before. "I wonder if this means Amber is going to go on a diet. She told me she would be listed as the book's co-author. Maybe she'll be another *Before and After* story, like her mother and stepmother before her."

Paul shrugged. Clearly diets did not interest him. "What's the story on your husband? You think he's a real suspect here?"

"Probably not. Rob is more greedy than threatening. I

could see him trying to get the furniture back, but not painting a sign on the door."

"How's Rob's grammar?"

"What does that have to do with anything?" Was he arguing that only the grammatically challenged would write "Watch Your Back, Bitch" on my door?

"You're not an editor, so you probably didn't notice, but whoever wrote the message knew enough to add a comma after 'Back'. A lot of people would have left out that comma."

I tried to recall Rob's punctuation skills, but couldn't. "He probably would have put in the comma; he's a very precise person. 'Watch Your Back, Bitch' doesn't sound much like him, though."

"Too colloquial?"

"You might say that." Suddenly I was tired of the topic of who hates Lauren. I knew Paul meant to be helpful, but the discussion was only making me more nervous. How could I combat an enemy I didn't know and an agenda I didn't understand? "But we need to talk about my article, don't we?" I said, getting up to refill our coffee mugs.

Paul stood too, picking up the plates and silverware and bringing them to the sink. He handed me the manila folder he'd brought along. "This is the edited article. Why don't you take a look at it? Most of the changes I suggested are pretty minor."

I glanced at the article. The changes didn't look all that minor to me.

My editor suddenly looked inexplicably sheepish. "How about I paint your front door while you look through the article?"

I could feel my mouth drop open. "That—that really isn't necessary."

"I know it's not, but I like to paint. I worked summers as a painter when I was in high school. Look at me. Why did you imagine I came dressed like this—think I was going to cut down a tree on my way home?"

"I thought it was your idea of office casual," I said. "A Friday kind of thing. You do know that I am capable of painting too?"

"I know you are. Consider this a neighborly gesture. Also I'm fast."

"Okay—thanks." Who was I to turn down a neighborly gesture?

"You want to keep the door the same color?"

I envisioned the now-gray door streaked with crimson letters. "No, I think I'd like it to be black, a glossy black."

"Good choice. I'll pick up the paint and get right at it." Before I could change my mind, he smiled and headed out.

I had just locked the door after him when the phone rang. It was Meg.

"So have you called my lawyer?" she asked.

Oh, Lord, it had completely escaped my mind. "Not yet, but I will," I said. Meg had not seen the painted message on my door last night, and I didn't feel like telling her about it. There was just so much mother-henning I could take in a day.

"You know I was thinking when I drove home last night that you really should change your locks. I bet Rob still has his house key. You don't want him sneaking back and stealing all your furniture again while you're out."

"Good idea," I said.

"A good idea that you're actually going to do?"

"Sure." Eventually. "Listen, Meg, let me call you back later, okay? I have to finish polishing my article this morning. Paul O'Neal gave me the edited copy and I told him I'd finish the revisions soon."

160

"Sure, call me when you're done. And Lauren, please call the lawyer and the locksmith today. Being single is a different world than you're used to, sweetie. You're going to have to learn to watch your back."

Sixteen

Paul hadn't been kidding when he said he was a fast painter. I'd only just finished adding the editing changes to my story when he knocked on the back door to say he was done.

There was a smear of black paint on his right hand. "For now. I think it's going to need another coat. I'll come back tomorrow to do it." He hesitated, looking for an instant like a shy high-school boy. "Well, I guess I'll go then. Don't touch the front door for at least the next few hours."

"Wait!" I said as he turned to leave. "Won't you at least stay for another cup of coffee?"

"I don't want to keep you from anything," he said, looking embarrassed.

"No, really, I'd like the company." Was I imagining it, or was the man actually attracted to me? It had been such a long time since I'd thought of a real man (as opposed to men in novels or movies) in any kind of romantic way; Rob had stopped being flowers-and-whispered-endearments romantic about ten minutes after our honeymoon. And while I liked Paul, in a safe, platonic kind of way, I wasn't at all sure how I felt about him in a more sexual context.

Of course maybe he wasn't attracted to me at all. Didn't men his age—my age—invariably go for svelte blonde cuties twenty years their junior? And here I was, not blonde, certainly not svelte, looking more like a potential grandmother than a potential date.

While Paul washed up in the bathroom, I retrieved two

clean mugs. Would he want another bagel with his coffee? Or maybe he'd prefer a sandwich.

"What can I do to help?" Paul's unexpected voice, from right behind me, made me jump. "Sorry, didn't mean to startle you."

"No problem. I'm just kind of jumpy today." Particularly when I'm mulling over whether or not you have a crush on me. "Are you hungry? Would you like something to eat?" Good God, was I blushing? It was high school revisited—except this time the raging hormones came with hot flashes.

"No, coffee's fine."

I managed to pour our coffee and bring it to the kitchen table. "It was very generous of you to paint the door."

"It's no big deal. I like to paint and I wouldn't want the vandal to think he was getting away with it."

I put down my mug. "You mean you think he or she will come back to see my reaction?" Not at all a nice thought.

"Not necessarily," he said a little too quickly. "But in case he does, I want him to see that you painted over the message and moved on with your life."

"Wouldn't that make this person want to write another message on my newly painted door?" Or—I thought, but didn't say—do something worse?

He studied me with his gorgeous Newman-blue eyes. "I hope not."

Me too. I swallowed a mouthful of coffee that suddenly seemed tasteless.

Tactfully Paul steered the conversation toward Stan Harris and my article. "I really liked your story, by the way."

"Thanks." I was genuinely pleased. Even if he did like me, Paul would not flatter me about my writing. The magazine was too important to him.

"If you still want the staff writer's job, it's yours. Though I can't pay you much, unfortunately. The best I can do is twenty-five thousand."

"That—that's great! The job, I mean." The salary wasn't great, but it was twenty-five thousand more than I had right now. "When do I start?"

He grinned. "Didn't have to mull that over for long, did you? You can start on Monday, if you want."

"Monday's fine." Probably two months from now, I'd be mourning all my lost free time, but right now I was elated. A real writing job, with a regular salary. Maybe, if I budgeted carefully, I'd even be able to keep the house.

"Good. I'm glad that's settled."

Suddenly I heard a noise. Was that someone unlocking the back door?

"Mom?" Em's voice called. "You home?"

I put my hand over my racing heart. "In the kitchen, honey," I called.

"Hey, Mommy!" The smile on my younger daughter's face froze as she glimpsed the stranger sitting at our table.

Paul stood up when he saw her.

"Paul, this is my daughter Emily. Em, this is Paul O'Neal, my editor at *City Magazine*."

A look of palpable relief crossed Em's face, an oh-okay-he's-only-Mom's-professional acquaintance look, as they said hello.

"I didn't expect to see you so early."

"I decided to skip my morning class." Em picked up a duffel bag that I knew from experience was stuffed with dirty clothes and headed toward the laundry room. On another day, without an audience, we would have had a discussion about that decision.

"It's time for me to get going," Paul said.

164

Before I could reply, Em yelled, "Hey, we got our furniture back!"

Then the front doorbell rang.

Before I could warn her about the wet paint, Em was opening the front door. Meg walked in. "What prompted you to paint the door?" she asked me.

"Oh, I just wanted a change. I like the black better than the gray, don't you?" I had no intention of telling either Meg or Em the real reason for the paint job.

"I guess." Meg turned her attention to Em, giving her a long hug. "Emmy-Bear, what a nice surprise!"

I left them to return to the kitchen. "Don't want to keep you from your company," Paul said, moving toward the back door. "I'll drive by tomorrow to check if the door needs another coat of paint. If it doesn't, I'll see you at work Monday morning."

He was halfway out the door when Meg's voice stopped him. "Why Paul O'Neal, is that you?"

Paul turned around. "Well, hello. Meg, isn't it?"

"Meg Peters," she said. "We met at the Graftons' dinner party a few months ago."

"Of course," he said, grinning down at her. "You were about to take a cruise to Tahiti, if I recall. How was it?"

"Divine," she said, looking up at him through her long, mascara-thickened eyelashes. "Incredibly relaxing. I spent most of my time on board either lying by the swimming pool or getting massages."

Paul's blue eyes widened slightly. No doubt he was envisioning Meg in her bikini stretched out by the pool—or wearing even less clothes lying on the massage table.

"Well, I know you have to leave," I said, wanting very much to shove him out the door.

"You're right. Nice meeting you, Emily, and enjoyed seeing you again, Meg."

Meg smiled coquettishly at him. "Me too. Hope to see you again sometime."

I wanted to strangle her. Neither of us spoke until Paul had closed the door and headed toward his car. "You didn't tell me he was here at the house," she said, making it sound like an accusation.

"I don't have to tell you everything, do I?" I said, trying to keep my tone light, but not quite succeeding.

"Yes, you do. You owe me."

I turned to stare at her. "Well, I've got a job now, so I can start paying you back. Paul hired me as a staff writer."

Meg shook her head. "You know that's not what I mean. What's gotten into you, girl?"

What had gotten into me? I was way too old to be acting like a jealous teenager. "Sorry. I'm just tired I guess."

"Well, congratulations on your new job." Meg patted my shoulder. "That's great news."

"That's terrific, Mom!" Em joined in. "When do you start?"

"Monday morning."

Em grabbed a bottle of water from the refrigerator. "Now let me tell you my good news."

I poured Meg a cup of coffee and we all sat down at the kitchen table. Em's news, we knew, could drag on a bit.

"A friend of mine, who's a hacker, told me he'd help me find stuff in computer records to track down Dad," she began. "Seth is really good at it, much better than me, but he couldn't find any new credit card listings for Robert Prescott. Finally, though, he asked me what Grandma's maiden name was." She paused and, very much like her grade-school self, asked, "And guess what?"

"What?" Meg and I asked.

"Dad has an American Express and a MasterCard under Grandma's name—E. Morris Prescott."

"How do you know that it's your father's card?" Meg said. "Maybe it's your grandmother's."

Em shook her head. "For one thing, they're both new cards. For another, Grandma always hated credit cards. Dad gave her one once but she refused to use it. So." She beamed at us. "Guess where Dad is having the credit card bill sent?"

I was not in the mood for a guessing game. "Tell us."

"Grandma's nursing home! The bills are sent to Grandma there."

Which meant that either Rob gave his mother enough money to pay all his bills—a substantial amount of cash if he planned to be gone for a long time—or he had Mother Prescott forward the bills to his real address. And knowing Rob, King of the Skinflints, he wouldn't have wanted to hand over that much money to anyone, not even his doting mother.

Apparently Em had reached the same conclusion. "I bet Grandma gets the bills and then sends them on to Dad. But that's even better for us. It means we can find out where Dad is living."

Right. I looked at my sweet, bright, and achingly naive young daughter. Then pictured the squat, ferocious, white-haired woman who'd always resented sharing "her" Robbie's affections with anyone else. While Mother Prescott admittedly liked her granddaughters a great deal more than she liked me, her primary loyalty would remain with her son. Ellen Morris Prescott would guard Rob's address like a pit bull.

"Oh, I don't expect Grandma to tell me," Em said, as if

reading my mind. "But I figured with a few diversionary tactics and a little team work, we could find Dad's address."

"You mean like I could sneak into her room and rifle through her bureau drawers while you visited with Grandma in the sunroom?" I inquired sarcastically.

"Well, yes."

Meg caught my eye. "Might just work," she said. "And think of all the fun you'd have tricking that old witch."

"Okay," Em said, "this is the plan." She solemnly studied Meg and me, her two lieutenants, to make sure we were taking her seriously. Apparently reassured, she continued, "Stage One: I go to visit Grandma for a nice, long chat. I'll tell her I have to have more money for school and desperately need to get hold of Dad. She probably won't tell me anything, but at least I'll be able to keep her out of her room while Mom searches it."

Em turned to Meg. "Then, once I get Grandma out, it's your turn."

"Stage Two," Meg said.

Em nodded. "You need to get Mrs. Copeland, Grandma's roommate, out of the room. She likes to take an afternoon nap."

"So how am I supposed to accomplish this?"

"Mrs. Copeland is very sweet. She loves to visit, talks a lot about her two daughters—one is named Sara and lives in San Antonio, I remember that—and all of her grandchildren."

Meg had a mutinous look on her face. "Why can't your mother handle Mrs. Copeland while I search the room?"

"Because if you take Mrs. Copeland to the living room, where Grandma and I will also be talking, Grandma won't recognize you. But she would think it was pretty weird if

Mom was there visiting Mrs. Copeland instead of her." Em sent Meg a stern look. "Believe me, Mrs. Copeland is a lot more fun to talk with than Grandma."

"Anyone is more fun to talk with than Grandma," I said.

Em turned to me. "Now for Stage Three. After Grandma and Mrs. Copeland are out of their room, Mom, you need to get in there and search through Grandma's things for Dad's address or phone number."

"And try to talk my way out of a jail sentence if someone catches me going through her possessions," I muttered. "You do recall, I hope, how Grandma wanted that nurse's aide who pocketed a quarter lying on the floor arrested?"

Meg whistled. "There is something to that genetics stuff. Rob's just a chip off the old block, isn't he?"

"Let's get going," Em urged.

"I'm not sure that this is such a smart idea, honey," I said. "It seems like there's a lot of risk for not much potential gain. Mother Prescott has her faults, but carelessness is not one of them. She probably did a very good job of hiding Dad's address, if she even has it." Also, I didn't want to point out, our last information-seeking venture had ended up with Em, Katie, and me discovering Carol Quaid's lifeless body.

My daughter's lower lip jutted out in an expression I was all too familiar with. "Fine. If you're too scared to go there, I'll do it myself. I can look through Grandma's things when she's in the dining room eating dinner."

Sighing, I stood up. "Okay, let's go and get this over with." Maybe the outing would merely be a waste of time rather than an out-and-out disaster.

Meg and I waited in her car while Em headed into the nursing home. Emily had phoned her grandmother, who declined Em's offer to take her for a drive but said she'd like Em to come over to visit.

"So what the hell am I supposed to say to this Mrs. Copeland?" Meg asked me.

I shrugged. "She's a very friendly woman; she'll talk to anyone. I think she's starved for conversation living with Mother Prescott, who basically ignores her. It's like Pollyanna and the Wicked Witch of the West having to share a bedroom. It's possible that Mrs. Copeland won't even be in the room, in which case all you have to do is keep watch outside the door and warn me if anyone is coming."

"I'd rather be searching through the bedroom."

"I'd rather you search through the room too, but Em is right. Nobody will recognize you, and a lot of people know me."

I glanced at my watch. Em had said for Meg to wait ten minutes before entering the premises. "For the record, I think this whole thing is doomed to failure. My only hope is that it doesn't take too long, and none of us gets into trouble."

Meg looked at me and shook her head. "You are such a pessimist."

I glanced again at my watch. "Time to go, Nancy Drew."

Ten minutes later it was my turn. I'd considered wearing a wig to make myself less recognizable, but decided that if I were caught in Mother Prescott's bedroom, the disguise made me seem even more suspicious.

Unlike my elder daughter, I'd never been much of an actress. If anyone had been paying attention when I walked into my mother-in-law's unit, I'm sure they would have seen a woman radiating guilt. Fortunately, no one was around, and I made my way down the hall to her bedroom.

Cautiously I peered inside. No one was there. Taking a

deep breath, I stepped inside and closed the door behind me.

Now all I had to do was find Rob's address or phone number. Just in case Mother Prescott was less devious than I thought, I checked the obvious places first. Nothing of interest was on her nightstand or in the stack of papers on her desk. Her desk drawer was locked. I gave it a hard yank, but it didn't budge. Great! No doubt everything I needed was in there.

I decided to look through her bureau drawers, then leave. Carefully I lifted stacks of pajamas, underwear, socks. Nothing. Moving on to the bottom drawer, I ran my hand through piles of clothes that reeked of mothballs until I hit something large and cardboard. I pulled out a brown accordion-style folder.

Sitting on the desk chair, I peered into the folder and grinned. One entire compartment contained small bags of Fritos, Mother Prescott's junk food of choice, which she was forbidden to eat because of her high blood pressure. The other compartment looked as if it contained paid bills. Eagerly I splayed them across the desk. Maybe—

"May I help you?" an icy voice from behind me inquired.

I turned to see a nurse—one I didn't recognize—glaring at me from the door.

Oh, Lord. All the explanations I had come up with for just such a scenario suddenly seemed very lame. I glanced down at the bill in my hand and decided to improvise. "I—I just wanted to make sure that all of Aunt Ellen's bills are paid. You know how independent she is, doesn't want help from anyone, but sometimes she's a bit forgetful." I attempted a you-know-how-it-is smile.

The nurse didn't look as if she was buying it. "And you are?"

"Her niece, Lauren Prescott." If I was arrested, it would look less suspicious if I didn't lie about my name.

"You have any ID?" she asked, looking as if she was going to yell for security any second.

I pulled my driver's license from my wallet and handed it to her. She glanced at it and handed it back to me, looking marginally more friendly. "I guess it's okay then. I had to check, though, because Mrs. Prescott gets very upset if anyone violates her privacy."

"Yes, she's touchy about a lot of things. Believe me, I know."

She checked the hall behind her to see if anyone was coming, then, lowering her voice said, "When her son came to visit her, you would have thought it was some top-secret espionage mission. She insisted that we find a private room for them to talk—not in her bedroom or in the living room where everyone else takes their visitors. What's so private and important that they couldn't discuss it in her bedroom?"

The answer to that made me sufficiently irritated to consider turning over Mother Prescott's secret stash of Fritos. But since I didn't want her to know I'd been in her room, I decided to squelch my revenge impulses for the moment. Instead I nodded sympathetically at the nurse. "Aunt Ellen has always been a bit on the paranoid side. When did she pull this private-room stunt with Cousin Rob?"

The nurse cocked her head to the side, apparently thinking about it. "It must have been last weekend—Sunday, I think—because I was off the next day."

Rob was in Houston, less than ten miles away from our house, only six days ago? So where the hell was he right now? "Does Rob visit very often?"

"That was the only time I remember him coming,

though I've only worked here two months." She glanced at her watch. "I need to get going. If I were you, I'd get out of here before Mrs. Prescott gets back."

"I'll be gone in a couple minutes. I promise."

She left, closing the door behind her. Was she on the way to summon security to pick up the interloper in Ellen Prescott's room? I took a deep breath, told myself that one paranoid woman in the extended family was more than enough, and started scanning my mother-in-law's paid bills.

"Holy shit!" I said under my breath. Here it was: the American Express bill for E. Morris Prescott. And it listed a "$1,020" charge to a hotel in Matamoros, Mexico and, more recently, a "$589" charge to a motel in Del Rio. Was he still there? I pulled a piece of paper from my purse and jotted down the necessary information.

A frantic coughing outside the door made me freeze. "No, I'm fine," Meg's voice said loudly to someone in the hallway. "Just need a glass of water."

I only had time to push all the bills back into the accordion file before the door swung open. I jumped up as Meg marched into the room. "Under the bed," she mouthed, pointing to the floor.

I dove under the closest bed just as I heard Mrs. Copeland's voice in the room. "Do you want to get into the bathroom first, dear, for your water?"

"No, no, I'm better now," Meg said. "You go on in."

After what seemed like an interminable interlude, I heard a door close. Meg loomed over me, holding my purse. "Forget something?" she whispered.

I grabbed it. At least I'd taken the file with me.

"Get out," Meg whispered. "She wants to take a nap."

I glanced nervously at the bathroom door.

"Now!"

I ran to the bureau and pulled open the bottom drawer just as I heard the toilet flush. Oh, God, I hoped she was a hand washer. I shoved the folder under the clothes, pushed the drawer closed.

"Go!" Meg ordered, positioning herself in front of the bathroom door.

I sprinted into the hallway just as the bathroom door opened. "Maybe you should get a glass of water after all," Mrs. Copeland was telling Meg. "You look pale."

Clutching my purse, I strolled as nonchalantly as possible down the hall. Nobody tried to stop me. I kept walking until I reached the parking lot, crawled into the back seat of Meg's car and lay down. A security guard would have to look carefully before he found me.

I was doing deep-breathing exercises when the car door opened. "I thought I'd have a stroke when I walked into that room and saw you sitting there," Meg said.

"I thought you were supposed to keep Mrs. Copeland occupied."

"I did! For a very long time. But what can I do when she suffers from over-active bladder?"

It was a subject I didn't want to pursue. "At least you warned me. That was fast thinking."

"Which probably took ten years off my life." She peered over the seat at me. "Did you find out anything?"

"Amazingly, I did." I told her about Rob's visit last Sunday and the motel listed on the American Express bill.

Meg shrieked. "Now you can nail the bastard. When did you say you're talking to the attorney?"

"Tuesday. And before you go off into Vengeful Fantasy Land, I would like to remind you that we don't know where Rob is."

"But we're closing in on him. Aren't you going to ask me what I found out?"

"From Mrs. Copeland?" I couldn't imagine Mother Prescott confiding anything to her perennially cheerful roommate.

"It might just be gossip, but Mrs. Copeland says that the other residents think Rob is connected to the Mafia."

"Right." I snorted at the idea of Rob, who closed his eyes during movie torture, being connected to organized crime. "What was he supposed to have done? Filled a don's cavity?"

"She said she had it on good authority that Rob got into trouble for doing a favor for some Mafia guy."

"Well, that guarantees it's a lie. Rob doesn't do favors. But, come to think of it, it's kind of funny that someone started that rumor—Rob Prescott, world's most unlikely Mafia capo." The idea of it, combined with my tension, made me giggle.

Meg took one look at me, then began to laugh too.

We were still snickering when Em got into the passenger seat. "What's so funny?"

I wiped the tears from my face. "It's nothing. We're just a little punchy after our big adventure."

"Well, I'm glad someone had a good time," Em said. "Let's get out of here."

"So what did Grandma have to say?" I asked as Meg backed out of the parking space.

"That I needed to learn how to budget better and shouldn't expect Dad to pay for college; I'd appreciate my education more if I paid for it myself the way her children had to. She said she didn't know where Dad was, but if he ever happened to call her, she'd mention that I needed money. Then she gave me five dollars." Em pulled the bill out of her pocket and waved it at us. "I wanted to tell her to keep it, but I was afraid that might cut the visit too short." She looked at Meg. "At least you got to talk to someone who wasn't telling you how your parents spoiled you rotten."

"Now I really wish I'd turned over her stash of Fritos to the nurse," I muttered. "And, for the record, I was the one who put your father through dental school."

"She really is a bitch," Meg said. "Even Mrs. Copeland—a woman who has something nice to say about everyone—thinks so. By the way, I told Mrs. C that I was a friend of her daughter in San Antonio—that was how I got her out of the room. But when I left, she said, 'I know you never met my daughter, but whoever you are, I enjoyed talking with you.'"

"See?" Em said. "I told you she was a lot nicer than Grandma. Grandma would probably have called 911 and had you arrested."

"Well at least we got some valuable information," Meg said. "Let's go out to dinner to celebrate. My treat."

Celebrate the fact that my husband had been in town only a few days earlier—might, in fact, still be in town now? "You all can go out to eat," I said, "but I want you to drop me off at the house. I'm going to start looking for a locksmith who works nights."

Seventeen

Driving to my new job on Monday morning, I felt overwhelmed with elation. Here I was: a woman, who after years of unpaid work, now had an enviable, paying job that even used my long-dormant professional skills. My house once again resembled the home I'd spent so much time cleaning and furnishing. For someone who'd never considered herself materialistic, I was surprised at how much better I felt surrounded by my favorite furniture and my grandmother's cherished silver service. I even felt safer—at least from Rob. Thanks to an accommodating locksmith, the doors to my house and garage now held new, top-quality locks. Things, in short, were looking up.

The skinny receptionist with the nose ring was at her desk when I walked into the downtown office of *City Magazine*. Since the last time I'd been there her hair had changed from blue to stop-sign red.

I smiled at her. "Hi, I'm Lauren Prescott. Paul O'Neal hired me as the new staff writer."

It was clear from her expression that Paul had not bothered to inform her of this decision. "Yeah, I remember you now. You wrote the story about Stan Harris, right?"

When I nodded, she added, "I'm Caitlin Jones, by the way. God knows when Paul will get here, but I guess you can take the spare desk."

The spare desk was located in a tiny closet-like room that looked as if it had been most recently used for storage. Dismayed, I stared at the stacks of office supplies covering my desk. "Uh, when was the last time you had a staff writer?"

"About two months ago. That's when Eric left to go to law school." She followed my gaze. "Eric wasn't in the office very much. He liked to work from home."

I could understand why. While Caitlin made the coffee, I cleared the top of my desk. "Is there anywhere else I can put this stuff?" I asked, holding an armload of copy paper.

"Maybe I can find some cardboard boxes for storing things. You can stack them in a corner of your office or push them under your desk, I guess. Paul was going to see about getting us some bookshelves and storage cabinets, but he never seems to get around to doing it." She sent me an appraising look. "He works really hard to keep this magazine going and doesn't have time for the piddly details."

They didn't seem all that piddly to me, but now didn't seem the time to mention it. By the time Paul arrived, half an hour later, I'd stashed all the supplies into cardboard boxes and discovered that the aging computer on my desk did indeed function. I was ready to work.

Paul stuck his head in my office and muttered something that sounded like "mornin'."

"Good morning," I said, standing up and starting to follow him to his office. I'd only made it to the outer office when I spotted Caitlin shaking her head and holding up her palm.

I walked over to her desk. "What?"

"Paul," she whispered, "is not a morning person. You do not want to talk to him until he's had several cups of coffee."

Gritting my teeth, I returned to my office. I wondered how long Eric had been here before he ran off to law school.

I was reading back issues of the magazine when Paul finally emerged from his office. He sat down in the molded plastic chair next to my desk. "Glad you got settled in," he said, glancing at my cleared desktop. "Now we need some art for your story. Think you can locate some old photos we can use—Stan looking muscular, Stan and Terri at the gym, maybe something with Stan and the kids?"

"I'll get right on it," I said, glad to finally have something to do.

I phoned Jane Harris to see about the family photos, but, as usual, only her answering machine responded. Then I punched in Terri Harris's number, thinking how much I didn't want to talk to her.

She, of course, was home. "Sure, I have tons of photos of Stan and me. We had to have them for publicity purposes. I'll be home until late this afternoon if you want to come pick them up."

I said I'd be right over and then went to tell Caitlin that I was going to pick up the pictures and would be back after lunch.

"See you," she said, not looking up from her computer screen.

A wonderful smell wafted from Terri's house the minute she opened the door. "Smells like cookies," I said as I entered the hallway.

"I'm baking," Terri said. "Come and have a sample."

I followed her into the kitchen, noticing for the first time that she seemed to have gained at least ten or fifteen pounds since I'd first interviewed her. Well, she'd sold the gym and wasn't teaching exercise classes anymore. And not having the diet police in residence probably also was a factor.

So were her cookies. I took a bite of the sugar cookie Terri handed me, and said, "God, that's good."

She walked over to a wire rack where a batch of chocolate chip cookies was cooling. "Try one of these."

I did. "It's even better than the sugar cookie, though I've always been a sucker for chocolate. Did you make these yourself?"

Terri nodded. "When I met Stan, I was going to culinary arts school. I wanted to be a pastry chef." She watched me polish off the two cookies. "Think they're good enough to sell?"

"Definitely." I'd done my share of cookie baking myself, but Terri's rich, buttery cookies were a big step up from my Toll House standard.

"I'm thinking of opening my own bakery. I figure I have some name recognition from the gym. Maybe I'll call it Comfort Me With Baked Goods. Or maybe just Terri's Cookies."

"Low-calorie cookies? I bet there's a big market for that, particularly if they taste as good as this."

She shook her head. "There's nothing low-cal about these. I'm going more for the idea of 'You only go around once. Why not enjoy yourself?' "

I nodded, thinking of the mega-size bag of Baby Ruths in my pantry.

"Anyway, look at Stan," Terri said. "What good did all that starving himself and exercising do him? He tortured himself for nothing. I for one am never going to jog another day in my life. I'd rather die in bed eating a strawberry napoleon than gasping for breath on a treadmill."

Wasn't this the woman who just a few weeks ago was extolling the numerous benefits of regular exercise, like an evangelist to the sedentary? "Wait a minute. Didn't you tell

180

me how much you enjoyed exercising and that wonderful rush of endorphins? I remember you saying that you could eat whatever you wanted without gaining weight as long as you exercised every day."

Terri grinned. "I lied—unless, of course, what you want to eat is broccoli and celery sticks. I only told you that because I thought the article would come out before I sold the gym. I had to stay with the party line while I still owned it."

But now she could pig out on cookies and let those taut biceps atrophy into flab. "So it doesn't bother you that you're gaining weight?"

"Not enough to stop eating. Stan was the Puritan in the family, the one who got satisfaction from hunger pangs and aching muscles. I never did. I did enjoy looking great in a bathing suit, though." She picked up a large brown envelope lying on the counter and pulled out an eight by ten glossy of herself in a bikini. "I would really love for you to run this photo of me looking buff. I have a feeling it might be the last time I look like that."

I shrugged. "If I have any say in it, we'll run it."

She handed me the envelope. There were at least a dozen photos inside, most of them posed shots of Stan and Terri looking muscular and fit. And somehow sad, I thought. Always smiling, guts sucked in, looking like an aging Ken and a brunette Barbie doll.

I pulled out a photo of Stan sitting on a couch with Amber and SJ. "Oh, good. I'm glad you have one of Stan and the kids." Even though SJ looked supremely bored, Amber seemed sulky, and Stan, oblivious of anything except the camera.

"I took that last Christmas," Terri said. "The kids came over Christmas afternoon for their gifts."

I looked closer at the photo of Amber. She did, in fact,

look very much like her father—or the way he would have looked thirty years ago if he'd never dieted or exercised and was a girl. "I understand that Amber is going to finish writing her father's book."

"Yes, and if she handles it right, she could make a lot of money off it."

I wondered if that was what she told Amber, when she'd suggested Stan's manuscript could count as part of Amber's inheritance. "Wouldn't Amber also have to lose weight?"

"You mean you think the publisher would frown on a two hundred fifty pound woman writing a diet and exercise book?" she said sarcastically. "Of course Amber will have to lose weight—a lot of it. But that's what would make the book sell: another blimp-to-pretzel story mixed with some father-daughter sentimentality."

"And you believe that Amber suddenly can lose all this weight that she never could lose before?"

"Amber never had any reason to lose weight. Now she does. I always thought she was only doing the *Flab Power!* thing to piss off Stan anyway. She's a lot like her father—same fat genes, same ambition, same need to be the center of attention. Amber didn't get the money or publicity she wanted pushing fat acceptance. Maybe she'll get it by telling people how much happier she is starving herself."

I returned the family photo to the envelope. "What about you? Are you going to write a book about your change in eating philosophy?"

"God, no," she said, taking a bite of one of the sugar cookies. "No one wants to read a book about gaining weight, though they sure like to eat the food that makes it possible."

I thanked her for the photos and started to leave. Then I turned back. "This might sound strange, but did you

182

happen to paint a message on my door?"

I didn't expect her to admit it, but I thought I might get an answer from her reaction.

She stared at me. "Why would I do that?"

I shrugged. "Someone did."

"What did this message say?"

"Watch Your Back, Bitch."

She laughed. "Not me. I threaten people to their faces. Anyway, I got what I wanted—the sale of the gym is going through. Before that was finalized, I didn't want you printing anything about how bad our business was at the end. Sometimes those business types freak out about strange stuff. I could just see someone from National Gyms reading your article and suddenly deciding that maybe our gym's location was lousy or that people might not come to the new place because of negative associations with the old one."

I believed her. Terri was too in-your-face to sneak around at night spray painting doors. "What about Amber? Do you think she painted it?"

She shrugged. "I guess it's possible. She's thinking now about the spin on the book about her father, writing all this bull about how Stan's death inspired her to lose weight and how Stan always dreamed that she'd trim down." Terri rolled her eyes. "So needless to say, Amber isn't thrilled at the prospect of seeing her smart-ass remarks about Daddy printed in your magazine."

"I did cut out the worst paragraph," I admitted, "the part where she said that her father's fitness program seemed like an exercise in masochism."

Terri nodded. "It's true, but Amber will be pleased you took that out."

A timer buzzed and Terri hurried over to the oven to

take out another batch of cookies.

"The cookies were delicious, but I've got to get back to work," I said, picking up the envelope of photos.

"Any chance your magazine might do a story when I open my bakery?"

"I have to ask my editor, but I would think so."

"Great." She set down a sheet of wonderful-smelling chocolate chip cookies. "Oh, by the way, you should hope that it was Amber who wrote on your door. The girl has a big mouth and bad temper, but she won't hurt you. All talk, no action, that's Amber."

"That's reassuring," I said. There was something about the cold glint in her eyes that made me suspect that Terri would not say the same thing about herself. As I walked out of her house, I wondered how far Terri would go to ensure that she had sufficient capital to bankroll her high-calorie comfort-food venture.

Since I was out anyway, I decided to stop at my house for lunch. That way I could eat in a room with a window and pick up some photos for my article.

As I assembled my ham, cheese, and tomato sandwich, I mulled over my strange visit with Terri Harris. Her casually admitting that she'd lied about her love of exercise hadn't really surprised me; Terri had always displayed the questionable sincerity of a Miss America contestant declaring her dual passions for tap dancing and world peace. But for her to drop the pretense and veer so abruptly to the cookies-and-couch-potatoes camp did startle me. Perhaps, though, Terri was merely reverting to the person she'd once been, a plump, pastry-chef-in-training, when she'd come under Stan's charismatic spell. Maybe she'd given his fitness boot-camp lifestyle a trial run and then decided—after unloading Stan's gym—that she really preferred to be baking and eating cookies. Wishing I'd managed to finagle more of Terri's cookies, I ate my sandwich, appreciating the sunlight and peacefulness of my house. Would it be too early to broach the subject with Paul of me working from home, as my predecessor had done? I didn't want to appear ungrateful or unwilling to be part of the *City Magazine* team, but the cramped, dark closet laughingly called my office looked more like the space an orphan in a Dickens novel was shoved into as punishment.

But it was time to get back to that office. I walked up to my study to retrieve the photos. I found both the large glossy photo of Dr. Elizabeth and Amber's flyer for her *Flab Power! Workshop* in a manila folder. I inspected the posed picture of a smiling, confident Dr. Elizabeth, every blonde hair sprayed in place, her gold earrings and gold collar necklace both tasteful and expensive looking. I doubted if Paul would run the photo. My interview with Dr. E. had yielded so little in the way of either insight or interesting information about her good friend Stan that she was barely mentioned in my article. I wondered if the mind-over-disease philosophy espoused in the latest of her health books made her characterize everyone in her life in terms of upbeat platitudes, though, come to think of it, Stan Harris had a very similar power-of-positive-thinking outlook in his *Before and After* book.

The *Flab Power!* flyer had a grainy photo of Amber, looking proud and strong and very big. I wished there was some way that we could reproduce the picture in the magazine. I didn't mind deleting some of Amber's snotty comments about her father's obsessive exercising—they were adolescent and spiteful and eventually, when she grew up a bit, she would have regretted them. But I also didn't want to convey the impression that Amber was only a fat girl who was now using her father's ideas to slim down and rake in some money on his book. Although I didn't for a minute doubt that Amber was immature and manipulative, I knew that she was also bright and creative. I hoped that co-writing her father's book ended up being the great career move Amber obviously thought it would be.

After putting my dishes in the dishwasher and making sure that my front door did not contain any new messages, I drove back to work.

"You had a phone call, and Paul wants to see you," Caitlin said when I walked in. She handed me a yellow paper that said Jane Harris had returned my call.

I decided to telephone Jane first. When she answered the phone I explained about looking for family photos including Stan that we could use in our article.

"Sure, I have a few that you're welcome to use. Most of the recent ones are just of Stan and the kids. It's too bad that I don't have a new photo of Amber though. She's lost fifteen pounds in the last three weeks. You can really see the difference."

I'd seen Amber only a few days ago, but she'd been wearing baggy clothes that disguised her weight. "How did she manage that?" Never in my life had I been able to lose fifteen pounds in such a short time, and I'd tried every diet known to woman.

"Ironically, she's been following Stan's guidelines in *Before and After*. She exercises for a couple of hours every day and is eating only one thousand calories. And the weight is falling off her. She says she wants to lose one hundred more pounds before the book is published."

I had a sudden image of the fat flying off Amber and landing on Terri's hips: The musical flab game. "Well, I'm impressed," I said. "But I guess we'd want to run photos from when Stan was alive anyway, so the pictures you already have would be best." Before saying goodbye we made arrangements for me to pick them up on my way home from work.

Paul looked preoccupied when I walked into his office. He motioned for me to sit down on the chair in front of his desk. "So what have you got?"

I showed him the photos I had and said I'd be getting more family shots from Jane. I also told him about Terri's and Amber's new business ventures and the accompanying changes in their weight.

From behind his desk, Paul scowled at me. "You women are so damn obsessed about weight."

"We women?" I said. "Stan Harris, as you may recall, was one of the most fat-obsessed persons in the entire universe." My incredulity was rapidly being displaced by gender-based outrage. "And as far as 'we women' are concerned, do I look as if I'm obsessed with my weight?"

His eyes briefly scanned my size-sixteen body and returned to my face. "You look fine," he said in the dismissive tone of a man who isn't really looking.

I told myself that the pang of distress I felt was ridiculous. After all, he hadn't snickered and said, "That's for sure." What else could the man say? "Nice legs, but you could use some major work on those abs and that big butt"? What had I wanted him to say?

Paul cleared his throat. "I'm more interested in the angle of how Harris died. But no one is willing to go on the record about their doubts on the accidental death ruling."

"What do they say off the record?"

"That he had one hell of a lot of potassium in his body and that the accidental death ruling seemed premature."

"Do you mean someone is suggesting that the death wasn't accidental—that Stan committed suicide or was murdered?"

Paul sighed. "Todd, my source at the morgue, isn't speculating about that. I asked if there were any signs of violence on Harris's body—unusual bruising, that kind of thing. Todd said there was a bump on the back of his head, but that was consistent with the way he fell; Harris apparently hit his head on a rock when he collapsed on the jogging trail. So it's likely that Stan either purposely took the potassium or he was tricked—not forced—into taking it."

"If it was suicide, wouldn't he have left a note? Though, knowing Terri Harris, if she found a suicide note she probably wouldn't have told anyone about it. She'd figure the negative publicity might stop the sale of the gym."

Paul grinned. "You really are not a fan of Ms. Harris, are you?"

I shrugged. "She's ruthless, but she makes really good cookies."

I tried to remember what the various people I'd interviewed had told me about Stan's health. "Both Terri and Jane Harris said that Stan often took diuretics so he'd look thin for publicity photos and then took the potassium pills to balance the water loss. Dr. Elizabeth told me she'd warned him about doing so much self-medicating, taking massive doses of vitamins and minerals, but Stan insisted that the supplements were harmless and he was the best expert on what his body needed."

Paul nodded. "That was pretty much what she said at the hearing too. I got the transcript of the proceedings. She said Harris ignored medical advice and did a lot of things that harmed his health: fasting, the diuretics, too many supplements, and over-exercising. Apparently he didn't have a lot of confidence in physicians."

"It's strange that Dr. Elizabeth was the one who testified about Stan's health. She told me that she used to be his doctor, but she doesn't see patients anymore. She spends her time writing her health columns and her books. When I asked who Stan's new physician was, she said it was an internist named Thayer. I intended to call him, but I never got around to it."

"So why was she the one who testified as Stan's doctor at the hearing?"

I shrugged. "Maybe she saw Stan more regularly than his official doctor did. I gather they were friends. He could have come to her for unofficial medical advice."

Paul scanned a paper I assumed was the transcript of the hearing. "She also gave him a prescription for Dyrenium to reduce his blood pressure. The autopsy showed that in his body too."

"Several people mentioned that there was a strong history of heart disease in Stan's family. Apparently his father was very obese and sedentary—and died of cardiac arrest at age forty."

"And Stan, who was thin and fit, died of cardiac arrest at fifty-two."

"Maybe his lifestyle bought him an extra ten years." Though, considering the fasting and exhaustive exercising, I thought the price was awfully high.

"Maybe," Paul said. "And maybe I'm overreacting to the quick ruling. The fact that they rushed the investigation doesn't mean it's inaccurate." But he didn't look convinced by his own argument.

I wasn't either. "I think I'll call that Dr. Thayer tomorrow to see what he has to say about Stan's health."

Eighteen

When I arrived at Jane Harris's modest fifties-era ranch house, an elderly black Mercedes sedan was parked on the driveway next to Jane's Camry. Damn, I'd hoped to be the only visitor—the drop-in guest who coaxed Jane into a little girlish gossip about Stan's will and his not-very-grief-stricken widow.

But Jane, to my surprise, was more than happy to let me join the party. "It's only the two of us, SJ and me," she explained, gesturing to a slender, dark-haired young man who I'd talked to on the phone but never met. "We're celebrating SJ's getting accepted to medical school, and we'd love to have you help us eat the lasagna."

"Congratulations," I told him.

"Thanks." He regarded me with intense brown eyes that for some reason made me nervous. "I'm not sure that I'm ever going to actually attend med school, but thanks anyway."

So why had he bothered to apply if he didn't want to attend? I was tempted to ask but decided it wasn't high on the list of questions I wanted answered. Amber had implied that her father was scornful of his son's sexual preferences and his choice of a "female profession," nursing. Maybe SJ had applied to medical school to impress his father, and now that Stan was no longer around, he didn't want to bother with the additional years of education.

"But I don't want to intrude on your party," I said to

Jane. "Let me just pick up the photos and I'll get out of your way."

"Oh, we'd like to have you join us—really," SJ said. "Amber was supposed to come, but she decided that Mom's cooking was too much temptation for someone trying to starve herself. So you can eat her share."

I hesitated. The food, in fact, did smell wonderful, and the only things I had to eat at home were eggs or canned soup. And wasn't I much more likely to pick up valuable information over a nice, leisurely meal? "You've twisted my arm," I said with a smile.

"Wonderful. Let me set another place," Jane said, leaving me alone with SJ.

He looked uncomfortable. "I wanted to apologize to you. I was rude to you on the phone. It was a bad day, and the last thing I wanted to do was discuss my father with the media."

I nodded. "That's okay. You really weren't rude, just a bit abrupt."

He didn't say anything, but looked marginally more relaxed. Looking at him—the delicate features, long eyelashes and large, expressive eyes—I suddenly saw what I imagined Stan Harris envisioned every time he'd looked at his children. SJ had the face and bone structure of a very attractive woman, while Amber had her father's strong features and the beefy body of a linebacker. For someone as macho, homophobic and grossly insecure as Stan, this realization must have been like a slap in the face.

Jane called us to come to the table then. She'd set the table with gold-rimmed china and crystal wine glasses, an arrangement of white and pink carnations in the middle—a real celebratory dinner.

"So when is your story about Stan coming out?" she

asked as she poured red wine into my glass.

"In about six weeks, I think. My article is finished and I'm collecting photos for it now. I got some from Terri this morning."

I was hoping that the mention of Stan's widow would trigger a reaction from one of them, but neither took the bait. Instead they both seemed focused on eating what turned out to be delicious vegetarian lasagna, buttery garlic bread, and a tangy green salad with artichokes and hearts of palm.

"You can't tell me this is low-calorie cooking," I said to Jane. "Everything tastes wonderful."

She laughed. "I stopped doing low-cal cooking when I left Stan. Unlike him, I believe in eating reasonable portions of normal food. Not many people can keep on eating the tasteless diet foods Stan subsisted on."

I nodded. "That's what Terri said too. When I was over there this morning she was baking cookies. I think she's even considering opening a cookie business."

This time I got a reaction. "Cookies?" Jane asked. "That's certainly a change from the Fitness Nazi role she was playing a few weeks ago."

I shrugged. "She said she'd been training to be a pastry chef when she met Stan."

Jane's brown eyes flashed. "A money-hungry chameleon is more like it. If Stan had wanted her to be anything from a sumo wrestler to a lady jockey, Terri would have tried her damnedest to become it. She was in the market for a wealthy, successful husband—which at that point, Stan was—and she'd do whatever was necessary to reel him in. What Stan wanted just then was someone who'd be as consumed by his fitness business as he was. So that was how Terri Harris, fitness nut and aerobics instructor, evolved."

"And now she's moving on to a new role." SJ said. "Did Terri happen to mention how she's going to fund this new business venture?"

"Not really. When I was at her house she was just testing cookie recipes." It did not seem like the right moment to mention how scrumptious those cookies were. "What I assumed, though, was that she was putting her share of the gym profits into her new business."

SJ gulped a mouthful of wine, looking as if he was trying to medicate himself. "According to my dear step-mother, we shouldn't be counting on much in the way of profits from the gym sale. She claims Dad had some business debts that first have to be paid off. And then we still have to wait until the will is probated before Amber and I collect our inheritance—whatever inhcritance is left."

"So we're wondering," his mother said, "how Terri would have enough cash to open a business."

"She didn't give me any details. I don't even know when she intends to start it. Maybe it's a long-term plan."

"Or maybe not," SJ said. "I know I sound bitter, but Terri is the person who just told me that there's probably not going to be enough money available to fund my entire medical school education. I wasn't asking her for a gift, damn it, only my rightful inheritance."

I shook my head. "Oh, that's terrible. Have you talked to an attorney? Maybe there's more money than Terri is letting you believe."

Jane sighed, the look of celebration stripped from her face like a gaudy mask. "We will. But of course the real issue is that Stan told me he meant to change his will. He intended to leave everything to Amber and SJ and cut Terri out of the will altogether. So even with Stan's business debts, there probably would have been more than enough money left to fund SJ's education."

"But legally isn't a wife entitled to a share of her husband's estate?" I asked. Terri, I was sure, would have sued in a second if Stan had left nothing at all for her in his will.

Jane shrugged. "I'm just not sure. I don't think Stan had thought it all through, and certainly changing his will didn't seem urgent. He had no reason to believe that he would die anytime soon."

This was my opportunity, my opening line. I took a deep breath, debating with myself about whether I wanted to be a polite dinner guest or a tacky and insensitive reporter. Journalism—and my innate ill-bred curiosity—won out. "Are you sure about that—that Stan didn't think he might die sometime soon?"

"What do you mean?" Jane looked puzzled.

"I mean he had a family history of heart disease, high blood pressure, and was doing a lot of things—fasting, taking diuretics, exercising too much, popping huge amounts of vitamin pills—that were dangerous to his health."

"Stan had high blood pressure? Where did you get that idea?" Jane asked.

"At the cause-of-death hearing, Dr. Elizabeth testified that he was taking a drug called Dyrenium for high blood pressure. The drug was found in his system during the autopsy."

Jane shook her head. "His blood pressure was fine."

"Mom, Dad probably developed blood pressure problems and didn't tell you. You didn't see him that much."

"Well, maybe." Jane hesitated. "It was just that he was such a hypochondriac, so obsessed with his health, that it seems like the kind of thing he would tell me."

"If he was a hypochondriac, he didn't visit his doctor very much," I said. "I called the internist he got when Dr. Elizabeth stopped seeing patients. Dr. Thayer—the new doctor—said he hadn't seen Stan in over a year and a half. He had no idea about the potassium pills or diuretics Stan was taking."

"Dad probably didn't tell him. He was a hypochondriac, but he didn't trust doctors to cure his illnesses. He believed in his own self-prescribed cures, crazy as they sometimes were."

I felt like a bloodhound following a scent that suddenly disappears. Thinking, very briefly, about what a nice person I used to be, I inquired, "So you didn't suspect that Stan might have committed suicide?"

They stared at me.

"After all he was having business reversals, marriage difficulties, and apparently some health problems. For someone who so valued being youthful and fit and, well, macho, might not all of that have pushed him into"—I searched for a less awful way of saying it—"a desperate act?"

I could tell from the look of distaste on Jane's face that she wished she hadn't invited me to stay for dinner. I didn't blame her.

SJ rolled his eyes. "You're not suggesting that Dad was purposely jogging himself to death? Adding the potassium, I guess, for good measure so, one way or another, he'd go into cardiac arrest? I can think of a lot easier ways to kill myself."

"But what if you didn't want it to look like suicide? Overdosing on potassium could seem like an accident. In fact it was ruled an accident."

"Stan would never have tried to kill himself," Jane said, her eyes flashing. "Why, he was looking forward to expanding his business and finishing his new book—he told me so. And he was involved with—maybe even in love with—some new woman. He didn't tell me who it was, but I gather they were quite serious."

A voice behind us, from the kitchen, said, "It was Carol Quaid, Mom. The woman who was murdered a few weeks ago."

I turned to see Amber Harris. Apparently she'd come in the back door without any of us hearing her. She held up a baggie filled with carrot and celery sticks. "I've come to join the party."

"How do you know that your father was seeing that Quaid woman?" her mother demanded.

"I saw them together at a movie theater. They were whispering into each other's ears, kissing. It was quite embarrassing, actually. Fortunately, they didn't see me, so I didn't have to talk to them."

Carol Quaid and Stan Harris? I remembered now that Mrs. Quaid had mentioned that Carol had started working out and how proud she was of her newly muscular physique. But I'd never imagined that Carol and her trainer were having an affair.

Suddenly I shivered. What if there was some connection between their deaths? And if so, how could I figure out what it was?

After a moment of silence, Jane said, "Let me get you a plate, Amber. At least you can eat some of the salad."

Amber sat in the empty chair next to me. "Didn't expect to see you here," she said, sounding curious rather than unfriendly.

"I didn't expect it either. I came over to pick up some photos, and your mother invited me to stay for dinner." And then I ruined the celebration for her by asking a lot of upsetting questions. The guilt that I hadn't felt before was starting to seep in. More out of contrition toward her mother than anything else, I added, "By the way, I took out the paragraph in my story where you put down your dad's exercise philosophy."

"Thanks." She looked grateful. Amber was wearing a loose black sweat suit, so I still couldn't see much change in her body. But I could see the weight loss in her face. The first time I'd met her, Amber's face had been round and fleshy, but today high cheekbones were emerging, and large eyes like her brother's were more noticeable. She looked as if a sculptor had been remodeling her face.

Her mother set a plate, silver and glass of water in front of her.

"Maybe I should be going," I said to Jane. "I'm sorry to have intruded on your celebration."

"Don't be silly," she said. "You haven't even finished your meal."

I finished it, the once-delicious food suddenly tasteless. To my relief, the three Harrises started chatting easily to each other. I let the words flow around me, not really listening, biding my time until I could leave.

Amber, I noticed, was eating a large serving of salad and, at her mother's insistence, a tiny serving of lasagna. I watched her drop an orange tablet into her glass of water; the tablet started to foam.

"What's that?" I asked.

"K-Lyte," she said nonchalantly. "I need the extra potassium now when I'm dieting, and Dad drank it all the time."

I stared as she took a big gulp.

The minute I got home from Jane Harris's I put on a pot of coffee then sat down at my kitchen table to make notes. I felt overwhelmed by tidbits of information that might—if only I managed to arrange them correctly—add up to something important and, possibly, sinister.

Carol Quaid and Stan Harris: Was there some link connecting their deaths? Perhaps there was none, but it seemed awfully coincidental that Stan, the woman he'd been having an affair with, and her mother all died within weeks of each other. I stared at my blank paper, feeling as if I had one of those maddening jigsaw puzzles in which all of the pieces are the same solid color. Where did I begin?

Because I couldn't think of anything else to do, I wrote headings for two lists, one labeled "Who Killed Stan Harris?" and the other, "Who Killed Carol Quaid?"; I was assuming that whoever killed Carol had also killed her mother.

I started with Stan. My suspect list included: Terri Harris, who possibly realizing that Stan was about to divorce her and cut her out of his will, could have decided she'd better get rid of him quickly to maximize her share of his estate; Amber Harris, who seemed to know an awful lot about her father's potassium intake and, at least the first time I talked to her, appeared very hostile to Stan; Jane Harris, who may have believed her ex-husband had already changed his will in favor of her children and wanted them to at least get something valuable from their lousy father; and SJ Harris, who also had seemed angry with his father and, like his mother, might have thought that he'd be inheriting a lot more money.

I moved on to Carol Quaid. This list was a lot harder; I didn't know Carol very well nor had I interviewed people for an article about her. While I'd never thought Carol was well liked, I still wasn't sure who would want to kill her. Nevertheless, I made my list: Rob, my dear husband, because Carol was keeping information about him in her safe-deposit box and told her mother to use it if she died suddenly; anyone else Carol had included in her safe-deposit box hit list—Mrs. Quaid had indicated that there were several others; Terri Harris, if she knew Stan was cheating on her with Carol Quaid; and Jane Harris, who might have been a lot more jealous of Stan's new love than she was letting on, particularly if she had been harboring any fantasies of reuniting with Stan now that his marriage with Terri was falling apart.

The only people on both lists were Terri and Jane Harris. As suspects in the Quaid murders they were very "iffy." I had no indication that either of them had ever met Carol. Jane claimed she hadn't known the identity of Stan's new girlfriend. And just because she and Stan had seemed to be on good terms didn't mean Jane was romantically interested in him.

Terri seemed a more likely criminal candidate. While I couldn't picture calm, composed Jane driving to Carol's cottage and shooting her in her bed, Terri seemed to have the ruthless, self-centered temperament required to kill three people. She also had more of a motive: getting rid of both the husband who'd cheated on her and the woman he'd cheated with—and inheriting a big hunk of Stan's estate to boot.

Rob, I was quite sure, hadn't known Stan Harris at all. But that didn't necessarily mean that he hadn't killed Carol Quaid and her mother. I really didn't see Rob as a murderer, but there were a lot of things about Rob that I hadn't seen. And if Carol had some kind of incriminating information about Rob, maybe he would feel forced into violence, particularly if the information adversely affected his cash flow.

Of course Carol apparently was keeping information on other people as well, according to Mrs. Quaid. Was Carol a blackmailer? Or was she keeping this information as some kind of protection for herself? Perhaps she, as office manager, had figured out that Rob was doing some kind of illegal billing—charging an insurance company for patients he hadn't seen or billing for procedures that he hadn't actually performed. In that case, the X-rays she'd kept might have been for a non-existent person—perhaps Rob had duplicated someone else's X-rays to establish a phony patient file. And Carol might have kept them in case of a later lawsuit—or to extort money from Rob.

The problem, of course, was that I didn't know Carol well enough to guess her motives. So who could tell me more about Carol? When I'd talked to Iris, the receptionist Rob had replaced with his bimbo girlfriend, she hadn't seemed to know much about her. Iris, in fact, had thought that Rob and Carol had been having an affair. But if they hadn't been sexually involved, why had the two of them been whispering together and eating private lunches? Although Rob had always respected Carol's intelligence and hard work, he'd never seemed to like her much. So were they discussing problems with Rob's practice, information he didn't want others in the office to overhear?

A few years back, Rob's practice had declined. Too many longtime patients suddenly moved out of town or changed to cheaper dental clinics. But that decrease in revenues was hardly a secret. In the last eighteen months Rob had seemed to find new clients, and business improved. So what were Rob and Carol whispering about?

I had too many unanswered questions and no one to answer them. I needed to talk to someone from Rob's old office. Iris probably didn't know any more than she had already told me, but I couldn't think of anyone else to call. I dialed her number and let the phone ring six times. I was about to hang up when she answered.

"Oh, I was just walking in the door," she said when I identified myself. "What can I do for you, Mrs. P?"

For starters, you could stop calling me Mrs. P, I was tempted to say. But I restrained myself. "I know this sounds a bit strange, but can you tell me what you know about Carol Quaid—like, for instance, who her friends were?"

"She didn't have any friends that I know of. She wasn't a very friendly person, if you know what I mean, and I don't think she had any time for a social life. She was always going to night school or studying, and then, after she finished school, she was doing freelance accounting jobs on the side. Though I do remember that she went out to lunch a few times with that doctor newspaper columnist—what's her name?"

"Dr. Elizabeth?"

"Yeah, that's the one. I said to Carol that I'd seen her, Dr. Elizabeth, interviewed on TV. Carol said they had gone to MBA classes together, but said Dr. Elizabeth was 'book smart, but dumb about money.' I thought it was a funny thing to say, but then Carol always was real interested in money." She paused. "That's about all I know."

"Thanks." I knew she was wondering why I was so interested. "I guess I was just curious. You know the girls and I were the ones who discovered Carol's body."

"Oh, yes, that must have been terrible for you."

"It was." I was relieved that she seemed to be satisfied with the explanation. We chatted for a few minutes about the new job she'd found in a doctor's office and then, promising to stay in touch, we said goodbye.

I remembered Dr. Elizabeth saying at the memorial that

she and Carol had been in night school together. Maybe tomorrow I'd call her at her office with some request for my article. If I played my cards right, I might even coax her into telling me what else she knew about our mutual acquaintance, Carol Quaid.

I walked back to the table and glanced at my two suspect lists. Talk about amateur night! My list reminded me of brainstorming exercises I'd had to do in high school—write down every thought that came into mind, no matter how stupid it is. I needed a lot more facts before I could make reasonable suspect lists, and I wasn't sure that I'd ever get them.

Feeling restless, I paced around my house, trying to figure out what would make me feel better. A phone conversation with Meg or one of my daughters? A long, hot bath? An hour of mindless TV? None of the options seemed appealing.

I needed to get out of my too-quiet house, go someplace with other people. I considered which nearby stores would still be open and decided on the drug store. I could pick up some cosmetics I needed and maybe page through a few magazines. When I got home, I might feel tired enough to take a bath and go to sleep.

I drove to the drug store, feeling vaguely pathetic, like some elderly widow who gets into long conversations with store clerks. At the cosmetics department I picked up gray eye shadow and mascara—a first-day-of-work present for myself. I started for the checkout counter, then reconsidered. Since I was already here, why not do a little investigating? What better place than a pharmacy to learn about the effects of potassium?

I started out at the vitamin section. I found potassium pills, but no K-Lyte.

The pharmacist, a friendly-looking young woman, did not look that busy, so I stood at the counter until she saw me. "I'm wondering if you stock a potassium supplement called K-Lyte," I said.

She nodded. "But you need a prescription for that. You can get potassium tablets, though, without a prescription."

Okay. Stan and Amber must have got a prescription from someone, unless, of course, Amber was using Stan's leftover K-Lyte.

I decided I'd need to level with this woman if I wanted to get any useful information. "Actually, I don't want to buy potassium. I'm a journalist and I'm doing a story about a man who may have died from an overdose of potassium."

To my relief, she looked interested. "Oh, that can happen. When I was working at a hospital a pharmacist sent too high of a dose of potassium—they usually piggyback potassium with another medication they're injecting. But particularly for diabetics and heart patients, getting too much potassium can be life-threatening."

"What happened to the patient in the hospital?"

"I'm not sure. All I heard about was the pharmacist. He got fired."

"So potassium can be injected?"

She nodded. "Some forms of it. Potassium chloride and potassium acetate, for instance, can be injected."

I thought of Stan with the injection between his toes. "Who else could die from getting too much potassium?"

"It depends a lot on the dose of potassium. And the other medications the patient is taking could also have an effect. I heard of one woman who was hospitalized after taking high blood pressure medication with her potassium supplement—the medication greatly increases the level of potassium in your body."

I was aware that another customer had walked up and was waiting behind me. "You don't remember the name of that blood pressure medication, do you?"

She shook her head and looked pointedly at the customer behind me.

"Thanks for your help." I sensed that she had been a very big help indeed.

I paid for my purchases and then drove home, feeling increasingly excited. How had Stan got a prescription for K-Lyte? Had he known that too much potassium could be dangerous for people with heart problems or that blood pressure medication could increase the amount of potassium in his body?

I pulled into my driveway. As I waited for the automatic garage door to open, I thought I caught some movement from the corner of my eye. Was there someone in the bushes by the back door? Someone who was waiting for me to come out of the garage?

Heart pounding, I backed out of the driveway and onto the street. No one ran after me. But then he wouldn't have to. He could wait until I came back home.

I'd read somewhere that a woman who thought she was being followed should drive to a police station or to a crowded, well-lit place. I went back to the drug store.

Had I been imagining the movement? Could it have been the wind just rustling the bushes? I'd feel like an idiot bringing a police officer to my house and then discovering nothing—or a stray cat—behind the shrubs. But still, if there actually was someone there . . .

I pulled my cell phone from my purse and dialed Meg's number. "Listen, I'm probably being ridiculous," I said when she answered, "but there is a slight possibility that someone is hiding behind my bushes."

"Where are you? Do you want me to come over? I have a revolver, you know."

No, in fact I hadn't known. "No, I want you to stay on the phone with me. No, wait. First go get your cell phone, but stay on this line."

I drove home slowly. By the time I was back to my garage, Meg, cell phone in hand, was ready to call 911 if I screamed.

"Do you see anything?" she asked as I pulled the car into the garage.

"No." Not yet anyway.

"Tell me what's happening!" she demanded as I got out of the car and walked toward the house.

"Nothing! I'm at the back door." I inserted my key with shaking fingers. Any minute I expected a hand on my shoulder or a hissed command to get off the phone.

But no one emerged from the bushes. I stepped inside, slammed the door shut and immediately locked the new deadbolt.

"I'm inside. I'm okay."

"Go look around the house first. I'll stay on the line."

I did as I was told, feeling my heart thud at every step. "Everything seems to be okay. No broken glass or kicked-in doors."

"Thank God."

"I probably over-reacted. But thanks for holding my hand, Meg. I really appreciate it."

"What are friends for?" She yawned. "Do you want to talk?"

"Not now. Go back to sleep. I'm all locked in, safe and sound."

But as I hung up the phone, I didn't feel safe and sound. Not at all.

Nineteen

Dr. Elizabeth answered her office phone herself, sounding preoccupied, only mildly interested when I said I was collecting photos for my article.

"I don't think I have any pictures of Stan and me," she said. "Can't you use the photo from my book jacket that I sent you?"

I wanted to say, "Hard as it apparently is for you to believe, this article isn't about you." But since I wanted information from her, it didn't seem like a smart move. Instead I said, "Right now I'm just collecting family photos and snapshots of Stan. I guess I thought of you because of our conversation at Carol Quaid's funeral. Was she a close friend of yours?"

If she thought it was a strange juxtaposition of topics, Dr. Elizabeth did not let on. "We were friendly classmates in some MBA courses. I wouldn't say we were close friends. Both of us were extremely busy with our careers."

I ignored the hint and plunged on. "After Carol died, I always wished I'd gotten to know her better. I didn't really have much of a sense of what she was like personally. I only saw her as Rob's office manager."

"I don't mean to be rude, but I'm on a deadline and have to finish my column."

So much for that. She probably didn't know any more than I did about Carol anyway. "I'll let you go then. Thanks."

"If I find any photos of Stan and me I'll phone you," she

said. "What's your number again?"

I gave her my office number. "I'm working now as a staff member at *City Magazine*."

"Oh really? You have to let me take you to lunch. I have a lot of ideas for stories you might want to do."

"We have to do that sometime."

"How about tomorrow?"

"Uh, great." Maybe I could extract some information about Carol between Dr. Elizabeth's pitching articles about herself.

I spent the next several hours writing back-of-the-magazine fillers that I extracted from the pile of news releases that public relations offices sent to the magazine. Then I got myself another cup of coffee and studied all the photos I'd collected of Stan Harris. In almost every one he looked as if he was too busy sucking in his gut and flashing his very white teeth to reveal much of himself to the camera.

"Any of the pictures usable?" Paul O'Neal asked from the doorway.

"You judge." I spread the photos across my desk.

He walked over and leaned down to inspect them. "God, he looks like a model for a denture-whitening ad—the same fake grin in every shot. No wonder his kids hated him."

"Looks more like a grimace than a smile. But we can run some of the photos, can't we?"

"Sure. The ones with his family and the posed muscle-man shot are good enough." Not looking at me, he added, "Would you like to go to lunch? You can tell me what else you learned about Harris then."

"You mean right now?"

"Well sometime in the next couple of hours. Does that mean you do or do not want to dine with me today?"

Dine? "Uh, yeah, I'd like to." I had, in fact, packed a

peanut butter sandwich and a banana for lunch, but this sounded more appealing. "And I could eat now or later. I eat virtually all types of food."

Shut up! I told myself, feeling my cheeks burn. "I eat all types of food"? Lord, I sounded like a socially awkward sixth grader.

"Good, an accommodating woman."

I nodded and smiled when he suggested eating in half an hour at a Thai restaurant down the block, afraid of the words that might come tumbling out.

Fortunately, I seemed to have recovered my emotional equilibrium by the time we reached the restaurant, a dark, pleasant place that had a huge aquarium of multi-colored fish. I was even enjoying myself as Paul plied me with questions about my discoveries and then listened with focused attention to my answers—something Rob hadn't done for probably the last twenty years of our marriage.

"So let me get this straight," Paul said after the waiter took our order for chicken curry and pad thai. "Amber Harris was taking the same prescription medication, this powdered potassium that her father was using?"

"Right. When I saw her drink the stuff I realized that Stan wouldn't have had to pop dozens of pills to get so much potassium in his system. He—or someone else—could have mixed it all together into one glass of water. If someone else did it, maybe Stan wasn't even aware of how much he was drinking, particularly if the powder was mixed into some other drink. I read in his first book that he drank a lot of vegetable juices and protein shakes. Someone could have slipped the potassium into any of those."

Paul nodded. "If he kept bottles of the juices at work and at home, anyone who had access to his refrigerators could have done that."

I started to mentally list all the people who might have access to Stan's refrigerators when another scenario came to mind. "The pharmacist told me that if certain blood pressure medications are taken with potassium supplements they can cause a big rise in blood potassium levels that can be fatal. Remember that Stan was taking Dyrenium to reduce his blood pressure? So maybe he didn't need to take a giant amount of potassium to overdose. The pharmacist said something about too much potassium being especially dangerous for heart patients and diabetics—doses that wouldn't be a problem for healthy people. It's certainly possible that Stan had some undiagnosed heart disease—it ran in his family, after all—that could have made him particularly susceptible."

"You're saying maybe it really was an accident, the interaction of his blood pressure medicine and his standard dose of potassium pushing him into cardiac arrest?"

"Exactly."

"But I'd still want to know why his physician didn't tell Stan about the dangers of taking both medications, particularly for someone at risk of heart disease."

I shrugged. "Could be that Stan didn't tell Dr. Elizabeth about the potassium he was taking. He could have even got the K-Lyte from a different doctor."

Paul pulled a little notebook out of his pocket and jotted something in it. "You mentioned before that Dr. Elizabeth wasn't his official doctor. Do you know who is?"

"An internist named Thayer—Mark Thayer. He told me it was over a year and a half since Stan had been to his office."

"I think my friend at the morgue needs to call Drs. Elizabeth and Thayer to get some more detailed medical information about Stan. Doctors are much more likely to give out that kind of stuff to other doctors than to journalists."

Our food arrived then, and for a few minutes we ate in companionable silence. "This is really good," I said, after sampling both the entrees.

"I've been coming here for years. Alice, my ex-wife, introduced me to the place. She used to work near here."

Briefly I questioned the wisdom of proceeding any further with a possibly touchy topic, then decided what the hell, journalists always ask questions. "What kind of work does Alice do?"

"She's an editor too. Right now she edits a medical journal in Philadelphia."

"So you don't see a lot of each other?"

He shook his head. "Occasionally we run into each other, but since we never had kids, there's no real reason to stay in touch."

"How long have you been divorced?"

"Nine years." He set down his fork and looked me in the eye. "It was not an especially acrimonious divorce. We'd been married seven years and just kind of drifted apart. When Alice was offered the job in Philadelphia—a really good job—I'd only been at *City Magazine* a few months. I wanted to stay here and she wanted to go. We tried for a while to make that work, flying back and forth between Texas and Pennsylvania. But eventually it seemed like too much effort, more like constantly entertaining weekend visitors than being married." He raised an eyebrow. "Anything else you'd like to know?"

"Nope, that about covers everything." I wondered if he was really this matter-of-fact about his divorce or if this was his for-public-consumption explanation. Nine years from now, what would I be saying about Rob? Nothing that benign, I'd bet. More on the order of "I thought my marriage was fine—not great, but okay—and then the shit-heel left me after I refused to apologize to him for eating some Baby Ruths."

"What about you?" Paul asked. "Have you filed for divorce yet?"

"I'm working on it. I talked to a lawyer last week. The fact that we don't know where Rob is complicates things a bit."

Fortunately he didn't pursue the topic. Talking about Rob tended to depress me.

"How does your front door look?" he asked instead. "I was going to come around on Sunday to see if it needed a second coat, but something came up."

"What could possibly be more important than painting my door?"

His eyes widened, then he grinned. "Oh, you're kidding. For a minute there . . ."

I smiled back, declining his offer to come next weekend to give the door a second coat. But as we got up to leave, I realized that I very much wanted to know what Paul O'Neal had been doing last Sunday—and I was appalled that I was so interested.

If I wanted to hold onto this job, I decided as we drove back to the office, I was going to have to keep a more professional distance from my attractive boss.

I managed to stay busy the rest of the afternoon and left work a few minutes early so I could pick up some groceries for the dinner I'd promised to make for Meg. It was the least I could do after all the help she'd given me, and I was also looking forward to having some company in my too-quiet house.

The spaghetti sauce was simmering, the salad made, and

garlic bread in the oven when Meg arrived with two bottles of Chianti.

"Oh, no," I said, looking at the wine. "The last time I drank that much with you I had the hangover to end all hangovers."

"You really do have a rather prissy streak." Meg opened the first bottle and poured us each a glass. "Has anyone every told you that?"

I thought about it. "Not lately." I dumped the pasta into a colander. "Let's eat."

"Fortunately, your cooking skills compensate for your prissiness," Meg said after finishing a plateful of spaghetti and three pieces of garlic bread. "Now tell me about your new job. How do you like being a working woman?"

"Except for the fact that my office is a closet, I like it just fine." I told her about getting the photos from the cookie-baking Terri Harris, having dinner with Jane Harris and her children and about Dr. Elizabeth's lunch invitation thirty seconds after I mentioned I was now on the magazine's staff.

"You haven't said anything about Paul O'Neal. What's he like to work for?"

"Nice. Of course I don't see that much of him. We're lucky if he gets there by noon, and he's just getting into gear when I'm leaving for the day."

"I always thought he was kind of cute, if you like that big, hulking type."

The phone rang then, saving me from having to respond. I was going to let the answering machine take a message, when I saw on the caller ID that the call was from the magazine.

It was Paul. "Lauren, I just talked to my friend at the morgue. He was lucky enough to catch Dr. Thayer this afternoon."

I could hear the excitement in his voice. "And what did Dr. Thayer have to say?"

"He said he never prescribed any medication for Stan Harris, and the last time he saw Stan—about a year and a half ago—his blood pressure was normal, though his cholesterol level was high. He was very surprised that Stan had been taking Dyrenium to reduce his blood pressure, though he did say that Harris was a classic Type-A personality who was at high risk for heart disease."

"So maybe Stan developed high blood pressure within the last year and another doctor prescribed the Dyrenium." The information didn't seem all that surprising to me, and I wanted to get off the phone. "But thanks for calling to tell me."

"Wait. I haven't told you the best part. I was telling my friend about our idea of someone slipping some extra potassium in Stan's breakfast protein shake, and he said it wouldn't work that way unless maybe Stan drank it on the jogging trail. Apparently death from a potassium overdose is quick, one to five minutes after taking it. So if Stan drank the stuff at home he certainly wouldn't have been able to start jogging."

"Very interesting," I said, aware that Meg was hanging on my every word. "I want to hear all about it tomorrow, but my friend Meg is here for dinner."

"Oh, sorry to interrupt your dinner. Tell Meg hi."

I hung up the phone. "Paul says hi."

"Hi back to him," Meg said with a big smirk. "You know what I think?" She didn't wait for me to reply. "I think that Paul O'Neal is hot for you."

"Don't be ridiculous." I turned away from her to get the coffee cups.

Twenty

My lunch with Dr. Elizabeth was just about what I expected: boring as hell.

After suggesting that *City Magazine* run a "personality profile" of her to coincide with the publication of her next book, *Dr. Elizabeth's Guide To Preventive Medicine*, Dr. E. confided that her father, a physician, had wanted a son. "But when it became clear that it wasn't going to happen, he decided that I'd have to be the family carrier of the medical flame. My writing genes came from my mother. She was a journalism major and encouraged me to get summer jobs on our local newspaper. So I guess you could say that I combined both of my parents' interests in my choice of career."

Fascinating. I wished I was drinking wine rather than iced tea. The shrimp salad was good and the restaurant's signature biscuits delicious, but neither was good enough to make listening to Dr. E. prattle on about herself a fun experience. What was there about the woman that evoked such a negative reaction in me? Sure, she was self-involved, narcissistic, a blatant publicity hound, and her smiley Texas sorority girl mannerisms—a combination of fake intimacy mixed with a big dollop of arrogance—set my teeth on edge. But was that any reason to want to toss my iced tea in her face?

I nodded and chewed and pretended to listen. It was her condescension that was getting to me, I decided—the fact that Dr. Elizabeth sincerely believed I was placed on this earth to serve her. I tuned in long enough to hear the end of her story about a recent "hilarious meeting" of her Mensa group.

"I think it might make a fascinating feature, Lauren. You'll be surprised. We Mensa members are not remotely like the humorless nerds we're reported to be."

I promised I would mention the idea to my editor. "But before I forget, Elizabeth, I wanted to ask you a few questions about Stan Harris. I know you prescribed the blood pressure medication for him, but did you also prescribe the potassium powder K-Lyte that he was taking?"

I could see that she was trying to stomp down her feelings of irritation. "I didn't prescribe any K-Lyte. Maybe Stan's internist prescribed it."

"He said he didn't. He also said that Stan didn't have high blood pressure."

"Do you know when he last saw Stan?"

"About eighteen months before Stan died."

She nodded. "That explains it then. Blood pressure changes, particularly as one ages. The last time I saw him, Stan mentioned that he was under a lot of stress. He was always very worried—almost like a hypochondriac—about the possibility of heart disease. To reassure him, I took his blood pressure. It was quite high, and, at his request, I prescribed the Dyrenium. I also strongly suggested that he get a complete workup from his physician, which he apparently didn't do."

"When was this?"

She thought about it for a minute. "In early December, maybe a month before he died. Stan was in my office giving me advice on the exercise chapter of my book. He's had impressive results helping chronically obese people lose weight through exercise. Weight loss is such a complex issue. Over ninety-five percent of dieters regain the weight they've lost plus some additional pounds." Her eyes swept over me. "But then you already know that, don't you?"

I shrugged. "Most of us middle-aged women, unfortunately, are all too aware of it." Pointedly I studied her own not-so-svelte body. Unfortunately, it was a good twenty pounds more svelte than my own.

Why was the bitch suddenly trying to antagonize me? Minutes ago she'd been acting as if I were her new best friend. It didn't make sense. Either she was extremely touchy about anyone questioning her medical judgment or she was attempting to divert my attention from a topic she didn't want to discuss. That made me, of course, all the more eager to purse it. "When you prescribed the Dyrenium, you weren't concerned about the dangerous interaction it might have with his potassium supplements?"

She looked confused, then after a moment said, "I wasn't aware he was taking K-Lyte."

Was it possible that she didn't know about the combined effect of the two medications? She had admitted, after all, that she'd stopped practicing medicine several years ago in order to focus on her writing. "Really? I recall you telling me before that you'd advised Stan to stop taking so many vitamins."

She glared at me. "Yes, I did suggest that, but I wasn't aware of which supplements he was taking. Not that Stan ever took my medical advice. He always felt he knew more about his body than any physician."

I nodded. "Stan seemed to do a lot of harmful things—fasting, over-exercising, popping vitamins, using diuretics indiscriminately—to keep himself in shape."

Dr. Elizabeth sighed. "Stan was a very stubborn, headstrong man. He believed that his father, who died at forty of a heart attack, had received poor medical care, and that made him distrust the entire medical profession. The only reason he trusted me was that we became friends when I started working out at his gym."

"You mentioned he said he was very stressed. What was bothering him?"

She frowned. "He didn't really go into it with me, but I knew it bothered him that his business wasn't doing as well as it used to."

"Were you surprised that Terri Harris sold the gym so quickly after Stan died?"

"Not really. From what Stan said, quite a few of his old clients had started going to new gyms in the area. Terri probably felt lucky to find a buyer." She glanced at her watch. "Oh, I need to get going. I have an appointment in half an hour."

My mind raced over all my unanswered questions. "Did you know that Carol Quaid was having an affair with Stan?"

She stared at me. "What are you talking about?"

I repeated the question.

"I had no idea they were"—she searched for the right words—"personally involved with each other. I knew that Carol was Stan's accountant. The three of us had discussed Stan's business."

"Why?"

She blinked. "Because several years ago I invested in Stan's gym."

"So you must have been upset that business was declining."

"No, I had faith that Stan would turn things around eventually. He was a shrewd businessman." She glanced at the bill the waiter had brought and laid two twenties on the table. Standing, she said, "I've enjoyed chatting with you, Lauren."

"Thanks for lunch. It was very informative."

"Glad to hear that. We must keep in touch." Her lips curved, but her eyes were not smiling.

Caitlin was at her desk reading her horoscope when I returned to the office. "Have a good lunch?" she asked.

I'd told her how much I was not looking forward to eating with Dr. Elizabeth. "The food was pretty good."

She grinned, reminding me of Em, if Em had spiked hair and a nose ring. "That bad, huh? I like her column—told me what to do about my disgusting yeast infection. Though when I saw her interviewed on TV one time she came across as kind of a diva."

"That's a pretty accurate impression."

"Come to think of it," Caitlin said, "she was being interviewed with that fitness guy you wrote an article about."

"Stan Harris. The two of them were interviewed together?"

"Three of them—him and his wife, this buff aerobics instructor, and Dr. Elizabeth—all talking about how to get fit. Both of the women, though, seemed really pissed off with Stan. They kept on shooting him these lethal looks."

"That's interesting. Could you tell why they were angry?"

Caitlin shrugged. "He was this old macho guy—like really sexist. He kept talking as if he was the only expert there. I figured the women just wanted to tell him to shut the hell up. I mean Stan might have been hot once, but it was a long time ago, and he didn't get that. He was like one of those old movie stars who strut around, not realizing that they've gotten fat, their eyes are droopy, and their chins are just hanging there. Know what I mean?"

I sighed. "Yeah, I know what you mean." If I'd ever met him, I probably would have been pissed off with Stan too.

I had wanted to tell Paul what I'd learned from Dr. Elizabeth, but when he came into the office an hour later it was pretty clear that he was not in the mood to hear it. Caitlin, my source of all office gossip, told me that Paul had had a major argument with the publisher yesterday over the direction the magazine was heading. From the grim look in his eyes, I could believe it.

"I want you to get started on the article about pollution control," he said, from the doorway to my office. "Don't spend any more time on the Harris article."

"Sure, I've already lined up the interviews." I hesitated. "We're not going to do the sidebar about Stan's death?"

He shook his head. "We don't have anything concrete, just speculation—which could, my boss reminded me, result in big-time libel suits. Don't worry, I'll still run your story."

"Okay." I was not, in fact, worried about my story. Unfortunately, what I *was* worried about—Caitlin's disclosure that Paul had received a job offer from a magazine in New York and she was afraid that he might accept it—was not something I felt comfortable asking him about.

When he left, I looked around my cramped, windowless office, which I had tried to personalize with a few photos of my girls and a dish of midget Baby Ruths. How could I be so attached to a job in only a few days? The pay was lousy, there was a lot more grunt work than I'd anticipated, and I spent my workday in a closet. Yes, there were some compensating factors. I liked doing journalistic writing again. I loved feeling competent, professional. I enjoyed having a place to go, somewhere I had to be, five days a week. And I liked the people I worked with: gossipy, spiky-haired Caitlin and unpredictable, rumpled Paul. Granted, I liked one of them slightly more than the other, but being sexually attracted to one's boss seemed an embarrassing, middle-aged cliché, particularly when said supervisor was contemplating leaving his job.

I tried to direct my attention to a more profitable topic. I needed to plod through a lot of background information about Houston's pollution problems before I interviewed anyone. I got another cup of the bitter office coffee, doctored it with powdered cream and fake sugar, then started plodding. Or tried to.

So what if Paul was abandoning the sidebar on the cause of Stan's death? I asked myself during frequent breaks from contemplating the ozone layer. As the publisher had pointed out, we could only speculate about the high level of potassium in his blood, the possibly fatal interaction of his blood pressure medicine and his potassium supplements, the quick verdict of "accidental death." In fact, it was likely that his death had been accidental. He'd been a middle-aged man with a family history of heart disease, a stubborn, over-stressed fitness nut who exercised obsessively, often starved himself, and indiscriminately took mega doses of vitamins and diuretics. It was probably a miracle that he lived as long as he had.

"Lauren?" I looked up from the EPA documents to see Caitlin standing in the doorway. She looked uncharacteristically solemn. "There are two guys here who want to talk to you. They say they're police officers."

I walked into the waiting room. "Officer Watts and Sergeant Wolfe, what a surprise. What can I do for you?"

"We need to talk to you. Privately," Watts said, glancing meaningfully at Caitlin.

I mentally measured my cubicle, wondering if the three

of us could squeeze in. "Why don't you go into Paul's office?" Caitlin suggested. "He's out for the afternoon."

"Thanks, I think we will." I ushered the men into Paul's office, letting them take the couch while I sat across from them in a leather chair.

Watts, always the more aggressive of the two, leaned toward me. "This look familiar to you?" He held up a large brown envelope on which someone had written "Carol's Safe Deposit Box."

"It looks like the envelope I told you about, the one Mrs. Quaid brought to my house. The dental records and X-rays from Rob's office were inside it, along with some other things I didn't see."

"Only two dental records and X-rays are there now. What made you think there were other things as well?"

I tried to remember exactly what Mrs. Quaid had told us. "I think she said something about there being additional items in the safe-deposit box that she didn't understand and she was going to see some other people to try to figure out what the stuff meant. Apparently Carol had told her mother that if she died, Mrs. Quaid should use the information in Carol's safe-deposit box. But Mrs. Quaid didn't see the significance of the things from Rob's office or how she was supposed to use them. Neither did I. I looked at the records and the two X-rays, but nothing seemed very remarkable about any of them."

The officers looked at each other. "I'm guessing that the remarkable thing about them is that these were the records and X-ray of a Mafia bigwig who supposedly died in a car crash last year," Watts said.

I stared at him. "Rob—my Rob—had a patient who was in the Mafia?"

"He had several."

"Of course there's no crime in that," Sergeant Wolfe said. "The Mafia deserve good dental care too."

I was not amused. "So let's cut to the chase. What are you trying to tell me?"

The detective returned my glare. "What we're telling you is that your husband falsified dental records he provided to the FBI. He claimed that, according to his records, the charred body found in a burned-down warehouse was that of Leonardo Lorenzo, a Mafia lieutenant about to be charged with racketeering."

"So whose body was it?"

"According to the X-rays from Carol Quaid's safe-deposit box, it was another one of your husband's patients, a scum bag named Vinny Scalia."

"You mean Rob or someone in his office got the two men's X-rays mixed up?"

"We don't see it as an innocent mistake, Mrs. Prescott. More like a cover-up. Lorenzo probably paid your husband a bundle to say that he was the one who died."

I must have looked confused, because Sergeant Wolfe leaned forward to explain. "It was actually Vinny Scalia, a small-time drug dealer with delusions of grandeur, who took the hit. Lorenzo is probably enjoying himself right now on some tropical island, thinking that he and your husband pulled something over on the Feds."

I stared at them, trying to take it all in. So had Rob known that this Vinny Scalia was going to die in a warehouse fire? Had he and this Mafia lieutenant discussed the scheme in detail? "You cover for me, Rob, just give the Feds the wrong X-ray, and I'll make it worth your while." And was this, rather than Rob's marital dissatisfaction, the reason he'd closed his office so abruptly and disappeared?

"I didn't know," I almost whispered. "I had no idea."

The detective's face was dispassionate as he asked, "Do you know where your husband is? Has he tried to contact you?"

I shook my head. "He used to be in a motel in Del Rio— I saw the credit card bill. But he isn't there now." I gave them the name of the motel and then my mother-in-law's name and address. "If anybody knows where Rob is, it's his mother. Not that she's likely to tell you."

A few minutes later, apparently convinced that they'd gotten every crumb of useful information from me, the officers turned to leave.

"Hey, wait a minute," I said. "You didn't tell me where you found that envelope. I thought you said before that you'd never laid eyes on it."

"It just surfaced today," Watts said.

"Surfaced? Surfaced where?"

"Someone sent it, anonymously, to the police," Wolfe said.

"Who would—" I began when Watts interrupted.

"Let us know if you hear from your husband, Mrs. Prescott. We wouldn't like to see you get dragged into this, out of some old, misplaced loyalty. Don't kid yourself. Dr. Prescott is a very dangerous man. He's possibly killed two women, and there's no reason to think he'd hesitate to kill anyone else who gets in his way."

Twenty-One

"You look sick," Caitlin told me.

Sick? I stared at her, feeling unable to think clearly, unable even to move from Paul's office. Certainly learning that your husband of twenty-seven years and the father of your children had covered up a Mafia hit and very possibly murdered several people himself might make anyone ill.

"Maybe you should go home," she added in such a gentle voice that I wondered if she'd overheard the police officers' bad news.

"Yes," I finally managed to say. Going home would be good. "But first I need to make a phone call."

She nodded, pointing at the phone on Paul's desk, then closed the door behind her.

The phone rang five times before my husband's former office receptionist picked it up. "Iris, hi. It's Lauren Prescott. Listen, I know this must sound weird, but I need to ask you a couple of questions about two of Rob's patients. Do you remember someone named Leonardo Lorenzo or Vinny Scalia?"

"I don't know about the last guy, but I sure remember Mr. Lorenzo," she said with more heat than I expected. "He was the reason your husband fired me."

"What? What did Lorenzo have to do with it?"

"When I complained to Dr. P. about Mr. Lorenzo—how loud and crude he was, always telling dirty jokes to the girls in the office—he told me I needed to try harder to fit in with the 'new office environment'—that's what he called it.

I said that ever since Mr. Lorenzo referred a bunch of his friends, the new environment seemed to include a lot of lowlifes. Then Dr. P. said these were his new patients, and if I didn't like them, maybe it was time to leave. A few days later he replaced me with that bimbo. I bet she didn't mind the new patients at all. She probably fit right in with them."

"Probably. But about Mr. Lorenzo—did he have a lot of dental problems?"

"Not really. I mean he came in occasionally to have work done, but most of the time he just wanted to talk to Dr. P. in his office." She paused. "But why are you interested in Mr. Lorenzo?"

A good question. "Oh, someone just told me that a patient of Rob's recently died in a fire."

"Oh, yeah, that was Mr. Lorenzo. He was in some warehouse when it burned down—probably doing something illegal. That happened after I left, but I heard that Dr. P. had to provide dental records to identify him."

I thanked Iris for the information and said that as much as I'd love to chat, I needed to get back to work. Then, feeling sick to my stomach, I told Caitlin I was going home.

But when I got there, I couldn't muster enough energy to get out of the car. I just sat in the driveway, staring at my large pseudo-Tudor brick house, remembering how thrilled I'd been when we moved into it: the lovely home in a nice, safe, tree-lined neighborhood where children walked to the library for story hour and to the community pool for swimming lessons. The perfect comfortable setting for our perfect little nuclear family.

Except now I felt as if I'd been acting a part in someone else's play—and I'd been too blind to even realize it. I used to think sometimes that my life seemed as if it should be part of a fifties sit-com: the *Donna Reed Show*, perhaps, though without Donna's high heels, pearls, and unremitting cheerfulness. But in actuality I'd only had a bit part in *The Godfather*—the pathetic, naive wife of the Mob's dentist-on-retainer. What an idiot I'd been!

I don't know how long I sat there. Only the constant ringing of my cell phone from inside my purse finally roused me.

"Where are you?" Meg's voice asked when I said hello.

"Sitting in my car."

"I called your office, and a woman told me you'd gone home for the day."

"I did. I'm in my driveway right now."

"Do you want to have dinner tonight? We could go out or I could get carryout."

"Okay."

"Okay what—restaurant or carryout? What are you in the mood for?"

"You decide."

"Oh, come on, Lauren. You have to have some opinion."

"Do I?" I could feel the fury rising in me, like a silent, unseen army suddenly marching over the hill for battle. "I seem to have spent a good half of my life having no opinions at all, certainly no awareness of what was going on around me. What was I doing, Meg, sleepwalking through my life? Or maybe a better analogy is those monkeys who see no evil, hear no evil, and speak no evil."

"Did something happen today?"

"You might say that. I just learned that, among other things, Rob was falsifying dental records for his Mafia clients."

"I'll be right over," Meg said and hung up.

By the time she arrived, I had managed to move from my car to my house. I still felt numb but at least I no longer had a steering wheel sticking in my ribs. Opening the door, I inspected the grocery sacks she was carrying. "What did you bring?"

She walked inside, taking what she probably assumed were surreptitious, assessing looks at me. "A little of everything: brandy, amaretto, cheese potato chips, double-fudge brownies—all the first-aid basics."

Over cheese potato chips and our liqueurs of choice, I told her what I'd learned. For once even Meg was too shocked to say much more than "Holy Shit!"

"This is what I don't get," I told Meg. "What happened to the other information that Mrs. Quaid said she'd gotten from Carol's safe-deposit box? And who sent the envelope to the police?"

Meg set down the potato chip she'd been about to pop into her mouth. "Maybe there wasn't any other information. Maybe Mrs. Quaid was just telling you that."

"But why would she lie to me?"

"Maybe she did realize the significance of Rob's X-rays and patient records and just wanted to see if you knew about it too. It doesn't make sense that Carol would tell her mother to use the information in the safe-deposit box without telling her how to use it. Maybe Mrs. Quaid came over here hoping you'd tell her where Rob was, and then she planned to blackmail him. Or who knows? Maybe she was hoping you'd pay her to give you the stuff."

I tried to remember everything Mrs. Quaid had said that day. All I really recalled was how upset she'd been about Carol's death and how eager to hear any information we had about the police investigation. "I don't think she asked about Rob, though I probably mentioned I didn't know where he was when she took out his dental records. And if Mrs. Quaid wanted to blackmail me, walking through my furniture-less house must have clued her in that I had no money for bribing anyone."

I took another sip of amaretto. "Though the police seem to think that she somehow found Rob—or he found her—and then he killed her." I shook my head. "It's so hard for me to imagine him—I mean Rob is many things, but a murderer?"

Meg didn't seem to think the question required a response. Instead she pushed the plate of brownies toward me. "Eat."

I took a bite, but even the chocolatey richness didn't have an effect. I was past the place where food—even chocolate—could comfort me, though the amaretto seemed to be making me less agitated.

"Let's say, for the sake of argument," I said, "that Rob killed Mrs. Quaid in order to get the X-rays and to prevent her from ratting him out to the cops. But what possible reason would he have for mailing the information to the police? I mean the man is cheap and ruthless, but he's not dumb."

"Maybe Mrs. Quaid herself sent the records," Meg said. "Maybe she was afraid of Rob, afraid that he'd killed her daughter and intended to kill her, and she made copies of the records: one set for Rob and another for the police."

It certainly was possible. If nothing else, Mrs. Quaid would have wanted revenge against the person she suspected of killing her daughter. But when she was at my house, she seemed to be searching for information on what had happened to Carol. In the few remaining hours of her life, had Mrs. Quaid somehow determined who the killer was?

"But if she mailed the envelope before the killer showed up, how come it took so long to get to the police?"

Meg shrugged. "Maybe it got lost in the mail. Or maybe somebody else—a cleaning lady or a relative who inherited her car—found the envelope and, knowing that Mrs. Quaid had been murdered, mailed it to the police."

"But I don't see why a cleaning lady would think Rob's X-rays and dental records should be sent to the police. It wasn't as if the envelope contained a death threat or anything sinister. When Mrs. Quaid showed the stuff to me, remember, I thought it was insignificant."

Meg sighed, looking as if she was growing tired of playing Twenty Questions. "Who knows? The police may have asked the cleaning lady if she'd seen this big brown envelope you'd told them about. The cleaning lady says no, but then later she finds it—under the couch or in a drawer she's emptying. She wants to help find the killer, but doesn't want to get involved in the investigation, so she sends the envelope to them anonymously."

I sipped my drink while I thought through what she'd said. "That's certainly a possibility. Mrs. Quaid could have put the envelope somewhere for safekeeping before the killer showed up. But another possibility is that her murderer sent the police the envelope after first taking out the items that incriminated him."

Meg rolled her eyes. "You mean the killer personally knew Rob and, realizing what a cheap, lying, amoral, greedy bastard he is, decided to set him up as the killer?"

I laughed. "If I didn't know better, I'd think that you sent the police the envelope."

"Me turn in my good friend Rob?" Meg inspected me through narrowed eyes. "I think you've had enough amaretto. I'm going to go order some takeout. You want Chinese or pizza?"

"Don't care." I sniffed as she picked up the amaretto

bottle on the way to the telephone. "You're not exactly the person who should get prissy about other people's drinking," I called after her.

"Shut up," she yelled back. "I'm ordering our moo-shoo vegetables."

When she returned she brought me a can of Diet Coke. "You know the only good thing about this is that now the police might get serious about finding Rob. And once they arrest him, you might be able to get some of your money back."

"Dream on, Meggy. Knowing Rob, he's already stashed our money into a Swiss bank account. Maybe some of his Mafia buddies helped him hide it." I shook my head. "Can you believe that—Rob doing deals with the Mafia!"

Meg's face turned grim. "In a minute."

It was almost ten by the time she left. "You sure you're okay? I could spend the night," she said as she threw the empty take-out containers into the trash.

"I'm fine. There's no reason for you to stay. You've done more than enough already."

"Well, be sure the doors are locked."

"Yes, Mother." I tried to smile as she walked out into the cold, windy night. I watched until she got to her car, then started to close the door.

"Hey, wait," Meg called to me. "You have a shutter hanging loose up there." She pointed to an upstairs window.

"Okay, I'll have to get it fixed." Sometime. At this point the shutter was the least of my problems. I waved goodbye to Meg, then locked the door and headed upstairs.

After a quick shower, I crawled into bed, hoping that all the amaretto I'd drunk would at least put me to sleep. But despite my feelings of exhaustion, I stayed awake, my mind racing with unanswered questions. Outside the wind made the loose shutter bang against the house, a noise too much like someone pounding furiously on my front door. Why hadn't I let Meg be the gallant, nurturing friend and spend the night in the guest room? With someone else in the house I probably wouldn't be feeling so edgy.

Then I heard glass shatter downstairs.

Oh, Lord! Had the wind broken a window? Grabbing the portable phone from the nightstand, I held my breath and listened for more sounds from downstairs. Nothing.

Before I phoned for help I needed more information. Sticking the phone in my pajama pocket, I tiptoed to Katie's bedroom. In the dark I rummaged through the paraphernalia on her closet floor, finally finding what I needed. Katie's softball bat would have to be my weapon.

Shaking, I crept down the stairs. And stopped. The light in the kitchen—I had turned it off before going to bed.

I started back up the stairs.

"You changed the locks," said a voice behind me. A familiar, accusing voice.

I glanced over my shoulder. At the foot of the stairs stood my scowling husband.

Twenty-Two

I stared at Rob, too petrified to move or even say anything.

He flipped on the hall light. "I had to break the damn den window to get in. I'm lucky I didn't cut myself."

Same old whiny Rob. But this balding, jowly, incredibly ordinary-looking man was not at all the person I'd imagined him to be. He only looked the same.

"What—what do you want?" I finally managed to ask.

"The police are after me, Lauren." He shook his head, looking astonished by the news. "They think I killed Carol and her mother."

"Did you?"

"No!" Rob's face reddened, the color creeping up his neck, coloring even his ears. "I didn't kill anybody."

"Not even that patient of yours—Vinny the Drug Dealer—who died in the warehouse fire? The guy whose dental records you said were Leonardo Lorenzo's."

His eyes narrowed. "Who told you that?"

"The police. Someone sent them copies of Vinny's and Leonardo's dental records and X-rays."

"Shit!" His eyes darted down the hall, as if he were looking for the nearest exit. "Mom told me the police were looking for me, but she didn't say anything about X-rays. Who the hell even had all those records? I destroyed—"

He didn't complete the sentence, but I could guess the rest of it. "Carol Quaid apparently made herself some copies before you destroyed them."

232

"That lying bitch! I paid her for those records. I thought she handed over everything."

"Apparently she wanted some personal life insurance. She kept your records in her safe-deposit box and told her mother to use them if she had an untimely death."

"I should have known not to trust her," Rob muttered, more to himself than to me. "I pay her twenty thousand dollars, and then she gives the stuff to the cops anyway." Correctly interpreting my skeptical expression, he glared at me. "And I did not murder her after she gave me the records. The last time I saw Carol was the day I closed the office. She was walking off, counting her blackmail payoff. I told myself good riddance, happy I'd never have to lay eyes on her again."

Twenty thousand dollars! Apparently threats and strong-arm tactics were the only ways to get money from the old skinflint.

Sighing, I sat down on the stairs. I believed Rob when he said he hadn't murdered Carol or her mother, but I still wanted to keep my distance from him. He might not have killed anyone, but he had perpetrated a good number of criminal acts—helping a Mafia goon falsify his own death, not paying his employees, stealing money from our joint accounts and hauling off most of our furniture and art. And he'd shacked up with a girl young enough to be his daughter, which while not criminal, was definitely disgusting.

"You still did not answer my question about what you're doing here," I said. "Have you come back to return the money you stole from me?"

"Stole from you? What the hell are you talking about? I left you the house."

"Big deal. You didn't leave me enough money to make a

single mortgage payment. You took every cent we had—and it was a lot more than the equity on our house. And if that wasn't greedy enough, you had to come back to steal our art and furniture. You even took my grandmother's silver service, you cheap bastard."

"Greedy?" Rob bellowed. "I took my fair share—less than my fair share. Who do you think earned the money in those bank accounts? Whose money paid for this house? It wasn't you, Lauren. You haven't contributed a dollar to our net worth since the girls were born. The way I see it, I was giving you a free ride for years. You're lucky I left you the house as a sentimental gesture."

I gripped the bat. Who would blame me for taking a few swings at him? Hell, the police would probably be grateful that I'd incapacitated this felon-on-the-run long enough for them to catch him.

I stood up, holding the bat so he could see it. "Get the hell out of my house or I'll call the police." With my free hand I pulled the phone from my pajama pocket to show him I wasn't kidding.

Rob seemed to deflate before my eyes—the arrogance and bullying aggression seeping out like toxic gases. "Lauren, you've got to let me stay here. I don't have anywhere else to go. The police are looking for me and Lorenzo is after me too. He even found out where I was staying in Mexico. I barely got out in time."

"Why would Lorenzo come after you? You already told the police he was dead. What more does he want?"

Rob looked as if he might be sick. "What he wants is no witnesses. The way Leonardo views things, if there's no one around who can testify that he didn't die in that fire, the less chance he'll have of ending up in the penitentiary."

I couldn't help myself. "And this possibility—that Lethal

Leonardo might decide to get rid of you too—didn't occur to you before? You just expected him to be eternally grateful for your little favor, maybe send you unsigned Christmas cards from his tropical hideaway?"

"So I made a mistake, okay?"

"Some mistake." I suddenly remembered the sinister-sounding man who'd called the house demanding to know where Dr. Prescott was. Could that have been Leonardo looking for a private consultation with his favorite dentist?

Rob shook his head. "You are such a nag, Lauren. You know what? It was a relief to leave you. I probably never would have done it if Leonardo hadn't started getting so nervous that the FBI would show up to question me about his dental records, and it suddenly seemed like a very good idea to get out of town. But ditching you—well, that was an unexpected bonus."

I waved my bat. "Get out NOW."

He backed away, raising his palms. "Wait! I'm sorry. I didn't mean it. I'm just so tired—and scared. I should never have let Leonardo talk me into falsifying those X-rays. And he only told me about his idea after Vinny was dead—I didn't have anything to do with that. Leo begged me. If the Feds thought he was dead, he could start a whole new life somewhere. He said it was zero risk and I'd get a very nice bonus just for changing the name on the X-ray."

"How nice of a bonus?"

He hesitated, then shrugged. "Two hundred grand." He looked as if he was going to cry. "It was so damn stupid of me. I had to pay Carol twenty thousand to keep her from turning me in to the authorities. I lost all the revenue from my practice, and moving around all the time costs a lot more than I thought it would. And that isn't even mentioning Leo trying to kill me and the police trying to put me in jail."

I shook my head. "You are pitiful. I should have left you years ago."

"Oh, please, Lauren. I know I'm greedy and selfish and maybe I wasn't such a great husband. But I'm so exhausted, haven't slept for days. The cops won't look here. They know you hate me, and I've hid my car so they won't see it."

I stared at him—a totally self-centered, amoral, and rather pathetic man on the brink of old age. "Why should I let you stay here, Rob, after everything you've done to me? If the police find you with me, I could go to jail too."

"Because you're a better person than I am," he said softly.

More like a gullible, softhearted idiot, I thought—a bone-weary idiot who probably was going to regret her kind impulses in the morning. "Okay, you can spend the night— just this one night—but you have to leave first thing to-morrow."

"Oh, God, thank you. I'll leave in the morning. I promise." Smiling, he started up the stairs.

"Oh, no, no, no, no." I gripped the bat handle with two hands to reinforce the message. "You can sleep downstairs tonight, on the couch. There's a pillow and blankets in the linen closet." He seemed to hesitate. "You remember the linen closet. It's that cabinet I kept going to for sheets and towels during my stint of unpaid labor as your housekeeper, cook, and child-rearer." Not waiting for a response, I turned and headed for my bedroom.

After briefly considering the possibility that Rob might sneak in and murder me in my bed, I surprisingly fell into a deep, dreamless sleep interrupted only by the blaring of my clock radio at seven in the morning. I hit the snooze button, then remembered my visitor downstairs and groaned. Was it possible that Rob, always an early riser, had already left for his next hiding place? Certainly 4:30 a.m. would be a nice safe time to slip out the door—no nosy neighbors up and about or cruising cops likely to spot you.

But as I padded down the stairs, I heard the unmistakable sounds of someone in the kitchen. Seated at the table, drinking coffee, Rob scowled at me. "What happened to that Swiss muesli we always used to have?"

"The person who used to eat it no longer lives here." I walked past him to pour myself a cup of coffee. "You can have a bagel before you leave."

He wrinkled his nose. "I noticed there's not much food in the house." He pulled out his wallet and extracted two fifty-dollar bills. "Here's some money for groceries."

"Thanks." I took the bills and shoved them into my pocket. I could tell from Rob's expression that he expected me to be grateful. Probably so overwhelmed with gratitude that I'd jump up and rush to the store to buy him some muesli.

I sat down across from him and took a deep breath. "You clearly don't get this. I want you to leave. The police have come to see me twice already, and undoubtedly they'll return. They told me to be on the lookout for you; they expect you might show up here. This is not a safe haven, Rob, and you're endangering me by being here."

Whatever he was about to say—and he clearly was getting ready to argue the point—was cut short by loud knocking at the back door. I glanced at the clock. Who the hell showed up at 7:25 on a Saturday morning?

Rob looked as if he was going to pass out. "The police! Where should I go?"

I scanned the room. "The pantry!" I pointed to the large walk-in closet with louvered doors. "Get in there, and don't come out until I tell you to."

For once he followed my directions. Heart pounding, I made sure the doors were tightly closed, then checked the rest of the kitchen. Two coffee cups! I shoved one of them into the dishwasher.

The knocking continued, loud and insistent. "Okay, I'm going to the door now," I hissed in the direction of the pantry, then, taking a deep breath, I went to see who my early-morning visitor was.

I glanced out the peephole. Dr. Elizabeth, of all people, stood there, dressed in a long, dark trench coat and a big matching rain hat. I opened the door.

"I apologize for barging in on you so early," she said, "but we have some important business to discuss."

"This isn't the best time," I began when she shoved me aside and stepped in.

"I'm afraid that's not a negotiable point." She pushed the door shut and locked the deadbolt.

I stared at her. "What the hell are you doing?"

Dr. Elizabeth didn't say anything, but the revolver she pulled from her coat pocket effectively answered my question.

"I need to sit down," I said.

Dr. Elizabeth seemed to hesitate. My God, did she just want to step in the door, blow my brains out, and leave? Kill Lauren—Task One on the day's To Do List. "What the hell," she said. "I guess a few minutes won't hurt. It's not your fault that you're a born meddler—a good trait for a journalist, dear, but unfortunate for you personally."

We headed for the kitchen table, close enough to the pantry for Rob to hear what was going on and come to my

238

rescue. Unless, of course, he chose to stay in his hiding place, waiting until my killer left to hightail it to his next hideout.

My knees were shaking as my mind raced through all the possibly threatening questions I had asked her—and came up blank. Clearly I was missing something.

We sat down, Dr. Elizabeth's back to the pantry and me facing her. "Would you like a cup of coffee?"

She shook her head. "I don't use caffeine. It's detrimental to your health, you know."

And aiming loaded guns at people wasn't? Though maybe Dr. E. would argue it wasn't her health that was at risk. "How about some herb tea then, or orange juice?"

"No, thanks, I'm not staying that long."

I could feel my heart thudding double-time. "What is this all about?" I said a little too loudly. "I don't even know what terrible questions I asked."

"Really?" She shook her head, looking rueful. "And here I thought you were figuring it all out."

I wanted to say, "Well, I didn't, so let's forget the whole thing." But somehow I didn't think she'd buy it. "What was it I was supposed to have figured out?"

She smiled again, clearly enjoying herself. "Why should I tell you?"

To brag about your clever scheme (whatever it was), to show me how damned smart you are, how your Mensa buds would be so proud. "Why not? At this point what difference does it make if you tell me?"

She seemed to consider it while I stared, transfixed, at her revolver. And suddenly I knew. I envisioned Mrs. Quaid opening her door, just as I had, and finding Dr. Elizabeth there—Elizabeth and her trusty sidearm.

"You shot Mrs. Quaid, didn't you? Carol must have left

something in her safe-deposit box about you, and Mrs. Quaid contacted you, the same way she did me."

She pretended to clap. "See? I told you that you knew more than you thought."

"So it must have been you who sent Rob's dental records to the police. You took the envelope of stuff from Carol's safe-deposit box when you killed Mrs. Quaid. But then when I started asking questions about how you knew Carol, you decided you needed to implicate someone else—Rob—in Mrs. Quaid's murder."

"And in your death too, I'm afraid, dear. That bad Rob has been doing a lot of naughty things lately."

She raised her gun.

What the hell was Rob doing—taking a nap?

"That was very clever of you," I said quickly. "Won't you tell me how you did it?"

She tilted her head to one side. "I do realize, dear, that you're playing for time, but I guess I can give you another five or six minutes. I suppose I at least owe you that."

She lowered the revolver to the table. It was still pointing at me, but at least it wasn't leveled at my head. "Carol was trying to blackmail me. Apparently she did the same thing to your husband, but I was, shall we say, less tolerant."

"Why was she blackmailing you?"

She scowled, glancing down at her gun.

Maybe I needed to lay off the annoying questions if I wanted my whole six-minute reprieve. "Hey, Rob," I wanted to yell. "Time is running short out here."

After a martyred sigh, she said, "Carol knew that years ago I invested a significant amount of money in Stan Harris's business. For a while, right after his book came out, the gym was doing well, but in recent years it was just bleeding money. Unfortunately, I was having some financial problems of my own—I lost a bundle in tech stocks and was desperate for some cash. When Stan got an offer for the gym, both Terri and I encouraged him to sell. It was a good offer, a sound business move, and would have made all of us a nice little profit. But Stan wanted to keep his gym, and Carol—his CPA as well as his girlfriend—agreed with him. She even said he should expand the business. It was insanity, but Carol kept telling him what a big success he was going to be again, that the new Stan's Gym was going to corner the market on aging exercisers. What a crock! So instead of finally receiving a return on my investment, here's Stan asking for more money that he can lose for me."

I couldn't help myself. "So you killed Carol because she gave Stan bad business advice?"

She shook her head impatiently. "No, I told you, Carol was blackmailing me. Somehow she figured out that Stan had not"—she paused, apparently searching for words—"died of natural causes."

She killed Stan too? And I would be her next victim if I didn't come up with an escape plan pretty damn fast. I tried to look interested. "How did Carol realize that?"

"Well, at first she suspected Terri—the person with the most obvious motive. Everyone knew that Stan intended to divorce her, and Terri the widow was a lot wealthier than Terri the divorcee ever would have been. Unfortunately, Terri also had a whole aerobics class vouching for her whereabouts at the time Stan died. Then Carol talked to some smart-ass at the medical examiner's office who mentioned that Stan had one hell of a lot of potassium in his system. I guess Carol concluded that while Terri was certainly ruthless enough to have killed Stan, she wasn't smart enough to do it without being caught."

"But you were."

She nodded. "I still don't think Carol would have figured it out if that coroner's report hadn't mentioned the bump on the back of Stan's head and the puncture mark between his toes—the place where I injected him with potassium chloride after he was unconscious. I thought I had everything covered when I testified at the hearing: Stan accidentally hitting his head against a rock when he fell on the jogging trail, his special vulnerability to heart disease because of his family history and all the potassium supplements he was taking along with the blood pressure meds. The man, in fact, was a coronary waiting to happen. I just made it happen sooner."

From the corner of my eye, I thought I saw the pantry door open. At last! I forced myself to keep looking at Dr. Elizabeth. "So that was what Carol used to blackmail you?"

The doctor looked annoyed. "She had the coroner's report and copies of e-mails I sent Stan—telling him I needed the money and to sell the damn gym when he still had a chance to unload it. And she claimed she had pharmacy records tracing the potassium chloride back to me, which turned out to be a bluff. If she hadn't mentioned the pharmacy records, I probably would have shrugged off her threats—and Carol and her mother would still be alive today." She sent me her condescending teacher look. "Now isn't that a lesson in lying-doesn't-pay?"

Was she totally nuts? Involuntarily I glanced toward the pantry and saw Rob take a tentative step into the kitchen. I needed to keep her talking. "What I don't understand is why Carol, who was supposed to be in love with Stan, didn't just turn this information over to the police."

"Instead of extorting money from me, you mean?" When I nodded, she said, "I can only guess. Probably she realized that everything she had was circumstantial evidence—she couldn't prove that I did anything. She also could have learned that Stan had no intention of marrying her after he got rid of Terri—he told me was through with marriage. So maybe Carol wasn't feeling all that kindly toward old Stan, and when she saw a money-making opportunity, she grabbed it."

Rob moved one step closer.

"So this whole thing—Stan's death, Carol's blackmailing, Carol's and her mother's murders—was just about money?" I asked, in a much-too-loud voice.

Dr. E. shrugged. "Everything is about money. Everything. Though I guess, to be fair, you and Mrs. Quaid could be seen as innocent victims." She picked up the revolver. "If that makes you feel any better."

Actually it didn't. In a detached, movie-watching kind of way, I saw Dr. Elizabeth point the revolver at my head, heard Rob starting toward us.

I threw myself on the floor, expecting to feel a bullet whiz past my head.

Instead I heard Dr. Elizabeth's maniacal laugh. "Well, well, well," she said. "It's Dr. Prescott and his lethal can of pineapple chunks."

I peered up to see Dr. Elizabeth aiming her gun at Rob. Slowly he raised his hands above his head, and the aluminum can he'd been holding thudded to the floor.

Twenty-Three

From my seat on the floor, I lunged for Dr. Elizabeth's legs. If she was going to kill us, we might as well go down fighting.

She wasn't expecting any under-the-table action, so the impact of my body slamming into her knees took her by surprise. I heard a shot, then a loud thud as she hit the floor.

Faster than I'd ever seen him move in his life, Rob was on top of her. "Get her gun," he yelled to me as he pinned her hands to the floor.

The revolver, which she'd dropped on her descent, lay about ten feet from me. It looked obscene and deadly. Nevertheless I crawled over and picked up the weapon that probably had killed Carol Quaid and her mother—and had almost killed Rob and me.

Carefully, feeling as if I was holding an angry rattlesnake, I hoisted myself to my feet. With trembling hands, I pointed the gun at Dr. Elizabeth's chest.

"Were you shot?" I asked Rob.

"No. You okay?"

"Yeah." More or less. My flying tackle had done a number on my right knee, but under the circumstances, I wasn't complaining.

From the floor Dr. Elizabeth shot me a look of pure hatred. But there was something else in her steely gray eyes, a cold, assessing look that wondered, is she ruthless enough to shoot me—or is she too gutless?

Rob turned to me. "Get me some duct tape from my tool box."

I'd started toward the utility room when Rob shrieked. Heart pounding, I swiveled around. Dr. Elizabeth's teeth were clamped onto Rob's right ear!

For a horrified minute I just stared at them, hearing Rob's screams, watching his arms flailing, trying to get hold of his attacker. Then I lifted the gun. "Let go of him or I'll shoot you!" I yelled.

She seemed not to have heard me. Or, more likely, she chose to ignore me. Taking a deep breath, I leveled the gun at Dr. Elizabeth. But she and Rob were rolling around so much that I was afraid I'd shoot him by mistake.

Finally, though, in one fluid motion, Dr. Elizabeth released Rob's ear and shoved him off her.

Rob lay on the floor, holding his ear. "Shoot her, Lauren!"

I turned to Dr. Elizabeth who was pushing herself onto her feet. She faced me, Rob's blood smeared across her mouth, grinning as she caught sight of my shaking hands. "You don't even know how to use that gun, do you, Lauren?"

I gripped the revolver and, stepping forward, slammed the butt of it into her head. "No, but I can improvise," I muttered.

Wordlessly she slumped to the floor.

I squinted down at her, feeling my stomach lurch. "She's not dead, is she?"

Cupping his bleeding ear, Rob barely glanced at her. "I doubt it. Can you get the damn duct tape? I want the bitch tied up before she tries to take off my other ear."

I found two rolls of the tape in Rob's old toolbox. "We need to bandage that ear."

"Later. Help me get her into the chair."

I took Elizabeth's legs and Rob took her shoulders, and together we hoisted the not-very-light doctor into a kitchen chair. Then Rob positioned her hands behind her back, and duct-taped them together while I taped her ankles. For good measure, Rob looped tape around her waist to tie her to the back of the chair.

Standing up, I shuddered. There was something about the woman—something evil, unquenchable—that made me expect her to leap up, biting and clawing at us.

I handed the gun to Rob. "Watch her while I get something for your ear."

She still seemed unconscious while I swabbed Rob's ear with peroxide and Neosporin, then bandaged it. "It doesn't look too bad," I told him.

"Easy for you to say. The woman is a cannibal."

Hesitantly I walked behind Dr. Elizabeth and felt for a pulse on her neck. "Thank God, she's alive!"

"Oh, what a relief." Gingerly Rob touched his bandaged ear. "I would have taken her down myself if you had some heavier cans in the pantry, but all you had were a few little sissy cans."

I shook my head. Let it go, Lauren, I told myself. But I couldn't. "As I mentioned before, I didn't have the cash to stock up on food supplies, due to your siphoning off every penny in our accounts."

"I just gave you a hundred bucks."

"And that's good for two weeks of staples and a couple pounds of hamburger."

"I noticed that you managed somehow to scrape up the money to spring for a bag of Baby Ruths."

"You selfish, hypocritical, self-important shit-heel!" I shouted. I would have continued the discussion, but I suddenly saw Dr. Elizabeth's thin lips move. She was smirking.

Mid-rant, I stopped myself and marched to the kitchen phone.

"What are you doing?" Rob said.

"Calling the police."

"Hey, wait!"

I shook my head as I punched in the numbers. "I don't want that homicidal maniac in my house." Particularly when I was her next designated victim. "You won't be a suspect anymore when I explain everything to the police." At least not a suspect in the Quaid women's murders.

"Sergeant Wolfe," a gruff voice answered the phone.

"This is Lauren Prescott. Carol Quaid's killer just tried to shoot me." As briefly as possible, I explained about the early-morning visit of Dr. Elizabeth and her revolver.

"She still at your house?" I could hear the excitement in his voice.

I glanced her way. "Tied up in one of my kitchen chairs." And no longer smirking.

"We'll be right there."

I hung up. "The police will be here in a few minutes." I glanced down at my ratty pajamas. "Will you keep an eye on our visitor while I get dressed?"

"Sure, go ahead."

"If she tries to escape, shoot her. Someplace painful but not fatal."

I hurried up the stairs to my bedroom where I pulled on slacks, a sweater, and loafers, and brushed my teeth in record time.

I could hear the sounds of sirens in the distance as I entered the kitchen. Damn, there was a bullet hole in the bottom cabinet! But better the cabinet than our bodies.

"Rob?" I didn't see him, but Dr. Elizabeth was still

there, tied up in her chair. It looked as if Rob had duct-taped her mouth shut as well as adding an extra layer of tape around her hands. He had never liked hearing from lippy women.

Dr. Elizabeth sounded as if she was trying to say something, but I couldn't understand what it was.

"Rob," I yelled. Where the hell was he?

Then I saw Dr. Elizabeth's handgun lying on the kitchen counter. A note in Rob's familiar scrawl lay next to it. I walked over and read the note: *Sorry, babe. Not ready for the cops yet.*

It looked like I would be facing the police alone.

Dr. Elizabeth started jabbering the minute Officer Watts removed the duct tape. Pointing at me, she said, "She and that Mafia dentist husband of hers kidnapped and assaulted me. They want to pin the murders her husband committed on me."

His face expressionless, the detective turned to me. "Your husband was here?"

It was the part of the story I hadn't bothered to mention on the phone. I thought I'd wait until they got here to explain why Rob was at the house—after I first explained that he had not committed the murders of Carol Quaid and her mother. "He broke into the house in the middle of the night." I did not appreciate the skeptical look that passed between the two officers. "I changed the locks and Rob broke a window in the den to get in." Let them go check out the window if they didn't believe me.

"So why didn't you phone us when your husband first showed up?" asked Sergeant Wolfe in a stern voice.

A good question, one whose answer might determine whether or not I would still be at home this afternoon to get

the broken window fixed. "I did phone you. Eventually."
What difference did a few hours make? "When I called, I
had every expectation that Rob would be here when you arrived. After I phoned you, I went upstairs to change out of
my pajamas, and when I came downstairs a few minutes
later, he was gone."

"Because he knew the police would arrest him," Dr.
Elizabeth piped in, making a very big deal out of massaging
her wrists.

I ignored her. "I might have called you earlier if Dr. Elizabeth hadn't arrived at my house at 7:20 in the morning
and tried to shoot me."

"That's a lie!" she screamed. "Lauren and her husband
abducted me from my home. They brought me here to
make it look as if I'd come to their house to murder them."

Wolfe looked up from the notes he was jotting. "I don't
get it. Why did the Prescotts go after you?"

"We didn't!" I was practically shouting myself. "No one
in their right mind would go to her house, drag her back
here, duct tape her to the chair, and then call the police to
say she was trying to kill us. That's insane."

"Not any more insane than your claim that I was trying
to kill you," the doctor said. "Why would I want to do that?
I barely know you."

She made it sound as if it was a privilege to reap her
homicidal attentions. I glared at her. "You came here to kill
me and to set up Rob. You wanted the police to think Rob
murdered me as well as the two Quaid women."

I turned to the sergeant. "She was the one who sent the
police those dental records. After she killed Mrs. Quaid, she
took the envelope that Mrs. Quaid got from Carol's safe-deposit box. But Elizabeth sent you only the items about
Rob. She kept the information that incriminated her."

"That's ridiculous," Dr. Elizabeth said. She watched as Watts, using a tissue, gingerly picked up her revolver from the kitchen counter and placed it in an evidence bag. "You'll find Lauren's fingerprints all over that gun, Officer. She hit me on the head with it. I might even have a concussion." To prove the point, she probed the back of her head, wincing dramatically. "You can even feel the bump."

"If I hadn't hit you, I'd be lying on the floor with a bullet in my head."

The detective ignored us. "I'm going to take this evidence to the car," he told Wolfe. "Be right back."

The sergeant nodded, looking as if he badly wanted to be the one who got to go to the car. "You know where your husband went when he left here?"

I shook my head. "He didn't even tell me he was leaving. He just left a note saying he wasn't ready to talk to the police."

"Because he knew they'd arrest him," Dr. Elizabeth said. "If he's not guilty, why is he hiding? That's not the usual behavior of innocent people."

"Shut up!" I could just picture her as a motor-mouthed second grader, the know-it-all kid who snickered at other kids' mistakes.

"You shut up! I want the police to have an accurate and truthful account of what happened. They certainly haven't been getting that from you."

"Ladies, ladies!" Watts walked back into the kitchen, shaking his head. "Each of you will get her turn to make your official statement at the police station."

Dr. Elizabeth sat up a little straighter. "If you don't mind I'd prefer to give my statement here. I need to get to work. I have a newspaper column to finish, and I'm appearing on a television panel at noon."

"I'm afraid you're going to miss that," Watts said. "Would you stand up please?"

She stood, looking incredulous when the detective pulled out a pair of handcuffs. "My attorney is going to hear about this," she said as he snapped the cuffs on her. "Don't think for a moment that I won't sue."

"You can call your attorney from the station." The detective turned to me. "You have to come to the station too."

"You going to handcuff me?"

"I should," he said, "but acting stupid isn't an arrestable offense yet."

I decided that under the circumstances, it might be best not to argue the point.

"But I'm the victim," Dr. Elizabeth was saying as Watts led her toward the door.

"I'd find that easier to believe, ma'am, if I hadn't spotted a black Mercedes with the license plate 'Dr. E.' sitting right down the street."

She started to speak, but he cut her off. "I'm also curious how you knew that Dr. Prescott was a Mafia dentist. So give it a rest, lady. I'm not in the mood for any more of your bullshit."

Dr. Elizabeth did not look happy, but she shut up.

Trying not to look smug, I grabbed my purse and car keys and followed her and the two officers out of my house.

Twenty-Four

"Now let me get this straight," Paul O'Neal said. He measured the opening in my den window where a pane of glass should have been. "Dr. Elizabeth killed Stan Harris because she was a silent partner in his failing fitness business and she was annoyed that he refused to accept a good offer to sell?"

I nodded. "She needed cash and thought the money Stan was offered for his gym was the answer to her prayers. But not only did Stan refuse to sell, he wanted to expand the facilities—pour even more money down the drain. She figured the only solution was to get rid of Stan. Terri Harris was only too happy to sell the gym, and Dr. Elizabeth got her share of the million-dollar sale."

Paul jotted the window dimensions on a piece of paper. "But what's the connection to Carol Quaid and her mother?"

"Carol was Stan's accountant as well as his mistress. She was also the one person who encouraged him to expand the business. Apparently Carol somehow figured out that Elizabeth had been involved in Stan's death, and she used the information to blackmail her. So Elizabeth went up to the cabin where Carol was staying and shot her. She killed Mrs. Quaid because Carol had saved some incriminating information about Elizabeth in her safe-deposit box and told her mother to use it if anything unfortunate happened to her."

"So Carol's mother was going to continue the blackmailing?"

"I don't know what she was intending to do. Dr. Elizabeth only gave me the bare-bones account. She was kind of rushed. She had to kill me, get back to the office to finish her column, and then get to a TV station for a noon panel discussion."

Paul flushed. "God, I'm sorry, Lauren. Talk about insensitive. It must have been terrible for you."

I waved away his apology. "No, no, it doesn't bother me to talk about it. I just don't know anything else. And I do appreciate you fixing the window." Some people provided a sympathetic ear in times of crisis, some brought hot meals, and others, like Paul, showed their concern through home repairs. Paul had seen me on the TV news, walking with the hand-cuffed Dr. Elizabeth into the police station, and had called my home to see what he could do to help.

He got to his feet. "I need to go buy the glass. Want to come along for the ride?"

"Sure." I didn't want to mention it, but more than the prospect of his company was motivating me to accompany him. Even though I knew that the person who'd tried to shoot me in my kitchen was now in jail, and my spouse-on-the-lam was unlikely to return anytime soon, I still didn't feel safe alone in my house.

I followed Paul out to his car. "You're not leading up to suggesting that I write an article about this, are you? Something like 'Dr. Elizabeth's Unhealthy Surprise: The Nightmare Ordeal in My Kitchen.' "

He didn't laugh. "Didn't even consider it. In fact I've been thinking it would be a good idea if you write some light, up-beat piece next."

"Such as?"

He shrugged as he backed out of my driveway. "What are you interested in? Is there any quirky local person you've been wanting to interview?"

I thought about it. "How about Terri Harris and her new cookie business? I'd steer clear of Stan's murder and focus on life-after-Stan. It could be a great human-interest story: how this very plump pastry chef-in-training met a born-again fitness guru and then, under his guidance, became a buff aerobics instructor who wouldn't be caught dead even looking at a pastry. But then Stan dies unexpectedly, and within weeks Terri unloads his gym and starts baking cookies again—damn good ones too, I might add."

"And she's no longer so trim and fit?"

"She's gained a good ten or fifteen pounds but she said she didn't care. I thought that could be an interesting angle: Is she really happier fat than she was thin?" I sent Paul a sidelong glance. "A subject of obvious interest to me as well as thousands of other middle-aged women."

He turned to me, looking genuinely surprised. "What are you talking about? You're not fat."

A string of sarcastic retorts raced through my mind—everything from "You need to meet my husband and tell him that" to "Have you had your vision checked lately?" With great effort, I managed to keep them to myself. Instead I said, "That's kind of you, but you don't have to be so tactful. I am aware that I'm overweight."

To my horror, he pulled the car over and parked at the side of the road. "I am never tactful."

The man was running his eyes over me, as if he was checking out a brood mare he was contemplating buying. I could feel my cheeks burn. "I—"

He put one finger on my lips. "And you are not overweight. Granted, you're not skinny. But who'd want to snuggle up with one of those bony waifs you see in magazines and movies?"

"Practically every heterosexual male in America."

"Not me." Gently he traced his finger down my cheek. "And, for the record, I'm definitely heterosexual."

"I gathered that."

"Good. I hope you also have gathered that I find you very attractive as well as smart, funny, talented, forthright, kind, and maybe a bit insecure."

"Insecure?"

"Yeah, the kind of woman who sees a voluptuous body as a liability."

For a moment I felt as if I couldn't breathe. But finally I managed to gulp in some air. "It's a shame that you're going to be leaving town." Before you have a chance to become more familiar with said voluptuous body.

"Leaving?"

"I heard you got a great job offer."

"Which I turned down."

"What about your fight with our publisher?"

He shook his head. "Our Caitlin does have her ear to the ground, doesn't she? But in answer to your question, fortunately my job offer seemed to help my boss realize how much he needs me."

"That is fortunate."

"Yes." He leaned forward and very gently kissed me on the lips. "It is." Then he put the car into gear and drove us to Home Depot.

An hour and a half later he had expertly replaced the broken windowpane and was getting ready to leave. He was also, I suspected, having second thoughts—major reservations—about his impulsive kiss. From the moment we left Home Depot, he'd been unusually quiet, with the tight-jawed look of a stoic man with a toothache he doesn't want to complain about. I could almost hear the thoughts running through his head: Have you lost your mind, O'Neal? This is your employee who you're flirting with—your married employee whose felon husband is connected to the Mafia!

When we encountered each other at the office on Monday we probably would both pretend that nothing had happened. That his kiss had merely been kind and collegial, a comforting, Good Samaritan gesture to a suffering co-worker. And after that we would be friendly, in an entirely professional way, while quietly avoiding each other. It was, in the long term, probably the best arrangement. I needed a job, and liked this one. I was old enough to know that a fling with the boss was the quickest way, short of embezzlement, to derail my nascent career.

Pasting on a smile, I walked Paul to the door. "I really appreciate your fixing the window. I don't know where I would have found someone who was willing to come out on a Saturday."

He shrugged. "It was nothing. I like to do home repairs. I think I was a handyman in another life." He hesitated. "Call me if you need anything else."

"Thanks, but I think I'll be fine now."

We smiled awkwardly at each other for a minute, then he said, "Well, I guess I'll see you on Monday," and I said, "Yes, and thanks again for all your help." Then he left.

I poured myself a glass of the white Zinfandel I found in the refrigerator, not sure if what I needed most at the moment was a large shot of alcohol or of caffeine, or about sixteen hours of uninterrupted sleep. Within the last twenty-four hours I: had learned that my spouse was a dental consultant for organized crime figures; had my house broken into by my fugitive husband; had a crazed medical columnist try to murder me; and had been kissed by my boss, who found my figure voluptuous. Perhaps it was time to change identities and move to another country. I wondered if I could get CNN and Baby Ruths in some remote corner of Greenland.

A few sips of the wine convinced me that it was the wrong choice. I was edgy but exhausted, and the wine seemed to make me sleepier without doing much for my anxiety.

I checked my watch. I had two hours to kill before meeting Meg for dinner. I took a hot shower, which helped revive me, and then, on a whim, decided to phone Terri Harris to schedule our interview.

"I saw you on TV with Dr. Elizabeth and all those cops," Terri said after I identified myself. "I told Stan I never trusted that woman. She must have called me two dozen times to make sure she got every penny of her share of the sale of the gym. I finally told her to nag the probate lawyer and get off my back."

I made what I hoped was a sympathetic-but-not-interested-in-pursuing-the-conversation noise. Did everyone in Houston sit around on Saturdays watching the local news? Before she had a chance to ask me any questions, I said, "I'm calling to see if I can write a story about your new cookie business. How are things going with that?"

"Great!" Terri said, instantly diverted by self-interest. "I've found a little store near the Galleria so people can pick up some cookies for office events or stop by for a little sugar pick-me-up after a day of shopping. I'm hoping to open late next month, so getting some publicity would really be helpful."

"Terrific. Do you have time next week for an interview?"

"Oh, dear. I'm going out of town on Monday, and I

won't be back for ten days. Is there any way you could interview me before I leave—tomorrow maybe?"

"Fine." I'd planned on sleeping in, but I probably needed to get the interview before she went out of town.

"You could come any time after eight—come for breakfast, if you'd like. This morning the menu included scrambled eggs, scones, and oatmeal-chocolate chip cookies."

"Sounds like my kind of meal," I said. "You always eat cookies for breakfast?"

"Only if I feel like it—and some days I do. Yesterday I had cookie dough and an omelet for breakfast, take-out pizza for lunch, and cold cereal with strawberries for dinner."

"That's a lot different from the way you used to eat, isn't it?"

"I'll say. Stan would not approve. He looked at double-chocolate chip cookies in the way a teetotaler looked at a double martini. And he'd be appalled at all the weight I've gained."

"Oh?" I tried not to sound too interested. "Have you gained a lot?"

"I've thrown out my scale so I can't be sure how much, but I'd guess twenty pounds. My skinny clothes don't fit anymore. I went out and bought some loose smocks and pants with elastic waists."

"And you feel comfortable at this weight?"

She laughed. "Let me get back to you on that. The short answer is that I love eating what I want, love not being obsessed with the scale. When I was teaching four aerobics classes a day, my joints ached and my feet hurt, but my body looked great, the best it had ever looked. I'm not willing anymore to pay the price for looking like that."

She paused. "Oh, got to go; someone's at my door. I'm

expecting some deliveries. Why don't you come tomorrow at ten? I'll save some cookies for you."

"See you then." I hung up thinking fondly of her double–chocolate chip cookies.

I woke up Sunday morning in a good mood. No one had broken into my house in the middle of the night and I'd slept for ten hours straight after sharing a heavy Tex-Mex dinner with Meg: What more could one ask of life?

Meg had offered to spend the night at my house or have me camp out at hers, but I decided I needed to face my fears alone (aided by the two glasses of wine I'd consumed at dinner.) This morning, with the sun gleaming in the window and the smell of percolating coffee filling the kitchen, I was glad I had the place to myself.

Yesterday's visit from Rob had reminded me how difficult it had been to live with him, how often I'd accommodated to his demands to be waited on hand and foot, listened patiently to his constant complaints, and tried valiantly to jolly him out of his bad moods. For more than two decades I had tolerated his bossiness, his cheapness, and his relentless self-absorption. I wasn't willing to do it anymore. Seeing Rob had shown me something I hadn't realized: I preferred living alone. Granted, I could do without my constant worries that I wasn't going to be able to make the next mortgage payment, but other than that, life without Rob was a definite improvement.

I ate a bowl of cereal and made it over to Terri Harris's house by 9:55. I rang the doorbell, then waited for someone to answer.

No one did. Well, I was a bit early. I waited a few minutes and tried again.

Nothing. Could Terri have misunderstood the time or

date of the interview? Maybe she'd overslept or had had to run out on an errand. I fumbled through my purse for my cell phone and punched in her number. The phone rang six times, then Terri's voice mail kicked in: She could not come to the phone right now; please leave my name, number, and a brief message.

I did. "There seems to have been some mix-up about our interview time," I said, trying not to sound as annoyed as I felt. "Call me and we can reschedule."

I turned to leave but suddenly noticed a light shining through the blinds at the side of the house. Wasn't that the kitchen? Maybe Terri was at home, but for some reason couldn't—or didn't want to—open the door.

Feeling a bit like a voyeur, I headed to the side window. By pushing through some azalea bushes and standing on my tiptoes, I could barely peer through the window.

All I saw was a large, immaculate kitchen with the lights on. I sighed, wondering if some nosy neighbor had spotted me and called the police. But since I had already struggled through the azaleas, I decided I might as well check out the next window, which, if I remembered right, was in the breakfast room.

Trying to ignore the branches scratching my back, I moved a few feet to my right. Once again I stood on my toes and peered inside.

I wished I hadn't. Terri Harris lay slumped over the breakfast table, her dark hair resting on the bleached oak. From her posture and the pool of blood next to her head, I suspected that she might not be baking any more cookies.

Twenty-Five

I had just walked into my house after hours of police questions when Watts and Wolfe arrived.

"You seem to have a talent for discovering victims of violent crimes," the detective said when I opened the door.

"Tell me about it." I didn't want to invite them inside and most assuredly did not want to answer another question about Terri Harris, but I didn't see any way around it. "I've already told the police everything I know, which, basically, is next to nothing."

"Do it once more time," Watts said.

I sighed and stepped back for them to enter. "Want some coffee?"

"Sure, thanks," Wolfe said as they followed me into the kitchen.

We were still sipping our first cups when I finished my story.

"So you're saying this deliveryman who showed up at Ms. Harris's door on Saturday afternoon could have killed her," Wolfe said as he jotted down notes.

"I don't know that it actually was a deliveryman who was ringing her doorbell. She just said that someone was at her door and she was expecting a delivery." I studied him. "Was Terri killed on Saturday? Do you know that yet?"

"Did she say what kind of delivery she was expecting?" Watts asked.

"No. Do you know when she died?" Sharing information, I wanted to tell him, was a two-way street, but Watts,

I suspected, had never been very good at sharing.

"She probably died late Saturday afternoon or early evening," Wolfe said.

"That could mean that whoever was ringing her doorbell did kill her." I suddenly felt queasy. What if I'd stayed on the phone while Terri went to the door? Would the killer have decided to try again another time when no witness could overhear what was happening?

"That's why it's important that you tell us everything Ms. Harris said to you—maybe about her plans for the evening or someone she was expecting to see."

"The only thing Terri said about her plans was that she was going out of town—I don't know where—on Monday, and was going to be gone for ten days. And before you ask, she didn't tell me why she was going. I assumed that her trip had something to do with opening her new cookie store, but I could be wrong about that."

"Can you think of anyone who might have had a motive to kill Ms. Harris?" Watts asked.

"There's no chance that this was just some ordinary robbery?" I asked. "Someone without any personal motive?"

"Unlikely," Watts said. "So can you think of anyone?"

"I really didn't know her that well, so I'm just guessing here. The only people who even come to mind are Stan Harris's kids and his ex-wife, and only because they were annoyed that Stan left most of his money to Terri. But I don't really see any of them killing her because of it. And for all I know, the money Terri inherited might now go to her relatives or her favorite charity."

I searched my mind for other possibilities. "Terri laid off several people when she sold the gym and she lied to at least one employee, saying she didn't intend to sell. Maybe someone's mad about that—that Terri got a million for the gym and all they got was a week's severance pay. Or maybe it has something to do with her new business—some other cookie maker wants to eliminate the competition."

Watts looked as if he was trying not to roll his eyes. The two officers stood up. "Well, thanks for your time," the sergeant said. "You hear anything more from your husband?"

"Fortunately, no. Have you?"

"Not yet. Let us know if you think of anything else about Ms. Harris's murder."

I closed the door after them, thinking how much I did not want to recall the terrible images of Terri Harris's body. Unfortunately, I knew no way to stop thinking about them.

The phone was ringing when I returned to the kitchen. I glanced at the caller ID: Jane Harris. Was the woman psychic, knowing intuitively that I'd just ratted her out to the police? Surely they hadn't had time to call her already. "Hello?"

"Lauren, it's Jane Harris. I hope I'm not interrupting anything."

She sounded friendly enough. "No, not at all. I'm just sitting here drinking coffee." After discovering a dead body and making my statements to the police earlier in the day.

"I'm a little embarrassed about my reason for calling. I saw you on television yesterday with Elizabeth." She hesitated. "It's, well, it's important to me to know everything about Stan's death."

"Of course. But I really don't know that much. Elizabeth was trying to get rid of me too."

"But the reporter said she was being held for questioning about Stan's death. Do you know anything about that, anything at all?"

"She said she needed money and was angry when Stan

refused to sell his gym. Did you know that she was his business partner?"

"Of course." She paused. "I bet she prescribed that blood pressure medication just to push him into cardiac arrest. I knew he didn't have high blood pressure."

"I think she did more than that. She gave him an injection of something—potassium something—on the jogging trail that morning."

"My God, she was his friend! For years. She was at our house all the time. The kids called her Aunt Elizabeth. And she murders him because he wouldn't sell the gym? That's evil."

"Yes, it is."

I could hear her breathing, fast and loud, on the line. "Did Elizabeth say anything about Terri?" she asked in a harsh voice. "Remember how Terri couldn't sell the gym fast enough after Stan died? Maybe she was involved in his murder too. She and Elizabeth could have planned out the whole thing."

"She didn't say a word about Terri being involved in the murder." I took a deep breath. "Jane, I don't really know how to tell you this, but Terri Harris is dead. I, uh, discovered the body this morning."

There was a very long silence.

"Jane? Are you still there?"

"How—how did she die?" Her voice was barely a whisper.

"Shot. In her house."

"Was there a suicide note? If she actually was involved in Stan's death, maybe she felt guilty."

"Not that I know of," I said coldly. It wasn't that I expected her to wail in grief at the news of Terri's death, but her response seemed uncommonly mean-spirited. It made my own question easier to ask. "I was wondering, Jane, with Terri dead, who inherits her share of Stan's estate?"

"I know who *should* inherit—Amber and SJ, the ones who Stan wanted to give the money to in the first place. But as for who *will* inherit, I don't—Wait! There was something in Stan's will about in the event the beneficiary didn't survive Stan by thirty days, then the will would take effect as if that person predeceased him."

It took me a moment to grasp why she was sounding so excited. "How many days has it been since Stan died?"

"Not quite a month. If Terri died today, that would be twenty-eight—no, twenty-nine days ago. So my kids will inherit everything!"

She cut me off before I could ask anything else. "Sorry, I need to go now, Lauren." And she hung up—presumably to give a rousing victory whoop.

But as I replaced the receiver, I had to wonder. Was Jane Harris merely a very good actress? How many women, after all, knew precisely how many days it had been since their ex-husband's deaths—or were so aware of obscure provisions in said ex-husband's will?

But perhaps Jane was genuinely shocked by the news of Terri's death. If Jane herself had killed Terri, wouldn't she have been more discreet about her hostility toward Stan's widow? Why bother to plan the perfect murder and then go blab your motive to a casual acquaintance? Unless, of course, she had been trying to figure out if I knew anything that incriminated her. Perhaps Terri had mentioned that she'd been talking with me on the phone and Jane was afraid she'd said, "Oh, here's Jane at the door. I've got to go let her in."

And that was only one possibility. Maybe Jane and Dr. Elizabeth together had plotted Stan's death, and Jane's indignation was just an act for my benefit. Stan supposedly had told Jane he was cutting Terri out of his will; she had expected her children to be his heirs. Or—Option Number Three—Jane might be totally uninvolved in any crime, and she had correctly guessed that Dr. Elizabeth and Terri Harris had plotted together to kill Stan. Certainly Terri's fortunes had changed for the better after her husband's death. Without Stan in the picture, Terri was an independent, cookie-eating, entrepreneurial widow instead of a dependent aerobic instructor with a philandering husband. Or at least she had been until yesterday.

Suddenly I started to shake. A virulent wave of crime—murders and attempted murders, blackmail, robbery, and the cover up of a Mafia hit—had disrupted the placid little pool of my daily existence. I wanted my old life back, or rather my most recent old life, the one with my new job and without Rob or any dead bodies. A day ago I'd told myself that the danger was over: the killer behind bars, my fugitive husband departed for a hiding place other than my house. But there was no way I could believe that anymore. How many more people would die before the police figured out what was going on?

Shivering, I grabbed an afghan and curled up in a tight ball on the den sofa. I willed my mind to go blank, my body to ease into sleep. But it didn't work. All I kept thinking was that somewhere nearby a seemingly normal citizen—a person I might even know—was celebrating Terri Harris's death.

Never had I greeted a Monday morning with such enthusiasm. TGIM—an opportunity to leave my house, focus my attention on something other than recent homicides, and interact with co-workers who talked about things other than crime. When I got to the office I could talk to Paul about my next article (definitely not one about Terri Harris's murder).

I was locking my back door when something hard poked me in the back. A voice that sounded vaguely familiar said, "Don't scream, Mrs. Prescott, or I'll shoot you right now."

I knew I should scream or run to the street—do something—but the gun seemed to paralyze my will. All I could do was stand there, envisioning my spine severed, the life seeping out of me. "Mrs. Prescott," he'd said. The man, whoever he was, knew me.

"If you do what I say, I won't hurt you," he said. "Now open the door."

Desperately wanting to believe him, I unlocked it.

It wasn't until we were in the kitchen that I finally saw my assailant's face. "SJ?" I couldn't believe it. "What—what are you doing?"

The face I'd once thought delicate and rather feminine was transformed by hostility. The man in front of me today had an expressionless face with cold, remorseless eyes.

"I want to talk to you." He pushed me toward the table. "Sit down."

He pulled out a chair across from me. "This must be where you duct-taped Aunt Elizabeth."

I nodded. "How did you know that?"

His lips twitched into a mocking smile. "Why, she told me, of course. When I visited her in jail." He shook his head. "Aunt Elizabeth was not happy about the way you and your husband treated her. Not happy at all."

"Well, to tell you the truth, I wasn't thrilled about the way she treated me either. Did she mention that she was here trying to kill me?" As soon as I said it, I had a terrible thought, Had Aunt Elizabeth sent SJ to finish the job?

He didn't answer, instead looking around the room as if he was searching for something. "I need some paper and a pen."

"In the drawer by the phone." I stood up to get them, but he motioned with the gun for me to stay seated.

I watched him rummage through the drawer. Should I make a dash for the door while his back was to me? I turned slightly, starting to inch my body forward.

"Don't even think about it," SJ barked from across the room. "I'd shoot you before you ran five feet."

"And what's my alternative?" The hopelessness of the situation was turning me brazen. "Being shot while I sit here?"

"Oh, relax, Mrs. Prescott. Things aren't that grim." For a moment he sounded like the laid-back man I'd encountered at his mother's house, a man who was used to reassuring sick, cranky patients. "Now tell me where you keep your liquor."

Liquor? "There's a bottle of wine in the refrigerator."

"You have anything stronger—Scotch, gin, vodka?"

Did the man want a cocktail before he murdered me? "Only a bottle of amaretto in the pantry."

SJ made a face. "So which do you prefer, wine or amaretto?" he said as he pulled a pair of rubber gloves from his pocket.

What the hell? "I like them both."

I watched with growing apprehension as he put on the gloves, then collected the amaretto bottle and one glass. Did he want to make it look as if I'd drunk myself to death?

SJ sat down again and pushed my notepad and pen across the table to me. "You're going to write a note."

"What kind of note?"

"I'll dictate it. Write this down: 'I cannot live with myself and the knowledge of what I've done any longer.' "

268

Twenty-Six

"What?" I set down the pen. "What are you talking about?"

SJ's eyes glinted. "I am talking about the confession you are going to write, admitting to your loved ones—and the police—that your husband killed Carol Quaid because he was blackmailing her and you shot Carol's mother after the old girl tried to continue Carol's scam. Also you're going to admit that you and Rob tried to set up Aunt Elizabeth for the crimes you two committed, kidnapping her from her house and forcing her to drive her car over here."

I crossed my arms over my chest. "No one would believe that!"

"Oh, I think they will." He sent me a boyish grin that chilled me to the bone. "I have thought it through. At first I was going to have you admit to shooting Terri too, but I couldn't think of any plausible motive for you doing that. Of course you could have done Terri out of blood lust or just plain disliking the greedy bitch, but that didn't seem in character. You seem more like the naive, decent woman pushed into crime to protect her family—the kind of woman who'd later be overcome by guilt at the terrible things she did."

And then killed myself. I took a deep breath. "Did you—did you kill Terri and the two Quaid women?"

"Only Terri," he said cheerfully. "And you were right about the motive. I wanted my rightful inheritance and that bitch was going to blow every penny. Mom told me that you tactlessly inquired about who will now inherit Terri's

269

money." He shook his head, looking rueful. "Mom was really pissed that you'd smear the family honor. She, of course, never dreamed that her baby boy would be involved in Terri's death."

"So Dr. Elizabeth killed your father, Carol and her mother?" I tried to keep my voice calm, a disinterested party asking a purely factual question.

He nodded. "I helped her with Dad. It was her plan, but when the blood pressure medicine and potassium supplements didn't do the job, we had to use more drastic measures before National Gyms withdrew their offer. I knocked down Dad on the jogging trail and she injected the potassium chloride." He sneered at the memory. "Considering how the old man was always carrying on about what a little girl I was, he sure was awfully easy to overpower. Macho Man wasn't all that macho in his last moments. It was too bad he was unconscious when he got the shot. I would have liked him to see just how much I hated him."

I swallowed, trying to fight back a sudden swell of nausea. "You and Dr. Elizabeth must be very close." So close that you're willing to murder me, a virtual stranger, in order to protect her.

"Let's just say we understand each other." He leveled his gun at me. "Now that we've had our little chat, it's time to start writing."

"Why should I? You're going to kill me anyway."

"True. But I'm giving you the option to die peacefully, just drifting off into sleep." From his jacket he pulled out two boxes of pills that drug companies give to doctors. "If I'd had more forewarning, I could have gotten you your own personal prescription for these. But this will have to do. The police will assume that your physician gave you these samples to see if they help with your anxiety."

He gave me a minute to study the Valium tablets. Then he said, "Option Two is less pleasant. No signed confession, but you die slowly and very painfully. A bullet to the gut is not a nice way to go. Trust me."

I believed him. "But if you shoot me, you won't be able to pin Mrs. Quaid's murder on me."

He nodded. "I guess I'll just have to live with that. On the bright side, the police won't accuse Aunt Elizabeth of killing you, and you won't be around to testify at her trial. And there's a good chance that they'll suspect your husband was your killer."

I considered my options. Aside from the not-inconsiderable advantage of minimal pain, another benefit of going the Valium route was that I was buying myself time. People did not die instantly of drug overdoses, did they? It took at least an hour, and during that time help could arrive, a stomach could be pumped, and the name of one's killer could be whispered to the police. On the other hand, if I did in fact die from the pills, people—most specifically my daughters and friends—might actually believe that I shot Mrs. Quaid, conspired with Rob to kill Carol, and then committed suicide. Not only would I be helping SJ and Dr. Elizabeth to get away with multiple murders, I would also forever shatter my daughters' faith in their mother. Maybe it was better to die in agony than to risk that.

"Oh, one more thing I forgot to mention," SJ said. "If you decide to go with the homicide victim role, I will personally hunt down your two daughters and kill them too. As I recall, Em is going to UT-Austin, and the other one, Katie, lives in Dallas with her husband."

I gasped. I wanted to believe that he was bluffing, but I knew he wasn't. Killing one or two more innocent people would mean nothing to him.

"However," he said, "if you do what I want and write the confession, I will never go anywhere near your daughters."

I stared at him. "How can I be sure of that—that you won't hurt them if I cooperate?"

"You can't. But for what it's worth, I give you my word. I'd have no reason to kill them, and I won't. I'm a pragmatic killer, not a thrill-seeker or a sadist. On the other hand, if you don't write the note, you have my word that I will shoot them."

I pulled the notebook toward me. "Tell me again what you want me to write."

He nodded. "Good decision. Head the note anyway you want. To Whom It May Concern is okay."

I wrote down his words, hoping that whoever read the note would think it didn't sound like me.

He watched me write, then dictated: "I can't live any longer with the knowledge of what I've done. I conspired with my husband Rob to kill Carol Quaid, his former office manager who was blackmailing him. I myself killed Carol's mother when, after Carol's death, she tried to extort money from me, using incriminating evidence against Rob that Carol had left in her safe-deposit box."

He paused to make sure that I was writing exactly what he said. I was, except I omitted all commas, which I hoped would clue in my daughters—who used to call me the Punctuation Nazi when I edited their school papers—that I was not writing this of my own volition. Of course since neither of them had seemed to inherit my punctuation perfectionism, it was also possible they wouldn't notice the missing commas.

"Okay," SJ said, nodding for me to resume writing. "In addition Rob and I kidnapped Dr. Elizabeth Stevens from her home in order to implicate her in our crimes. We forced her to drive her car to our home and then tied her up in our kitchen. I told the police that Elizabeth had tried to kill us and that she admitted to murdering the Quaid women and Stan Harris. This was all lies."

I wrote his words as slowly as possible, wishing there were more opportunities to omit commas.

He checked what I'd written then continued his dictation. "I am now overcome with guilt at all the pain I've inflicted on others. I am horrified at what I've done. I ask only that my children, my friends, and the families of the innocent victims of my crimes forgive me." He watched me finish the sentence. "Now sign it."

For a moment I felt as if I were going to throw up. Surely no one who knew me would believe that I'd committed these crimes. They couldn't even think that I'd written the letter, could they? The writing was not my style. I was seldom horrified at anything and almost never overcome with guilt. But it would have been so much better if SJ was a member of the "I don't want no one to think Dr. Elizabeth done any of that viciousness" school of writing. My own style was leaner and more sardonic than SJ's, but the note was short, and most of it was straightforward enough for someone who wasn't paying attention to the niceties of composition to believe I wrote it. Oh, if only I'd added some spelling mistakes and changed my handwriting—given the reader more obvious clues that I hadn't composed this note.

"Wait a minute," I said as he leaned forward to take the note. "I want to add something—to tell my daughters that I love them." When he hesitated, I pleaded, "Come on, what can it hurt? It would be suspicious if I didn't mention them."

"Okay, but don't try any tricks."

I wrote one sentence more, a postscript to my beloved daughters.

SJ read it, then pushed a glass filled with amaretto and a handful of tablets toward me. "Time for your medication."

The phone rang as I put the first tablet in my mouth.

"Let it ring," SJ said.

I considered dashing to the kitchen phone, screaming "Call the police" into the receiver—hopefully before SJ shot me. But what if the call was from a telephone solicitor or, worse yet, a recorded message? I stayed put, taking a sip of amaretto as my voice on the answering machine instructed the caller to leave me a message.

She did. "Lauren, it's Caitlin at work. I was, uh, wondering if you were planning on coming in to the office today. Call me."

As she spoke, SJ, scowling, turned toward the phone. I used the opportunity to spit the Valium into my left hand.

"Maybe I should phone to tell her I'm too sick to go to work." I hoped that Caitlin would be able to pick up that it wasn't a bad cold keeping me at home.

SJ shook his head. "Start swallowing those pills. I don't have all day."

He watched closely as I put another pill in my mouth and took a slug of amaretto. "Now open your mouth."

I opened. His gloved finger probed around my teeth and under my tongue, making me want to gag. Thank God I had inadvertently swallowed the last tablet rather than squirreling it into a corner of my mouth.

Apparently satisfied that I wasn't trying to trick him, he pushed more pills toward me. "Take two at a time," he ordered. "I don't want this to take for-fucking-ever."

I managed to drop the pill I'd spit out onto my chair while I picked up the two new ones with the other hand.

Afraid that SJ was going to do another oral cavity inspection, I swallowed the new tablets, hoping that a lot more pills were needed before I went to sleep—permanently.

He kept his fingers on the table, but his eyes never left my face.

Feeling braver—or just more desperate—I pushed the next two tablets under my tongue, trying not to react to the bitter taste. Undoubtedly some of the Valium would dissolve in my mouth, but certainly less would get into my system than if I swallowed the pills whole. The question, of course, was how much was a lethal dose? Even if I managed not to swallow half of the pills SJ was constantly handing me, would the ones I did ingest be enough to kill me?

The phone rang again.

"Shit!" SJ said.

I listened to the message. "Lauren, it's Caitlin again. Please call the office. I'm starting to get worried about you."

Please, God, I prayed, let her be worried enough to call the police and insist they come over to check on me. It was 10:15, according to the wall clock. Normally I would have been at work for at least an hour and a half by now, drinking coffee and sitting in front of my computer. I could feel my eyes brim with unwelcome tears. Would I ever have another ordinary workday like that again?

Unfortunately this time SJ did not glance at the telephone when Caitlin talked. How could I get rid of the pills I wasn't swallowing if he never looked away?

Maybe I could fake being sleepy. I figured that SJ thought I'd swallowed six tablets. Wasn't that enough to put most people to sleep? Of course being a nurse, he would probably check my pulse or something to make sure that I actually was asleep. I'd read once about how some Tibetan monks were able to meditate for days at a time, sitting immobile, as if they were deep in sleep. Well, I'd taken a Transcendental Meditation class ten years ago and I still remembered my mantra. Closing my eyes, I mentally started chanting it.

I heard SJ's chair scrape across the floor. I willed myself to keep my eyes closed. "Sha-rim, sha-rim, sha-rim," I said over and over in my head, feeling anxious that I was not transcending my anxiety.

I yelped as SJ yanked my head back. "Open your mouth!" he ordered, his breath hot on my face.

I did as I was told, my eyes open now, frantically scanning the ceiling.

With his free hand he shoved a handful of tablets into my mouth and then clumsily poured in amaretto. "Now swallow!"

I started coughing, gagging on all the pills, gasping for breath.

"I'll get you some water," SJ said, letting go of my head to walk to the sink.

With his back toward me, I tried to cough out the pills still in my mouth. But only two half-dissolved tablets—the ones I'd been hiding under my tongue—came out.

He handed me the glass of water. "You look pale. Are you feeling nauseated?"

When I nodded, he said, "Take deep breaths and drink some more water."

I knew it wasn't concern for my well being that prompted the advice. He didn't want me to throw up all of the pills I'd taken. If only he'd leave now, maybe there was still time to stick my finger down my throat.

I drank some water. "So tired," I said, in a weak voice.

He nodded. "Don't fight it." He pushed the half-empty

glass of amaretto toward me. "Finish this up. It will make things easier."

Easier for whom? I wanted to ask. But since my goal was to get SJ to leave immediately, it seemed shortsighted to engage in what my loving husband claimed was my favorite hobby—"shooting off that wise-ass mouth of yours." I sipped the amaretto, doing my best to look groggy and out of it.

When the phone rang again I could barely focus on the message. Paul, this time. *Concerned if you're okay, blah, blah, blah.*

SJ refilled my glass. "Have some more." His voice sounded as if it were coming from a long way away.

If I rested my head on the table for a while, perhaps I could convince him that the pills were taking effect. And a short nap might actually help me to think more clearly. I closed my eyes. When I heard SJ's approach, I started meditating again. This time it seemed to be working. So calm . . .

He lifted my wrist and felt for a pulse.

Sha-rim, sha-rim, sha-rim. Breathing slowly and peacefully.

Abruptly SJ dropped my arm. I heard quick footsteps and then the sound of the back door closing. Or had the noise come from the front door?

Who cared? SJ was gone. Time for my rescue effort: First, Operation Deep Throat. Then get to the phone. Call 911.

I tried to raise my head, but it was too heavy. My hand wouldn't move either. "Lauren?" A too-loud voice in my ear. Someone shaking my shoulder. Hard.

"Stop!" I managed to open my eyes. Rob?

He was reading my letter. "Jesus Christ, Lauren! Jesus!" Shouting at me. So loud, so loud!

He shook my shoulder again. Harder, hurting me. "You bitch! Accusing me of killing Carol! You must really hate me."

I tried to speak. "No, not—" The words weren't coming out right. "Hospital," I tried to say, but Rob wasn't listening.

He finished reading. "Your daughters Emma and Katherine? Oh, shit!"

I closed my eyes and let the darkness surround me.

Twenty-Seven

Suddenly I saw a bright light overhead. My God, was I dead—moving toward that bright tunnel of light I'd always read about?

But then someone shook my shoulder and a too-loud voice commanded, "Lauren! Don't shut your eyes again. Open your eyes, Lauren." It seemed a pretty safe bet that the light I'd glimpsed was not celestial.

I managed to open my eyes.

"Good girl, Lauren." A sharp-featured woman in a white coat peered into my eyes. "You're in the St. Mark's Hospital emergency room. I'm Dr. Stein." She shook my shoulder again. "Stay with me, Lauren. Do you remember taking the Valium and the alcohol?"

I nodded. "SJ made me," I tried to say.

"Esjay? Is that something you took?" Dr. Stein asked. "What's Esjay, Lauren?"

I wished the woman would shut up. I wanted, more than anything, to go back to sleep.

"Lauren! You have to tell me what else you took." The woman's voice was loud and shrill. She was giving me one hellacious headache.

"Amaretto," I muttered. Now shut the hell up.

"That's what her husband said," another voice piped in. "Valium and amaretto."

"Lauren, we have to pump your stomach," Dr. Shrill said. She sprayed something in my throat. "I'm going to insert this tube now. It might feel a little uncomfortable."

A little uncomfortable? She reminded me of my Aunt Nelda who assured me when I was pregnant with Katie that childbirth involved only "minor discomfort."

A highly unpleasant interval followed, during which a tube was inserted through my mouth, into my esophagus and down to my stomach, and the entire contents were suctioned out. Dr. Shrill provided a running commentary. "Now we're going to wash out your stomach with lukewarm water, Lauren. We'll do that a few times until the fluids that come out of your stomach are clear."

Since there was a tube in my mouth, I wasn't able to respond. Every part of me seemed to hurt. I had a feeling, though, that even if I were able to convey this, Dr. Shrill would have shrugged and said, "Well, that's what you deserve for trying to kill yourself."

But at least I was alive. Alive to see my daughters mature and, I hoped, have children of their own: little grandbabies I could dote on and spoil rotten. Alive to make absolutely sure SJ Harris, that slimy bastard, didn't get away with trying to murder me.

Finally Dr. Shrill seemed to be done. "We'll be keeping you in the hospital for observation for a day or two," she said.

"No!" Despite my pounding headache, my incredibly sore throat, and a nausea so profound I might never choose to eat again, I knew I didn't want to spend the night here. SJ worked at a hospital—maybe, for all I knew, *this* hospital—and SJ would not be happy to learn I was not dead.

"You have to stay at least overnight," Dr. Shrill said. "We need to monitor you to make sure you have no toxic side effects." She sent me a stern look. "You were very lucky—this time. I think someone from Psychiatry will also want to talk to you."

I hoped my deeply malevolent look conveyed to her my opinion of her assessment. My throat hurt too much to put it into words. "SJ Harris," I rasped. "Tried to kill me."

But either no one could understand me or they assumed that my grasp on reality was slipping. The only response I got was from a nurse who watched as two orderlies rolled me onto another table. "We just want to make sure you're okay, hon."

"Me too," I muttered. Our visions on how to accomplish this feat, however, were radically different.

"I'm going to go get your husband to let him know that he can see you now." The nurse patted my shoulder. "He was really worried about you."

Rob worried? He must have been the person who got me to the hospital, and he obviously waited around long enough to tell Dr. Shrill what I'd swallowed. I had a vague recollection of Rob's voice yelling at me in the kitchen. But what was he doing there before he found me? And had he encountered SJ? The memories seemed to blur together, a disjointed hodgepodge of disconnected impressions: Rob screaming accusations at me; a hand shaking my shoulder; Dr. Shrill leaning over me as she inserted the stomach tube; one of the orderlies whistling softly as he pushed me, dizzy and queasy, down the corridors of the hospital.

The orderlies deposited me in my room, a double with the second bed empty. I was still trying to find a position that made me feel less uncomfortable when I had my first visitor.

"Rob!" I was both surprised and pleased to see him. I assumed he would have left the hospital as soon as they took me into the emergency room.

He sat gingerly on the edge of the bed. "You okay?"

"I'll live." I patted his hand. "Thanks to you."

"Who the hell did this to you? I thought that psycho doctor was in jail."

"She is. SJ Harris made me write the letter and take pills. And he helped Dr. Elizabeth kill his father."

Rob shook his head. "Jesus, Lauren, it seems like almost every day someone's trying to murder you. I know Mafia guys who lead quieter lives—or at least I used to know them."

I shrugged. At another time I would have liked to pursue the conversation about his Mafia buddies, but right then I wasn't up to it.

"And by the way, did you have to write in your letter that I killed Carol? I don't have enough trouble without being accused of a felony I didn't commit?" His voice had an all-too-familiar peevish quality that made me remember why I wanted a divorce.

"SJ told me if I didn't write everything he said, he'd shoot me and then find the girls and shoot them." Just saying it made my eyes well with tears.

"That bastard!" Rob's hands clenched into fists.

I took several deep breaths, trying to calm a wave of nausea. "I need to call the police, Rob. So if you don't want to talk to them, maybe you'd better leave now."

"I'm afraid it's a little late for that," said a deep voice from the doorway.

I watched the color drain from my husband's normally ruddy complexion as Officer Watts and Sergeant Wolfe entered the room.

My anger energized me. I sat up in bed, glaring at them. "Where were you a few hours ago when someone was trying to murder me?"

"I wish we'd been there," the sergeant said. "Why don't you tell us what happened, Mrs. Prescott?"

I told them. By the time the officers were through taking my statement, I was so exhausted that even displaced rage couldn't keep me upright. "How did you know I was here?" I asked, slumping onto my pillow.

"Your employer phoned us when you didn't show up for work or answer your phone. He insisted that we go to your house. When we got there, a neighbor told us she'd just seen an ambulance take you away."

Watts walked over to Rob and pulled out a pair of handcuffs. "You're under arrest, Mr. Prescott. You have the right to remain silent, the right to—"

"Hey!" I interrupted. "He saved my life. It's SJ Harris you should be arresting—a man who's still out there somewhere, possibly outlining his new plan for murdering me."

"Yeah, I got that," Watts said. As he led Rob to the door, the detective turned back to me. "Don't worry about Harris getting in here. I'll have an officer sitting right outside your door."

I might have been more reassured if I hadn't seen too many movies where the cop guarding the hospital room never once stopped even the dumbest killer.

I slept for most of the afternoon, and when I awoke it was dark outside. I phoned Meg, but only her answering tape responded. I left a message, telling her where I was, and then considered calling Katie and Em. But they didn't need to know tonight that their dad was in jail and someone had tried to kill their mother—at least not until I could tell them that the would-be murderer was behind bars. So instead I turned on the TV for company. At least it blocked out all the ominous sounds I kept imagining I heard in the hospital corridor.

I lived through the night, but I certainly didn't sleep

through it. I kept expecting to see SJ sneak up on me, lethal hypodermic needle in hand. Or maybe instead he'd be holding a scalpel or his handy gun. Now that he no longer had to convince anyone that I was killing myself, his homicidal options were almost endless.

For once I was delighted to glimpse the first morning light. Maybe now I could get out of this place. Although it might logically be argued that with a police guard outside my door I was safer in the hospital room than in my house—the site of two attempts on my life—I was willing to take my chances on home. At least no officious nurses would be bustling into my bedroom to wake me every time I managed to fall asleep for a few minutes.

But first I had to welcome a stream of visitors. Sergeant Wolfe and Officer Watts were the first to arrive. "We need your consent to send crime technicians to your house to collect evidence," Watts said without preamble.

I widened my eyes in mock surprise. "No 'How are you feeling today, Lauren?' Just 'Hand over your house keys, the crime technicians are on the way'?"

He had the grace to look embarrassed. "You look as if you're feeling better," he said almost sheepishly.

I nodded. "I do feel better. Though considering how god-awful I felt yesterday, that isn't saying a lot. Have you arrested SJ Harris? Is that why you want to check out my house?"

"Not yet," Wolfe said. "Harris wasn't at his apartment or at his job. But don't worry, we'll find him."

Before or after I turned up dead? Glumly I reached for my purse, which Rob had apparently brought along in the ambulance.

"Oh, we don't need your key," Wolfe said. "We have your husband's."

"He isn't supposed to have a house key that works. That's why I changed the locks." I narrowed my eyes. "Did Rob happen to mention what he was doing at my house in the first place?"

"He said he came to collect some of his possessions, but instead he found you slumped on the kitchen table next to a phony suicide note."

I nodded. "I guess I was lucky he happened to come by when he did." That was certainly true. The other true things—Rob obviously had pocketed my extra house key and come to re-steal the good furniture when he assumed I'd be at work—I'd leave for another discussion.

"The officer is still at the door," Watts said as they were leaving. "Maybe it would be a good thing if you stayed here until we take Harris into custody."

Fortunately another visitor arrived then so I didn't have to answer. "He's the guy who phoned you to come to my house," I explained as the officers gave my boss the once over. Apparently satisfied, they let Paul inside and departed.

"Well, it's nice to know you're well protected," he said, leaning down to kiss me gently on the forehead. "How are you feeling?"

"A lot better than yesterday." I told him the short version of events.

He shook his head. "I can't believe this is all happening to you."

"I know. I seem like such a mild-mannered woman."

"Not that mild." Paul grinned. "In any case, I'm glad you're feeling better."

We smiled at each other for a moment long enough to start bordering on awkwardness. "Oh," Paul finally said, "I brought these books for you. I remembered you said you liked mysteries."

I opened a bag containing three novels. "Hey, these are great—P.D. James, Laurie King, and Elizabeth George, my favorite authors."

He looked pleased by my reaction. "That's what I thought you'd said. I bought a copy of the P.D. James one for myself too."

For no apparent reason it crossed my mind that Rob would not have been able to identify my favorite authors if his life depended on it.

"So how long are you going to be in the hospital?" Paul was asking when Meg threw open my door.

"Could you please convince this policeman that I'm not going to kill you?" she said, sending my protector, a paunchy, gray-haired cop, a look of exasperation.

"She's harmless," I called to him. "Let her in."

Meg stalked into the room. "That fascist pig," she whispered as she kissed my cheek. "If I was carrying an automatic, I bet he would have pretended to be asleep."

"Now that's a reassuring thought."

My visitors exchanged greetings, then Paul said he needed to get to work, but he'd call to check on me this afternoon.

The minute he left, Meg said, "I am so sorry."

"That's okay, you weren't really interrupting anything."

She raised her eyebrows. "Actually I was referring to the attempt on your life. I kept thinking that if you'd been staying at my house, the way I wanted you to, this never would have happened."

I shrugged. "I'm not so sure about that. SJ seems like a pretty resourceful guy. He's managed to elude the police."

Her pale face turned a shade paler, but all she said was, "When are they letting you out of here?"

"Please God, as soon as possible. Right this minute would be good."

Meg stood up. "Stay here. I'll take care of it."

And, to my amazement, she did. Within ten minutes, Dr. Shrill appeared, and after a cursory examination, said I could go. "Alcohol and Valium can be a lethal combination. All things considered, Mrs. Prescott, you're lucky to be alive."

I didn't feel all that lucky, but I didn't think that was what she wanted to hear. Instead I thanked her for her help, pulled on my now-stained green wool dress, and followed Meg out of the room.

"I want to go visit Rob," I said. "He's in jail."

"Before you visit anyone, we're going to buy you some new clothes," Meg said, wrinkling her nose. "And that is not negotiable."

I managed to talk her into driving to my house instead. From the hallway she watched the crime technicians make a mess of my kitchen while I went upstairs to change my clothes and throw a few things into a suitcase. At Meg's insistence, I'd agreed to spend a few nights at her house, but only until the police picked up SJ.

"You want to get some lunch before we go to the jail?" Meg asked.

"What do you mean before 'we' go to the jail?"

Meg smiled. "As that doc said, it's your lucky day. You've got yourself a free body guard/chauffeur. And don't even try to talk me out of it."

I groaned. "Let's do the jail first. After that I'll think about what kind of food I might be able to keep down."

We ended up waiting for over an hour, but eventually, after a phone call to Sergeant Wolfe, I managed to see Rob.

We had to talk on phones, looking at each other through a glass partition. Rob wore a hideous, bright-orange jumpsuit that made the dark crescents under his eyes look even worse.

"So I see you lived," he said, not sounding all that happy about it.

"Thanks to you." When he didn't respond I said, "So what's happening?"

"They charged me with falsifying Lorenzo's dental records. Even though—get this—they told me that Leonardo actually died a week ago in some bar fight. They want to send me to prison for saying he was dead a few months before his actual death."

"You couldn't claim it was a simple clerical mistake—somehow the two men's X-rays got switched?"

"I wish." He looked, if possible, even glummer.

"You have a lawyer yet?"

The question seemed to revive him. "I think so. But there's a problem." He proceeded to tell me about the hotshot, cutthroat, just-what-he-needed criminal lawyer who had told Rob he'd take his case. "But he wants twenty-five thousand up front."

I stared at him. "And how do you propose to pay for that?"

"That's what I have to talk to you about. Do you have something to write with?"

"No, they only let me bring in my keys."

"Damn." He scowled at me. "How good is your memory?"

"Good enough," I said and listened to what he had to tell me.

Meg did not look like a happy camper when I rejoined her in the crowded, dingy waiting room. "You owe me."

"Big time," I agreed, following her out to the parking lot.

"You know I've never been fond of Rob," Meg said as we got into her car. "And after everything he did to you, I figured that he deserved to rot in jail. But even I wouldn't wish that place on him."

"I know what you mean," I began when my cell phone rang. I rummaged through my purse for it. "Hello?"

"This is Sergeant Wolfe. Where are you?"

"In a friend's car. We're leaving the jail. Thanks again for arranging for me to see Rob."

"No problem. Are you driving?"

"No. Why?" His questions were beginning to make me nervous.

"I just wanted to let you know that we've arrested SJ Harris."

"Great! Where did you find him?"

"St. Mark's Hospital. He, uh, shot a patient who'd been moved into your room. An orderly tackled Harris when he was running toward the stairs."

"SJ shot a patient who he thought was me?"

I didn't hear the answer. Instead, for the second time in forty-eight hours, I passed out.

Twenty-Eight

"I see you've regained your appetite," Meg said.

"Unfortunately, yes." I picked up another nacho. "For a few days there, I thought I might stay on a permanent diet of soup, saltines, and Jell-O, but that phase has passed." I took a sip of my margarita. "Anyway, we're celebrating."

Meg raised her margarita glass. "To your return to solid foods."

I laughed. "Actually we're celebrating several other things as well: SJ Harris's arrest, of course, and I just heard that the woman he shot in my hospital room is going to be okay."

"Wonderful." She lifted her glass again.

I held up my palm. "In addition, I officially filed for divorce yesterday." I pulled a check from my purse and handed it to Meg. "And at last I can repay your very generous loan."

Finally Meg got to deliver her toast. "To your freedom—from homicidal nutcases, your jerk of a husband, and financial destitution."

We drank to that.

"What did you do—sell your story to the *National Enquirer*?"

I shook my head. "Rob and I reached a private financial settlement."

Meg set down her drink. "You're kidding me. Skinflint Rob parted with his cash? How'd you manage that?"

"Basically Rob needed me to get money out of his Swiss bank account to pay his lawyer."

"He gave you his account number? I'm surprised he didn't entrust the task to his mama."

"I'm more mobile. I had to retrieve the money, get a cashier's check, and then deliver it to the lawyer's office. It's surprising how open Rob became about his finances once he thought he might be spending his golden years in the penitentiary."

"I hope you relayed all this information to your divorce lawyer."

"No, Rob and I worked out our own arrangements. In exchange for me not telling my lawyer how much money he has stashed away, I get what I want: a paid-for house, a trust fund for Em's education, and enough cash so I won't have to ever worry again about paying my grocery bills."

Meg's eyes narrowed. "I bet you didn't get half of his assets. It's still not too late to talk to your attorney."

"I got enough—certainly more than I expected. I'll probably have to keep working until I'm seventy, but at least I won't starve or be homeless. And Rob is going to need a lot of money for his legal bills. That cutthroat lawyer might very well get him off, but it's not going to be cheap. One way or the other, Rob is going to pay for what he did."

Meg's expression made clear that, in my place, she would not have made the same decisions, but she didn't pursue the matter. "What about Dr. Elizabeth and that Harris kid? I hope they're going to stay locked up."

I shivered. "I hope so too. Watts told me they found a Federal Express guy who saw SJ leave Terri's house, and a ballistics test matched up SJ's gun and the bullets in Terri's body. And get this: SJ's devoted Aunt Elizabeth tried to pin all the murders on him! Said she had nothing to do with any of them. When he heard that, he started telling the police how Elizabeth recruited him to help her kill Stan. She wanted him to kill Carol Quaid and her mother too, but SJ told her to do it herself."

I finished the last nacho. "I'm sorry to have to eat and run, Meg, but I need to get back to the house. The girls are driving in tonight and Paul's coming over this afternoon. He wants to dig up those big bushes by the back door where SJ was hiding." I took some bills from my wallet and left them on top of our check.

Meg raised her eyebrows. "How are Em and Katie handling everything?"

"You mean their father being in jail and two people trying to murder their mother? Actually, they're doing better than I expected. They're relieved I'm alive, and both of them said they want to visit Rob this weekend."

"And you and Mr. O'Neal—are you two an item?"

Grinning, I stood up. "Who knows?" I gave her a hug, then we walked together to the parking lot.

About the Author

Karen Hanson Stuyck is the author of three previous mystery novels: _Cry For Help_, _Held Accountable_, and _Lethal Lessons_. She has worked as a newspaper reporter, an editor, and a public relations writer for hospitals and a mental health institution. Her short stories have been published in _Redbook_, _Cosmopolitan_, _Woman's World_ and other magazines. She has a grown son and lives in Houston with her husband.